IT DEVOURS!

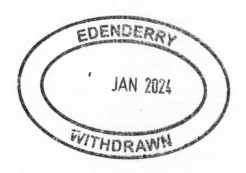

PRAISE FOR *WELCOME TO NIGHT VALE: A NOVEL*

"This is a splendid, weird, moving novel.... It manages beautifully that trick of embracing the surreal in order to underscore and emphasize the real—not as allegory, but as affirmation of emotional truths that don't conform to the neat and tidy boxes in which we're encouraged to house them"   **NPR.org**

"Fink and Cranor's prose hints there's an empathetic humanity underscoring their well of darkly fantastic situations. . . . As a companion piece, *Welcome to Night Vale* will be hard to resist. Though the book builds toward a satisfyingly strange exploration of the strange town's intersection with an unsuspecting real world, Night Vale's mysteries—like the richest conspiracy theories—don't exist to be explained. They just provide a welcome escape"   ***Los Angeles Times***

"The book is charming and absurd—think *This American Life* meets *Alice in Wonderland*"   ***Washington Post***

"Longtime listeners and newcomers alike are likely to appreciate the ways in which Night Vale, as Fink puts it, 'treats the absurd as normal and treats the normal as absurd.' What they might not foresee is the emotional wallop the novel delivers in its climactic chapters"   ***Austin Chronicle***

"*Welcome to Night Vale* lives up to the podcast hype in every way. It is a singularly inventive visit to an otherworldly town that's the stuff of nightmares and daydreams"   ***BookPage***

"All hail the glow cloud as the weird and wonderful town of Night Vale brings itself to fine literature. . . . The novel is definitely as addictive as its source material"

Kirkus Reviews **(starred review)**

"Take Conan's Hyboria, teleport it to the American Southwest, dress all the warriors in business casual, and hide their swords under the floorboards—that's Night Vale: absurd, magical, wholly engrossing, and always harboring some hidden menace"

John Darnielle, *New York Times* **bestselling author of** *Universal Harvest* **and** *Wolf in White Van*

"They've done the unthinkable: merged the high weirdness and intense drama of Night Vale to the pages of a novel that is even weirder, even more intense than the podcast"

Cory Doctorow, author of *Little Brother* **and coeditor of** *Boing Boing*

"This is the novel of your dreams, a hypnotic travelogue that shimmers and changes as you read. A friendly (but terrifying) and comic (but dark) and glittering (but bleak) story of misfit family life that unfolds along the side streets, back alleys, and spring-loaded trapdoors of the small town home you'll realize you've always missed living in. When it says 'welcome,' it's mandatory. You belong here"

Glen David Gold, author of *Carter Beats the Devil* **and** *Sunnyside*

"This small town full of hooded figures, glowing clouds, cryptically terrifying public policies, and flickering realities quickly feels more like home than home. You will want to live in Night Vale, even if that means you might be taken off in an unmarked helicopter or cross into a parallel universe by accident. There is nothing like Night Vale, in the best possible way"

Maureen Johnson, author of *13 Little Blue Envelopes* and *The Name of the Star*

"Brilliant, hilarious, and wondrously strange. I'm packing up and moving to Night Vale!"

Ransom Riggs, author of the #1 *New York Times* bestselling *Miss Peregrine's Home for Peculiar Children*

"I've been a fan of *Welcome to Night Vale* for years, and in that time writers Jeffrey Cranor and Joseph Fink have delighted me with stories that are clever, twisted, beautiful, strange, wonderful, and sweet. This book does all of that and so much more. It's even better than I'd hoped. I think this might be the best book I've read in years"

Patrick Rothfuss, author of *The Name of the Wind*

"Emotionally compelling and superbly realized. This seductive, hilarious book unfolds at the moment when certain quiet responsible people find they must risk everything on behalf of love, hope, and understanding. Not a single person who reads this book will be disappointed"

Deb Olin Unferth, author of *Revolution and Vacation*

"*Welcome to Night Vale* brings its eponymous desert town to vivid life. Those of us who have gotten to know Night Vale through Cecil Palmer's biweekly radio broadcasts can finally see what it's like to actually live there. It is as weird and surreal as I hoped it would be, and a surprisingly existential meditation on the nature of time, reality, and the glow cloud that watches over us. ALL HAIL THE GLOW CLOUD"

Wil Wheaton

BY JOSEPH FINK & JEFFREY CRANOR

Welcome to Night Vale: A Novel

Mostly Void, Partially Stars: Welcome to Night Vale Episodes, Volume 1

The Great Glowing Coils of the Universe: Welcome to Night Vale Episodes, Volume 2

It Devours!

A WELCOME TO NIGHT VALE NOVEL

IT DEVOURS!

JOSEPH FINK & JEFFREY CRANOR

www.orbitbooks.net

ORBIT

First published in Great Britain in 2017 by Orbit

1 3 5 7 9 10 8 6 4 2

Copyright © 2017 by Joseph Fink and Jeffrey Cranor

Designed by Leah Carlson-Stanisic

Illustrations by Jessica Hayworth

Title page design by Rob Wilson

The moral right of the author has been asserted.

A CIP catalogue record for this book
is available from the British Library.

HB ISBN 978-0-356-50864-1
C format 978-0-356-50865-8

Printed and bound in Great Britain by
Clays Ltd, St Ives plc

Papers used by Orbit are from well-managed forests
and other responsible sources.

MIX
Paper from
responsible sources
FSC® C104740

Orbit
An imprint of
Little, Brown Book Group
Carmelite House
50 Victoria Embankment
London EC4Y 0DZ

An Hachette UK Company
www.hachette.co.uk

www.orbitbooks.net

To Jillian Sweeney and to Meg Bashwiner

1

Not everyone believes in mountains, yet there they are, in plain sight.

Scientists insist, rather halfheartedly, that mountains are the bulging results of tectonic shifts along massive rocky plates. Mountains developed naturally over the course of many millennia, scientists say under their breaths.

Most people believe that mountains aren't there at all. Even when mountains are visible, as they often are, nonbelievers will explain that our minds create sensory illusions to help explain what we cannot understand, like the shapes of gods and monsters in the stars, or messages in tea leaves, or government codes in cloud patterns.

Mountains, real or not, ring this desert like the rim of an empty dinner plate. Scattered sparsely along the flat middle are small towns with names like Red Mesa, Pine Cliff, and, right in the center, Night Vale.

Above Night Vale are helicopters, protecting citizens from themselves and others. Above the helicopters are stars, which are completely meaningless. Above the stars is the void, which is completely meaningful.

Through this crowded sky, mysterious lights often pass. These are just alien spacecraft, or the auras left by interdimensional travelers, but these simple explanations are boring. The people of Night Vale often come up with elaborate stories to explain the lights to themselves. ("The sky once loved a certain rock. But millennia of erosion transformed the rock to dust. The sky, not understanding, still signals for its friend who abandoned it. The rock never knew about the sky. The rock only loved the wind that was slowly eroding it.") Sometimes it's okay to find something beautiful without correctly understanding it.

In the center of Night Vale, like in many cities, is its downtown, with the usual things a downtown has: city hall, community radio station, hooded figures, a library, a shimmering vortex blocked off with yellow police tape, dangerous stray dogs, and propaganda loudspeakers on every corner.

Beyond downtown is Old Town Night Vale, a residential and shopping area planned and developed during the booming economy of the early 1930s. After the war, the neighborhood fell into disrepair, but in recent years it has seen a regenesis of homeowners, neighborhood shops, tall metal trees, and predatory cats.

Beyond Old Town Night Vale are the sand wastes, which are exactly what you think they are. And beyond the sand wastes are the scrublands, which are sort of what you think they are. And beyond the scrublands is the used car lot, and Old Woman Josie's house, and finally, out on the edge of town, the house of Larry Leroy.

Larry had lived by himself for as long as he could remember. He owned a phone, which was broken, and a car, which sat wheelless atop four blocks of concrete out back. Hidden under the car he had an underground shed full of canned goods and bottled water and a year's worth of pork sausage preserved in animal fat. He used to have a shotgun, but he traded it for the car without wheels, figuring a car without wheels was safer than a shotgun. Despite the friendly reminders from the Night

Vale chapter of the National Rifle Association ("Guns don't kill people. Guns are the new kale. Guns are healthy as all get-out."), Larry never felt safe around guns.

When he was in his early twenties, Larry's father took him hunting. He didn't like his father. He didn't hate him, either. Once, when Larry reached into the back of his dad's pickup to grab the shotgun, a scorpion resting on the barrel had stung Larry's hand. He had distrusted guns ever since.

These days, Larry actually liked scorpions. After all, they eat squirrels, which he really hated. He rarely paid much attention to the illogical way in which the human mind develops certain phobias.

This evening, he bent over the shoe box on his desk. He was carefully pasting a tiny brown mustache he'd made from a sliver of tree bark to a tiny W. E. B. DuBois's face. He still needed to build the arm-mounted laser cannon DuBois was known for. Larry heard what sounded like the small claws of squirrels running around in his basement, and he hoped the scorpions were hungry. He turned his attention to his miniature version of the five-headed dragon named Rachel McDaniels that DuBois often rode when speaking. DuBois spoke from a place of moral and physical authority to the intellectuals and politicians who stood in the way of equal rights for black Americans. He also spoke from the back of a flying dragon.

Larry was building a diorama celebrating DuBois's famous defeat of the German army in 1915, depicting him and Rachel in their library, high-fiving above a copy of the declaration of surrender.

Larry adored this war hero and great orator of civil rights. He enshrined DuBois in fine detail in the cardboard shoe box. Larry's family never cared much for history, often telling him history didn't exist because it was no longer happening. The moment anything occurred, they would say every night at dinner, it was gone, relegated to the fiction of memory. They would say that with their heads bowed, and then they would begin eating.

Perhaps he had been a rebellious youth. Or perhaps he just wanted to explore the often wondrous, often tragic myth of human history. Larry adored his heroes: W. E. B. DuBois, Helen Keller, Redd Foxx, Luis Valdez, Toni Morrison. He believed it was his responsibility to help carry on their legacy by enshrining their great stories and deeds, so that they still felt present in the present. History is real, regardless of truth, Larry often said, not with words, but with his actions.

Tiny clothing, facial hair, painted set models, most pieces no bigger than any one of Larry's fingers. They took a steady eye, a steady hand. Unlike most men, he had grown more steady as he aged, more dextrous in his lack of speed. He expertly placed DuBois's mustache below the great intellectual's nose and set the tweezers down to begin working on the diorama's library backdrop.

Larry heard a whirring hum. He felt it throughout his body. There were undulations in the waves of the noise, smooth ups and downs, easily lulling the subconscious mind of a man hard at work. The troughs and crests of sounds accelerated, soon going from steady ululations to a bumpy roar. The metal plates and cups in his hand-built kitchen were the first to start rattling, followed by the creaking of the roof against the metal trusses.

He glanced at the earthquake calendar tacked to his wall. Agents from a vague yet menacing government agency delivered these calendars each month, sliding a manila envelope under the door in the middle of the night. According to the calendar, there was no earthquake scheduled for today.

He looked down at W. E. B. DuBois and Rachel McDaniels in their vast academic library. A drop of Larry's sweat the size of DuBois's head landed on McDaniels's back, smudging the paint and knocking off the freshly glued spines.

Larry wiped his brow. He didn't sweat often, even in the desert heat. "It's a dry heat," people from the desert often say to others, trying to disguise the fact that they're kidding themselves. But the heat today was unusual. He felt it not from the air, but from below his boots, and not the heat of the sun but of friction. The sand underneath his plywood floor burned, like two worlds rubbing together.

His sleeveless brown undershirt was drenched dark down its sides. He heard the crash of metal plates and cups falling out of the doorless cabinets. The ground, his house, his whole self shook. It was not the soft wobbling slide of a government-run earthquake. This felt like being punched from below. The desert was being pounded by a giant subterranean fist.

As he stood and staggered into the living room, there was another hard thump and shake of his house. Larry tripped forward, face-first, into the frame around his open front door.

He wasn't afraid but for his dioramas. He knew one day there would be an End to all of this, and long before that there would be an end to Larry. He was not so arrogant as to refer to his own death as The End, just one of billions of ends before The End. Death is only the end if you assume the story is about you.

He knew one day he would be found deceased in his home out on the edge of town. He was unbothered by this. He may not have had children, but the legacy provided by children is limited. Few people know the details of their family past their great-grandparents, and many people don't even remember that generation. Two generations of memory is all that children provide, and then everyone is forgotten. But he would leave behind stacks of writing, dioramas, and patchwork quilts. He had a handmade history, his attempt to offer immortality to his heroes, and perhaps extend his own story as well. Instead of a brief obituary in the *Night Vale Daily Journal,* he wanted his death to be a story of the discovery of his great collection, the work of his then-finished life.

He had already written letters for Sarah Sultan, president of the Night Vale Community College (instructions to donate his dioramas to the school's art department); Leann Hart, editor of the *Daily Journal;* and Cecil Palmer, host of the community radio station (an obituary he had written for himself, and also ones for Leann and Cecil); and Michelle Nguyen, owner of Dark Owl Records, who would no doubt be pleased to inherit Larry's vast collection of polka music, written, performed, and recorded himself using a concertina and a microcassette recorder. Michelle loathed any music popular enough to have been heard by more than her and the Dark Owl staff, so Larry's tunes would be welcome. According to his will, the letters were to be delivered and his belongings distributed accordingly.

His artistic and academic endeavors were his children, a legacy that would hopefully last for much longer than two forgetful human generations.

He could feel the bruise beginning to form on his cheek from where he ran into the doorframe. He turned back into the house. The pounding from below was bringing down his kitchen and living room. He watched as the walls and ceiling collapsed and twisted into dust and scrap. Pages of his books and personal writing scattered up toward the helicopters and stars above, and fluttered lazily in the wind, like unmotivated pigeons.

Lurching forward, arms straight out, using the walls for balance, he rounded the corner back into his art studio. His DuBois and McDaniels diorama was slightly damaged, but recoverable. He picked it up.

The wall of other dioramas was still there: decades of meticulous work and loving craftsmanship. His *Pride and Prejudice* diorama, which had been his first, still showed the inconsistencies of a neophyte but also the bravery of a young artist. Elizabeth Bennet's sword was soaked with blood (Larry had used his own). And for her eyes, he had used polished onyx. From wherever you stood in the room, Bennet appeared to be staring you down with the passion and vengefulness this dangerous literary villain was known for.

He set the DuBois box down on the worktable and walked toward his wall of dioramas. The long plexiglass windows were secured and locked over the displays. The thumping floor jostled him violently. He tugged a bit on each shelf, seeing they were safe but needing to touch them all to believe it.

Crack.

The floorboard below Larry split. He lost his balance but regained it against the support column next to the shelves. Another loud thump and half the worktable buckled into a sinkhole growing in the floor. He saw DuBois's box sliding down toward the opening. He jumped. He rarely jumped or did anything quickly, but now he did both. He grabbed the box, then, stepping with his right foot onto the sinking table, he pushed off, hurling himself, uncontrolled, into the far wall but managing to cradle the diorama of his favorite orator securely to his chest.

It was silent for a long moment, just Larry breathing. He heard a drop of sweat tap the floor below him. The earth was hot. His feet were beginning to cramp. His head was light. He took DuBois outside and set the box gently on the ground, safely away from the shaking building.

He grabbed his wheelbarrow out of the ditch and raced back into the collapsing house. He tossed any important documents he could find along with his letters to the people of Night Vale into the wheelbarrow. He grabbed the poems and plays he had written. He rushed back into his studio, his arms straining, wheelbarrow already half full. He set his dioramas carefully atop one another in the wheelbarrow, his life's work a delicate pyramid of paint, plastic, and paper.

He heard the ceiling creak. He placed Jane Austen's masterpiece on top of the others in the wheelbarrow. As he did, a loud pop and a harsh crunch. His ears were ringing immediately. He fell—or rather slid—to his knees. The floor buckled. The empty shelves collapsed. He glanced down into the hole. He saw dirt and wood and plexiglass falling. Falling, and hitting nothing. In that hole he saw a deep, endless nothing.

The floor tore away, the wood bending down into the hole below. He struggled to keep his boots' grip on the steeply angled floor. He gave the wheelbarrow a strong push, knowing if he didn't make it, he'd at least give the dioramas a fighting chance. The cart lurched a couple of feet and then began rolling back toward him. The pyramid of his life's work quivered, on the verge of tumbling.

His boots were sliding. Larry gave one more great shove with his calves, his knees unbent, his body thrust upward. He pushed up the sloping floor, straining but eventually gaining traction and then momentum. He rolled his cart off the top edge of the pit, leaping, as if from a ramp, into the living room, away from the growing hole behind him. He turned the corner and ran out the front door.

As daylight dwindled slowly across the desert, Larry emerged onto the patio. Out toward the sunset. Away from the collapsing home, and toward a collapsing earth.

The front lawn—mere pebbled dirt and leafless shrubs—was gone. Everything up to the ditch was an empty pit. The earth before him was completely gone, and with it, W. E. B. DuBois and Rachel McDaniels.

Larry barely had time to process what had happened when there came one more thump. He didn't know it yet, but it would be the last and the most terrible. The front few steps gave way to an implosion of sand. His palms burned as the wood handles of the wheelbarrow were wrenched from his hands. Elizabeth Bennet's eyes flashed an angry orange as she fell along with the other enshrined heroes into oblivion. He watched everything that proved he ever had existed fall into the nothing below.

Behind him, he heard the remainder of his house collapse into the pit as well. He stood on a patch of wood in an open doorframe surrounded by a growing, gaping nothing.

He stared at the earth dropping away around him. He stared at the stars and the void, which were falling upward away from him.

As the ground under his feet dropped away, as he started his fall toward the deep nothing below, Larry didn't believe what he was seeing. Of course, he didn't believe mountains were real either, yet there they were, in plain sight, if only for a few seconds more.

2

Nilanjana Sikdar stared at the bacteria. The bacteria did not stare back. They vibrated around, without sentience.

The experiment had to do with a by-product of the bacteria, a substance that had applications as a pesticide for industrial farming. But at this moment Nilanjana was more worried about why they seemed to mostly be growing on one side of the dish. It didn't mean anything necessarily, although it could mean something. Anything could mean something to someone. But it looked uneven. It was out of place. She wished she could nudge some of the bacteria to the other side of the dish, but that wouldn't be scientific and anyway bacteria are difficult to nudge. Maybe she could tilt the dish slightly. Just to get some of the bacteria colonies to the bare side of the dish. Then it would be more even. It would be no more scientific than before, but it would look neater. No, she couldn't do that. Manually altering the bacteria's behavior would be wrong. She sighed. The bacteria would be uneven. She would learn to cope with this, as she had learned to cope with everything else that she had encountered in her life.

Living as she had for nearly four years in a town like Night Vale, there was always a great deal to cope with. Hauntings by vengeful ghosts. Abduction attempts by curious aliens. Municipal holidays with startling casualty rates. She had learned to cope with it all. But still, the bacteria bothered her more than she would have been able to admit to anyone.

She tilted the dish. She just wouldn't tell anyone. The bacteria stayed stubbornly on the left side of the dish.

She made a few notes in her notebook, which was lined up so that the dish and microscope were exactly at its center line. Once she was done writing, she returned her pen to its place, flush against the sides of the pages. Her desk was otherwise bare. She didn't need anything but her experiment and her notebook in order to do her work, and if she didn't need something then there was no reason to have it around. Her table was a gratifyingly empty rectangle, with the microscope and notebook straddling the center line.

Also a thin dribble of the growth solution, snaking its way toward the edge.

"Shit," she said.

"Huh," said Luisa.

She had the table next to Nilanjana. Luisa's experiment had something to do with being visibly disappointed in potatoes, and she was, even as she cocked her head toward Nilanjana, keeping up a performative scowl at the pile of spuds on her own table. Her table wasn't messy, except that any table would look messy next to Nilanjana's. Luisa's table looked messy. There was a stack of paper toppling slowly over the entire desk, and her potatoes were in a haphazard pile, placement randomly assigned so as not to affect the outcome of the experiment, whatever that was supposed to be.

"No," said Nilanjana. "Nothing. Well, I just spilled. I mean, just a bit." She pointed.

"I'm extremely disappointed in you," said Luisa.

"What?"

"Sorry, that was for the potatoes. I have to provide a verbal reminder of my disappointment at set intervals along with the visual cues. Just in case they respond mainly to sounds."

"Do they respond to sounds at all?"

"Only one way to find out," Luisa said brightly. Her face was still stern and frowning. She shook her head. "You're not living up to your potential."

"Do potatoes have a potential?"

"No, not them. You, Nils. What is that experiment you're doing anyway?"

"Ah, see, that's actually interesting. I'm adjusting the pH level of this growth material by an incremental amount each—"

"Nils, is that even science?"

"Yes."

"Is it? Oh, I'm still not sure what science is. That sounded more like performance art."

She poked at a potato and it rolled off to the side of the pile. She either didn't notice or didn't care.

"In any case, you shouldn't be wasting your time on tiny experiments like that one. You should be working bigger, more prestigious projects. The kind of stuff that wins awards. Like the Best Science Award. And the This Science Was Good award from the Society for Good Scientists. Look at me and the potatoes."

She made a gesture that invited Nilanjana's gaze, but Nilanjana was already looking at them, so she widened her eyes to indicate that she was looking even harder.

"Do you know how many grants I've gotten for this potato thing? All goes according to plan, I can spend the rest of my career being disappointed in these potatoes, and getting all the big media attention that goes along with it."

Nilanjana didn't care much for scientific grants and awards. There were many wealthy, tabloid-famous scientists, but that was not why she got into science. She simply wanted to study the nature of the world. She was happiest coming to the lab every day, working on her bacteria, developing fringe, noncommercial things that benefit society, like pharmaceutical drugs or pesticides.

She had been studying these bacteria for the past three years to develop a natural pesticide. Up until then, farmers mostly got rid of bugs by setting them on fire, but this tended to have an adverse effect on the crops the bugs lived on. She had made some breakthroughs. Earlier this year, she managed to create a spray solution that kept wood-boring beetles off of trees, but the beetles tended to scream when in contact with the spray. They screamed a lot. It was off-putting. So she was trying to refine the formula.

For her, science was a process toward perfection. Every answer created new questions, branching out to more and more answers. She wanted to fill in the empty circle of human knowledge with facts and evidence, so we didn't have to explain the unexplainable with conjecture and legend. The less of life that belonged to the realm of myth, the better off humanity would be. If there were prizes or cash grants for all of this, great. But Nilanjana wasn't looking for approval. She was looking for scientific order and tidy knowledge.

"Right. But, Luisa. See. I like this experiment. It's interesting. And if it's interesting, it's important. That's what Carlos always says."

"Oh, Carlos. He's a great scientist, Nils, but he doesn't have the head for the career stuff. Stick with me. I'll help you get there."

"Okay, yeah, but." Nilanjana indicated her dish of bacteria, which was when there was a sudden, ear-crushing bang followed by a fluorescent flash, and her hand flinched right into the dish, knocking the whole thing over.

"Sorry!" said Mark. His station was behind them both, and he had invented a machine that was supposed to make a blinding flash followed by a startling bang, but it had been getting the order wrong for weeks now.

"Oh, now. Goddammit," Nilanjana said. "That was a month's work right there. I need a paper towel. Excuse me."

Luisa shrugged.

"Suit yourself. Let me know if you ever want more advice. I just want what's best for you, and you're letting all of us down."

"That's a bit strong, we barely—"

"No, I'm sorry, Nils. That was for the potatoes again."

Nilanjana stood to get something to wipe the spreading mess on her desk. There was growth solution on practically all of a small part of the table. It was overwhelming.

Mark winced apologetically as she passed him.

"Sorry about that. I should have sounded the warning air horn right behind you to let you know I was about to test this, but you know how it is. I got caught up in the experiment."

She nodded, waving the slight away with her hand. She knew exactly how it was. She liked Mark, and was sorry his experiment wasn't going well, even if his tinkering on it was liable to cause her serious psychological or physical harm.

"Don't listen to her," he said, as he unscrewed a hatch on his machine, trying to understand what the problem was. Its light weakly flickered and it let out an unstartling burble. He shook his head. "At least that was in the right order," he muttered.

"I can listen to her but not listen to her, you know?" said

Nilanjana. "I'm proud of my experiment. It's about something that interests me and it works. Or it worked. It worked until I knocked it over."

She opened up the lab's emergency station, which contained a roll of paper towels and nothing else.

"Or I don't know. I guess maybe that's what I do, you know? I work on small experiments by myself. Maybe that's just what's in store for me. That would be okay."

"Whatever makes you happy, Nils." He poked at the machine with a screwdriver. "Not being flippant. Really whatever makes you happy. Are you happy?"

"I'm fine." She glanced back at the small dribble of growth solution on the table, shuddered, and spooled a large portion of the paper towel roll around her hand, tearing it off with a hard tug. "I don't need to be happy when I'm fine."

As she wiped the growth solution up with the huge wad of paper in her hand, she considered whether she was even fine. How was someone supposed to know that? What was the objective test of happiness, let alone fineness? What data could be collected? Could "fine" even be demonstrated objectively?

She considered the other scientists. There were several tables around the large lab, each with a scientist working on their own experiment. Some of the experiments sparked or sang, others oozed or gelled. Only some of the experiments thought or felt. On one wall was a whiteboard with various project names and experimental observations. "Bees?" said one. "Hypothesis: Everything is frightening and we should hide," said another.

The lab was in the science district, a rough, industrial part of town, made dangerous by frequent feuds between rival groups of scientists. Astronomers and ornithologists in particular were always picking fights with each other, street corner ambushes that would start with the reading aloud of peer-reviewed research papers and end with the thrust of a broken bottle. Nilanjana stayed out of these disputes, but it was still unsettling walking by a faint bloodstain or the torn page of a thesis, marking the site of a particularly violent battle.

Still, she was fine with it. She was fine with her experiment. She was fine with Luisa and Mark. She was fine sitting in a large room full of smart people she respected, even if she didn't know them well. She was fine coming to work and talking about science, or maybe just life. She was fine going home alone at night and not being in a room full of people. She was fine limiting the people she knew to select hours of the day and then restricting them from other hours of the day when she could be by herself. She was fine being an outsider—the people of Night Vale regularly reminded her she was not from here. She had always been an outsider, and this was fine. She was fine growing up a girl who liked killing bugs and looking in microscopes and organizing microbes into even patterns. She was fine not having friends who understood or liked this. She was fine not being picked on or derided, but also not being invited to parties. Maybe she wasn't happy. Maybe what she was doing wasn't important or helping anyone. But it was fine. "I'm fine," she was fine with telling herself.

"Nilanjana?" said a smooth, oaky voice. She looked up from her table, which she had been wiping over and over with the paper towels, not even noticing the motion of her arm.

Carlos was standing in the door of his office. He looked frightened. No, concerned. No, frightened.

"Nilanjana, can you come in here? I need your opinion on . . . Just come in here please."

Carlos did not often call other scientists into his private lab.

That was where he did his own special experiments, ones that involved the saving of Night Vale from the various supernatural threats that besieged it, and also where he put together construction paper collage love notes for his husband. It was all important work and he preferred to not be disturbed. Nilanjana couldn't remember the last time she had been asked into his office.

If she had known all the events that would spiral out from the conversation she was about to have, she would have felt terrified, and maybe overjoyed, and terrified all over again. She would have felt so many things she hadn't felt since coming to this strange town where she didn't quite belong. As it was, she only felt confused.

"Sure," she said. "I'll be right in."

"Ugh," said Luisa, waving dismissively at her potatoes.

3

Nilanjana had no interest in Carlos and anyway he was married to the local community radio host, Cecil Palmer. Still, she couldn't *not* notice that he was, in his way, stunningly handsome. Even his frown was perfect, and he ran his hands perfectly through his perfect hair.

In science, of course, there's always a lot of pressure to look good. Appearances are a major part of a science career, and top scientists face all sorts of accusations of plastic surgery and unhealthy diets, a constant scrutiny in gossip magazines and tabloid blogs. But Carlos stayed out of all that. He was a beautiful person, but that never interested him much. He only cared about two things: his scientific work, and his family.

Nilanjana didn't know Carlos's family well. She knew his teenage niece, Janice, was born with spina bifida, and while her frequent checkups of eyes, kidneys, and spine came back healthy each time, Carlos would take days off work to be with her and his brother- and sister-in-law.

Nilanjana knew that his husband, Cecil, sometimes faced serious dangers as a reporter in a town as full of terrible secrets as Night Vale, and those dangers sent Carlos into a worried stupor. He would pace about the office, trying not to call the station to ask if Cecil was okay. Not much got done in the lab when Carlos fretted for Cecil's safety. She could tell when

Carlos had a date night planned, because he put gel in his hair and wore his most striking lab coat.

She was uncertain why Carlos wanted to talk to her now. She hoped that the problem was with his scientific work. She didn't have much to say on the subject of being in love. Not that she hadn't had boyfriends. She was a human being of adult age with an interest in other human beings, and she had been in relationships starting from high school. But she did not feel qualified to offer advice on the subject. She was just stumbling along, the same as anyone. It was occasionally fun and often lonely, whether she was with someone at the time or not.

Carlos interrupted this reverie by pulling down a chart that said in large letters SCIENCE.

"Today's topic of discussion is science. I've provided a visual aid."

Oh thank god.

He gestured for her to sit, but she didn't like sitting much, and so she gestured that she would rather stand, and there was some gesturing back and forth that neither of them understood. Finally, Carlos sat and she remained standing.

"I know you are aware of the house," he began.

"The general concept of houses?"

"No, uh, sorry, the house that doesn't exist."

He pulled down another chart. It had a picture of a house on it.

"Yes," she said, "I know that house. It doesn't exist. It looks like it exists. Like it's right there when you look at it, and it's between two other identical houses, so it would make more sense for it to be there than not, but . . ."

". . . it doesn't actually exist," he finished.

"Right. It's a weird house. Or it isn't a weird house. It's weird but not a house? Hard to know how to talk about it."

Everyone in town knew about the house that looks like it exists but doesn't. There was a common dare among scientists to knock on the door and then run away. Carlos himself had once entered the house. He didn't talk much about this. Anytime the topic came up, he would wave it off or try to change the subject.

What Nilanjana had learned from his research notes was that its interior was entirely different from that of the common prefab house it seemed to be when one peered through its windows. Seen from the inside, the house contained no furniture, and no decorations, except a small black-and-white photo of a lighthouse. The house was not a house but an entryway to a desert otherworld: vast and empty. There was a single mountain in that otherworld, and it was completely believable to all who saw it. At the top of the mountain was the lighthouse from the photo. There had been a cold light emanating from all around, though the sun was never visible.

Hypothesis: The desert otherworld had been cold and empty, and had made Carlos feel lost to the people he loved. Carlos cared more than anything about the people he loved, and so a place with no one and nothing in it had been traumatizing for him.

Ever since Carlos's return from the otherworld a few years back, everyone in the lab knew he had been obsessed with the house. And like most obsessions with the truth, this had made the City Council nervous.

"Your job is being a scientist," the council had told him via an empty-eyed child messenger who had helpfully lunged out at him from the shower when he had gotten up to pee in the middle of the night. "So look pretty and write papers. Don't go searching around for the 'truth.' You're a scientist, not a snoop."

"Man," said Nilanjana, as he told her about the message from the council.

"Yes, it was upsetting," said Carlos. "And then of course I was stuck with an empty-eyed child messenger, and you know how long it takes the City Council to come back around and pick them up. We ended up having to give her rides to school for the next three weeks. We're going to her eighth-grade graduation tomorrow."

"Oh cute."

"Supercute. But I won't let the City Council dissuade me from preventing anyone else from being hurt by that other-world. They've been trying to stop me."

It went like this.

Carlos had come up with the idea of performing measurements on the house that doesn't exist, using a wall-size machine in his office. The machine employed radar and microwaves and lasers to take measurements, spitting out numbers and making a high-pitched whirring sound.

Often, especially on hot days, the windows of the house that didn't exist were left open in the front living room, and he could try to get a reading of the distance between the house's nonexistent exterior and its parallel universe interior. A check for entrances into parallel universes and laser readings of their depths are common parts of any new home inspection, and so he had just applied this construction tool to his experimental problems. If one looked through the window, it seemed like a typical living room: armchair, settee, loudspeaker without volume control for the distribution of government propaganda, emergency backup settee. The usual stuff. But he knew this was only an optical illusion, which is a fancy, scientific phrase for a lie.

When he had switched his machine on, things had gone all wrong. There was a rumbling, deep from below the sand of the desert. It shook the ground. It was almost like an earthquake, but not human-made or scheduled on the municipal community calendar like a normal earthquake. The vibration and noise had made all of his readings useless.

Science was meant to be hard. After all, what was science but a bunch of bored human beings trying to challenge themselves when faith became too easy? So he had set up the machine again, carefully calibrating it, and then turning it on. Again, the moment after his finger hit the switch, there had been the rumble. The experiment was ruined.

"Someone is watching me. Every time I try to do the experiment, the rumbling starts up and ruins it. Someone doesn't want this house investigated. I think whoever is trying to stop me has their own counteractive machine to disrupt my research."

He pulled down a third chart, this one a map of where the rumblings had been concentrated. A series of orange blotches in the desert, surrounding the town.

"Along with the seismic action to throw off my numbers, there appears to have been violent displacement of earth. People have gone missing."

"But who would want to cover up the truth?" asked Nilanjana. "Besides the Secret Police, the City Council, the mayor, any number of world governments, and the invading forces from other worlds?"

"Exactly," Carlos said. "The City Council is the most likely, since they had already warned me."

Carlos had demanded an audience with the City Council, a brave move. Whatever multiform, extradimensional beast inhabited the council chambers, issuing forth smoke and brimstone and city ordinances, it had a ravenous taste for humans. But Carlos put science and his community before all other concerns, so he had taken a flame-retardant lab coat, slipped on a blindfold to keep him from the horror of seeing the writhing forms of the council, and gone to City Hall.

"Who is doing this?" he had demanded.

"Doing what?" the City Council had said in many-voiced, multipitched, surround-sound unison. "We've been on vacation recently. We haven't done anything. Just what are you accusing us of?"

"Ruining my experiments on the house that doesn't exist. Preventing me from understanding what I need to understand."

The council had hissed.

"You were told to drop this. Our patience is limited."

"So you *have* been disrupting my experiments with this rumbling under the earth?"

"Foolish scientist. Seeker of truth. You think you are the only one interested in that house? There are many who seek to exploit the power it holds."

"What power? What people?"

"We have said too much. We should devour you. But there are influential members of the media protecting you, and it wouldn't be worth the grief we'd get from them. Flee while you have your life."

"What is the power of the house? What do you know?"

The council had roared. A moist, spongy hand had slipped around his neck.

"The Wordsmith warned us of what is waiting to enter our

city. You are peeking through doors that should not be opened. Cease your research or it will be ceased for you."

The wet fingers had tightened. Carlos had backed away. The fingers had loosened as he stepped, letting him go. He was left with a smell like a leaking battery, an acid smell he tasted on the back of his tongue.

"The Wordsmith?" said Nilanjana. Despite herself, she was leaning on the desk, caught up in the story. "Who is that?"

"Have no idea," said Carlos. "Never heard that phrase before. Yet another mystery. Mystery upon mystery upon mystery."

He pulled a cord, and all three charts rolled themselves back up with a snap.

"It seems that these inquiries have hit a point at which I can no longer continue."

"You can't give up because the City Council says you have to."

"I'm afraid, Nils, that that is exactly what I have to do."

He sighed, and got up, looking out the window at the cracked asphalt of the strip mall where his laboratory was located. There were a few cars in the parking lot. Famished citizens stopping by for a slice from Big Rico's Pizza next door. Teenagers looking for a quiet place to make out or to stare in mutual fear at the vastness of the night sky. The unmarked black sedans full of bland-faced besuited government agents listening to every word anyone said.

"Science is a quest for truth, without compromise. But science must be done within human life. And human life is entirely compromised. Especially life here, in our watchful little town."

He tilted his head at the black sedans. He turned back to her. He mouthed, *Do you understand?*

She nodded.

"Nils, I would never ask you to help me continue this experiment. I would never ask you to try to find the source of the rumbling. It would be dangerous to push on this matter. If I did ask, you would have every right to walk out that door and go back to your bacteria."

"Why would you ask me, and not one of the other scientists?" she asked. "I mean, if you were to actually continue this experiment, which you are clearly not."

From outside his office, there was a sudden loud bang and a bright flash visible below the door. They could hear Luisa shout, "You're such a disappointment!" It was unclear if that was directed at Mark or at a potato.

Carlos glanced briefly toward the door and then back at Nilanjana. He smiled at her and held out his hand. She took his hand and gave a knowing nod.

An experiment that was being prevented. On a house that did not exist. A mystery the City Council was afraid of. And a person or entity going by the name Wordsmith. It seemed opaque, impossible.

But the study of science had taught her how to handle the impossible. Collect data. Form hypotheses. Test the hypotheses. Use what you learn to collect more data. And soon, the impossible would reveal itself to be a thin and pliable barrier.

She would start with the most objective, measurable part of the story. The rumblings out in the desert.

"I'm afraid I cannot help you," she said, going to the door. "If you'll excuse me, I need to get rid of my bacteria and go to the desert. I have some personal matters I need to attend to."

Thank you, he mouthed.

She swept her useless, ruined experiment off her desk into the bin—Luisa throwing her a confused sideways glance, briefly breaking her frozen expression of disappointment—and went out to her car.

Nilanjana found herself laughing as she turned on the engine. She laughed with real joy, without understanding why she felt that joy.

What was she getting herself into? She laughed happily. She had no idea.

4

Darryl Ramirez told the barista who overfilled his Americano that it was totally fine. It could happen to anyone, and he shouldn't beat himself up about it. But the barista glared at him and rolled his eyes, wiped away the coffee in a few quick, angry movements, and then thrust the cup at him. Darryl found himself apologizing even though it was his coffee that had been spilled.

Darryl was legitimately sorry. He had meant it all earnestly, but something in his demeanor made other people assume he was being sarcastic or false. What had been an honest attempt to make the barista feel better about his mistake had instead come across as a taunt about the barista's inability to correctly do what is, despite Barista Local 485's constant and loud insistences, a pretty simple job. He thanked the barista and then said, "Believe in a Smiling God, my friend," while making a circling motion with his upright fist. But the barista was already making someone else's drink.

It was his years in the church that had done it, Darryl thought. The church urged all its members to present a happy face to the world, which had the noble intention of spreading joy, but ultimately valued outside presentation over an honest connection to a person's feelings. Which meant that even when he actually felt a positive feeling, it tended to come off false to anyone outside of the Joyous Congregation of the Smiling God. Or maybe, he thought, he was just bad at connecting with people. At least, in person. He had early on in his life taken to writing notes when he had something important to say, so that his inflection and facial expression wouldn't affect the message he was conveying.

Nilanjana looked up when she heard his voice and, seeing the barista's reaction, assumed that Darryl had been yelling at him. Yelling at baristas wasn't uncommon in Night Vale. This was not because the baristas were bad at their jobs or unlikable people. Quite the opposite. Night Vale's barista district was densely populated with talented coffee makers and aficionados. There was a single block of Galloway Road that had six coffee shops on it. For a desert community, people took their hot coffee quite seriously.

It was because of the general politeness and the talent of the baristas that customers were so hard on them. With so many coffee shops, it was a consumers' market. Plus, it is basic human nature to treat polite people worse than rude people. It is easier to assert dominance over a person unlikely to fight back with much force. Rude people tend to fight hard, and it's not worth stirring them up.

Nilanjana watched Darryl, whom she was pretty sure she had met before, put a single drop of cream into his coffee and then carefully stir. She related to his level of exactness and order. She resented him for it as well.

She had gone to the desert directly from the lab, but the location where Carlos had detected rumbling recently was crawling with agents from a vague yet menacing government agency. This wasn't surprising. Agents from whatever agency it was tended to closely investigate and document any new activity in town. They would be done soon, and she would have the site to herself. In the meantime, she had gone to her favorite coffee shop, the Spikey Hammer, to get out of the heat and to sit doing nothing at a table so she wouldn't have to sit doing nothing in her car.

Her coffee was huge, a twenty-ounce filter coffee (espresso takes too long) with exactly two tablespoons of milk and three packets of sugar. Sometimes she would put in a half teaspoon of whatever spices the coffee shop had out: cinnamon, nutmeg, paprika, metal shavings, etc. She just wanted hot caffeine, and any extra flavors that could make the stuff drinkable were a bonus. She brought her own measuring spoons to coffee shops to ensure the precision of her routine.

The notes from this morning's meeting with Carlos were neatly set out in front of her, her pen lying across her hand, which was lying across the page as if writing, but she was lost in no thought, staring at no one thing. She had been watching Darryl, trying to decide whether she knew him somehow. His intense awkwardness with the barista, but then his kindness, and then his apparent religious zeal. Thinking about the myriad ways she might have previously met a stranger, her mind drifted. She had been looking at him, but now she was staring at the empty space where he had been: a series of flyers pinned to a bulletin board.

One of them read: LEARN TO PLAY THE GUITAR! And then in smaller print: "According to City Ordinance 12.546B, enacted on August 1, the crime of not knowing how to play guitar is punishable by a maximum fine of $12,000 and 3 years in prison. Learn to play the guitar today!"

There was another that had a picture of a bike on it: "Have you seen this bike? It never existed in this universe, in this time line. If you have seen this bike, please contact me immediately. I need to return home." There was no name or contact information.

She heard Darryl's voice again. He was talking to another patron in the cafe. He was making that circling fist gesture and then handing them a small brochure. He was smiling meaningfully. The other person was smiling without meaning. They said, "Stop it," and then covered their ears and shook their head until Darryl stopped talking and walked away.

He approached multiple people in the cafe, each time asking, "Do you know about the Smiling God?" and then doing the fist thing. One person made the fist gesture back to him. They made eye contact and hummed a single low note in unison for ten seconds before breaking off and continuing with their activities as if they had not seen each other at all. Darryl glanced at his watch and then started a conversation with another stranger.

The watch reminded Nilanjana of how she knew Darryl. About two years ago, she and a fellow scientist, Connie, were doing a study on time, examining clocks and watches they'd purchased at various stores across town. Darryl worked at one such store (Watch Yourself).

He had disagreed with her that time was weird. She had tried to explain the science to him, showing him charts and digital models which demonstrated that each unit of time stays the same, and that time moves forward for people in most of the world, but that in Night Vale, it was changing constantly, sometimes minutes going backward or skipping forward, moving differently for each person. Some people would stay nineteen years old for centuries without aging. Nilanjana and Connie had been studying a few such extreme cases, but Darryl was impervious to logic. He believed only what he felt was true: Time was totally normal.

She returned to her notes and plan of action for studying the rumbling in the desert, but she was still replaying those old, frustrating conversations about time in her mind. Distracted, she bumped her coffee reaching for her notes and let out a slight yelp.

People in the coffee shop looked at Nilanjana. She had been in this town four years. Or it had felt like four years. Time, despite Darryl's insistence, was weird here, and so she had no idea exactly how long it had been since her arrival.

"Interloper!" cried one person. Another followed suit. They were pointing at her. "Interloper!" came another shout.

The fuss didn't build much past that. It was a weekday morning. People had work, lots of things on their minds. Getting into a frenzied mob was not top of their list. Besides, a few of these people knew Nilanjana. She'd been to the Spikey Hammer many times. There was no way they hadn't seen her in the years she'd lived in Night Vale.

Still, even if they had recognized her, they had pointed and shouted. She had come to this town for the same reason all scientists came here: because it was the most scientifically interesting place in America. And it had not disappointed in that regard. But there was also a real sense of community. People belonged here, and loved each other, and knew their neighbors. And it was on this count that she felt she was not getting the full experience. Even after four years, she found herself confused by simple things that longtime residents took for granted.

"But why are writing implements outlawed?" she would ask, and Michelle at Dark Owl Records or Frances Donaldson, who owned the Antiques Mall, or whomever she was talking to at the time would give her a funny look and say, "Because they're illegal."

Then Nilanjana would ask why all the road signs had been replaced by tired city workers waving traffic instructions using semaphore flags, and the person she was talking to would sigh and say, "Why is the sky blue? Why is the moon fake? Why anything?" or else would just point at her and start chanting, "Interloper!"

She'd asked Carlos about it. "You're not from here either. You must get this interloper shit all the time. What's these people's deal?"

Carlos said he didn't get the interloper stuff much since he'd started dating Cecil, and once they had gotten married it had stopped completely. "Guess I'm finally one of them," he said, in an offhanded way that manifested in Nilanjana's chest as a pang of jealousy. He had gone on to explain that the "interloper" thing was their form of a friendly greeting. He had once sneezed in an ice cream shop only to be surrounded by a dozen shouts of "Interloper" followed by the small crowd picking him up and carrying him through the streets. He had been terrified, but then they got tired and set him down several blocks away.

It was kind of the Night Vale equivalent of "bless you," Carlos had told her. "Don't worry about it. I'm sure you'll be settled down here soon enough."

"It's been four years!" she had said. He had stopped what he was doing and turned to her, considering her kindly over his glasses.

"Maybe it's not about them accepting you. Maybe you have to accept them first."

She did accept them. Why else would she move here to study them? But, if she was honest with herself, the messy strangeness of the town, where any explanation given for an unusual event would be immediately contradicted by some other unusual event, was an affront to her need for order and neatness.

"I think I accept them," she had said. "It's pretty weird here though, right?"

He had nodded gravely.

"It is *super*weird," he had said, turning back to his work.

She was glad Carlos was so chipper about it. It must be easier, she thought, because men don't feel as threatened by shouts on the street as women do. Also, he has a husband, and the security of a relationship can make you feel at home, like there's someone who has your back. Carlos could have the worst day and still return home to Cecil. Someone would be there to at least hear you say, "Hey, I'm having a tough go of it. Can you just listen to me talk for a bit?"

That's worth something, Nilanjana thought. She herself still didn't even have a close friend in town. She and Connie had been on good terms when they were working together, but Connie had also been an outsider, and anyway later she had vanished while investigating a bizarre case involving plastic flamingos. Since then, Nilanjana hadn't talked much with anyone while outside the lab. No wonder people pointed at her and shouted "Interloper!"

The coffee crowd had quieted down. A few were still pointing and staring at her, but without the same zeal as before. As she turned back to her notes, she felt someone next to her. She saw the shadow cast across her papers and heard a bright sing-song voice: "Can I talk to you about the Smiling God?" She saw his shadow do that fist thing. There was something about the brightness in his voice that came off as false to her.

"Darryl, right?" She spoke quickly, hoping to derail his religious pitch.

He searched her face. He was still smiling, but it was all muscle memory.

"Yes, hi. I remember you," he said, almost convincingly.

"Nila——"

"Nilanjana, yes!"

"Interloper," someone else said.

"How nice to see you again." There was a pause where people would normally hug or shake hands, but they didn't do either of those things and so a couple of polite, empty beats passed.

"Anyone biting?" Nilanjana asked, indicating his pamphlets.

"Well, it's not about bites. I don't have a sales goal or anything. I just want to make sure people know about this great organization. Maybe it can save their lives like it did mine."

"Cool. Fight the good fight. Say, what time is it?"

He looked at his watch. "It's ten thirty. Am I keeping you?"

She wrote "10:30" in her notebook. "Not yet. So you come to coffee shops and hand out religious information for . . ."

"The Joyous Congregation of the Smiling God. Here." He handed her a tract.

In one smooth gesture, she took the booklet from his hand and placed it straight into her bag, never breaking eye contact with Darryl. "I'll give it a read."

"My parents were in the Congregation. I didn't like it much growing up. You know how it is when you're a kid. I got impatient listening to sermons and going to church camp and all that. But when my parents died . . ."

"Oh, I'm so sorry to hear that."

"It's fine. It's been twelve years. But after their accident, everyone in the church really helped me. Some of my friends and their parents let me live with them while I got through high school. My parents didn't leave behind much money, but the church got together to help pay for things like clothes and food and even college. I owe everything to that community. So I do what I can to help others find their way to it. It's a good church. Good people."

"Sounds like it."

"You can read about it more in that booklet."

"Well, cool to see you again, Darryl." She was putting her things into her bag. "I need to be going."

"Of course. Blessings." He did that circling fist thing.

"You too. Hey, what time is it?"

"It's ten twenty-eight. Hope I haven't made you late."

"Nah. I'll be fine." She grinned as she wrote "10:28" in her notebook, carefully placed it into its specified pocket in her bag, and stood up. Time is weird, Darryl, she thought. "Good luck with . . ." she said, indicating the room of potential converts in the coffee shop, "all this."

She walked out the cafe door to a few last noncommittal calls of "Interloper" and the ding of the door chime. The day smelled of juniper and pine. As she drove the empty roads out in the scrublands toward the desert, Nilanjana watched the clouds drifting backward under the morning sky.

5

Agents from a vague yet menacing government agency had finished going over the site, and had placed tape around the entire area that said, TOP SECRET! PLEASE DON'T GO NEAR OR EVEN LOOK FOR TOO LONG! Nilanjana pulled the tape aside. All of the agents would be off investigating the next new event in Night Vale, and none of them would stick around to enforce their cordon.

The pit was larger than she had imagined. Based on the data, she had been picturing a hole the size of a car, maybe a little larger. But the pit was at least the size of a house, maybe even larger than that. In fact, it was almost exactly the size of a house and a yard. She considered the mailbox, which was leaning steeply over the drop like a daredevil preparing to jump.

Looking around, she realized where she was with a feeling that wasn't grief but was adjacent to it. There was the used car dealership, and beyond that Old Woman Josie's house. Which meant that this was the house of Larry Leroy. Or it had been Larry's house. Now the house, and presumably Larry, was gone. She didn't know Larry well because she didn't know any of her fellow townspeople well. But he had always seemed kind and restrained. She had liked that he didn't seem to need anyone else's approval or disapproval to live. He just did his thing here on the edge of town, right up until whatever tragedy had occurred.

She unpacked her supplies from the stash of tools and materials she kept in her trunk: decibel meter, a number of glass jars to take earth samples, and a thick metal box with a series of blinking lights across the front and unmarked colored buttons on the top. In a place as scientifically interesting as Night Vale, she had learned that it was best to always keep her entire field kit with her in case, say, a time traveler appeared with a warning from the future, or a dog stood on its hind legs and began speaking, both of which had happened in front of her during her stay in town. Both times, she had no equipment with which to study the phenomena, and she had promised herself that a lapse like that would never happen again.

The box was not technically a computer. It was just a box with blinking lights that helped process data. The Night Vale government did not easily give out permits for owning computers, so scientists, mathematicians, computer programmers, and video game lovers had to do one of the following:

1. Try to do all of their work by hand. This was frustrating for computer programmers in particular.
2. Wait out the long, bureaucratic process for getting a computer permit. The several-month wait often ended in rejection based on some tiny paperwork issue.
3. Jump through the semantic loopholes of what is or isn't a computer. For example, a phone is not a computer, depending on how you use it. Nilanjana's metal box with blinking lights isn't a computer, just a novelty device. Some birds aren't computers, but, of course, most are, and only the government can own or produce birds.

Carlos circumvented his lack of computer permits by segmenting the computing process into dozens of esoteric machines, each of which could have been mistaken for something much simpler and less regulated, like a boom box, a homemade bomb, or a snow globe.

Nilanjana was from Indiana originally, where computers were legal. No government agency put any kind of restriction on what sorts of computers you had, or how many. That was left to the giant corporations who controlled the availability of information, helpfully colluding to fix prices for consumers, and thus keeping information freely available to those who could afford it. This had seemed the natural way of things, until she had learned about the town of Night Vale. She hadn't actually learned about it so much as suddenly knew about it. No one else in Indiana had ever heard of such a place, or could find any record of it online. But one day she knew it existed and that it was the most scientifically interesting place in America. Even though she had no map or directions to guide her when she left home, driving in no specific direction, she eventually arrived in Night Vale. This was a typical story for residents of Night Vale who had not grown up in the area.

There was no natural way of things here, only the capricious whims of competing global conspiracies. She was no more used to it now than when she had arrived. She supposed she never would be.

She set the metal blinking box on the sand at the edge of the hole and pressed a few of the colored buttons on top. The box shook almost imperceptibly, just a tight hum, like a bug zapper.

While the box did its analysis, she did a visual sweep of the site. The walls of the pit didn't taper much; they were nearly vertical. The pit floor was flat and looked damp. The pit itself was shallow for its size. Even if the house had fallen, debris from it should be easily visible. But it was as though the house had been swallowed whole. Or not swallowed. Swallowed seemed to assume something living, animal, and that was a bad assumption. She tried to think of a better word for *swallowed* and gave up around *consumed*. The house was gone, and she needed to figure out where it went.

She put on gloves and took some of the moist dirt from the side of the pit. The moisture felt viscous, dense. Not like mud. It wasn't so much that the soil had gotten wet, but that it had melted somehow. It was hot in her hands. Hotter even than the desert ground around it. She tried to write a note in her journal about this, but her latex gloves were sticky. The soil had fused to her gloves like tar.

Nilanjana gathered more dirt, some rocks, three lizards who were oblivious to the direction their lives were about to go, and a piece of cactus. As she worked, she thought she heard an intermittent noise mixed in with the wind. Like the gears of a machine, or like the scampering of a mouse. It seemed to be coming from below her, but every time she stopped to listen she would lose track of it. As a scientist, she had no choice but to doubt that she was hearing anything at all.

Hypothesis: The complete disappearance of the house, property, and body of Larry Leroy had set her on edge, and ordinary background noises that would usually be tuned out were being magnified and analyzed by her overactive mind.

She sat on a rock near the hole trying to write up notes for her report, but instead hovered her pen over the page, not certain how to frame her experiment. It was difficult to know what hypothesis these samples and anecdotes were supporting.

There was a house that didn't exist. It was a gateway to another desert world, where Carlos had once been trapped for a year. When he tried to investigate the house, or anything to do with the otherworld, these rumblings would start up, ruining the experiment and disappearing some part of Night Vale. Then city officials demanded he stop meddling.

Hypothesis: The City Council was using some unknown force to stop Carlos from investigating the otherworld.

Supporting evidence: The City Council had repeatedly told him to stop. They had connections with any number of government agencies and higher orders of the lizard people that could have caused the disaster, the aftermath of which she was currently sitting in. And then there was this Wordsmith who had provided some vital piece of information to the City Council, which had led them to order Carlos to stop his experiments. What was this Wordsmith's goal? Who did they work for?

"We will not let that thing into our city," the council had said to Carlos. What was "that thing"? Here she came back to words like *swallow, consume, devour*. These were not objective terms. They made assumptions she could not support. She tried to push them away. *We will not let that thing into our city.*

She looked across the empty scrublands, flat and drab, save the occasional newly formed hole caused by earthquakes or weapons tests or meteor showers or something. Or, she tried not to think, some Thing. But she had no evidence for that. She was looking at holes in the ground and her mind was showing her monsters. She heard the noise again, like hundreds of little legs, or like an engine right below her feet. No, she was being oversensitive to noise. The sound was just the helicopter overhead. There were always helicopters overhead. They were normal parts of everyday life.

The clouds had all disappeared and the wind was gone. The quiet of the desert and the endless sameness of the sky made the helicopter stand out. It made her stand out too. She tried to look casual, natural. It was important to not seem like she was looking at the helicopter, as that would be suspicious. But it would also be suspicious to not acknowledge the helicopter, as it was just the two of them together and alone in the scrublands.

She did what polite strangers do. She acknowledged the other. Shading her eyes from the bright sun, wincing under the cloudless white sky, she waved. "Hello, helicopter! How's it going up there?" she called, certain the person flying that thing could not hear her over the noise of the motor.

"Hello, Interloper. It's going fine up here. Thanks," came the call of an electric bullhorn.

Staring straight up toward the sky, the sun was too bright for her. She dug into her bag to get her sunglasses. When she pulled them out, some paper fell to the dirt below.

"What's that?" the helicopter called out. An antenna popped out of the helicopter's side, scanning the paper with a red laser grid.

She picked the paper up. It was the tract from Darryl's Joyous Congregation of the Smiling God. The metal box was still beeping, and Nilanjana knew it was quite a way from finishing its analysis, whatever it was. She knew she was far from understanding all of the evidence, whatever that might be.

"Just some religious tract a guy at the coffee shop handed me," she said.

"Cool."

"Just some guy," she said, unnecessarily.

"Oh."

Nilanjana opened the booklet. The pilot circled and descended, hovering behind her. Together, she and the pilot read about the Joyous Congregation.

| ARE YOU **SAD?** | ARE YOU **NOT** SAD? |

HOW DO YOU KNOW?

MANY OF US ARE **SAD** OR **NOT** SAD,
OR **DON'T KNOW** IF WE'RE SAD.

IF THIS SOUNDS LIKE YOU, THEN WE'D LIKE
TO TELL YOU A STORY. IT'S AN IMPORTANT
STORY, PROBABLY THE MOST IMPORTANT
STORY THERE IS.

THE STORY OF
THE SMILING GOD

BEFORE *ANYTHING,*

THERE WAS *NOTHING.*

THEN CAME EVERYTHING.

**BUT ALL ALONG THERE WAS
THE SMILING GOD.**

THE SMILING GOD HAS ALWAYS BEEN
HERE. YOU WON'T BE ABLE TO SEE IT
WITH YOUR EYES (NOT AT FIRST!) BUT
ALL AROUND YOU IS ITS POWER. THE
SMILING GOD LOVES YOU AND WANTS
YOU TO BE HAPPY.

WHERE DOES THE SMILING GOD LIVE?
TO ANSWER THAT, JUST
THINK ABOUT THE EARTH.

THEN THINK ABOUT
UNDERNEATH THE EARTH.

YES, THAT'S RIGHT!

THE SMILING GOD LIVES
UNDERNEATH THE EARTH.

THE SMILING GOD USED TO LIVE WITH US AND INTERACT WITH US DIRECTLY, BUT WE WERE NOT READY FOR ITS MANIFEST BLESSINGS, SO IT HAD TO GO AWAY.

BUT IT STILL SHINES ITS LIGHT ON US DAILY.

NO, NOT THE SUN!

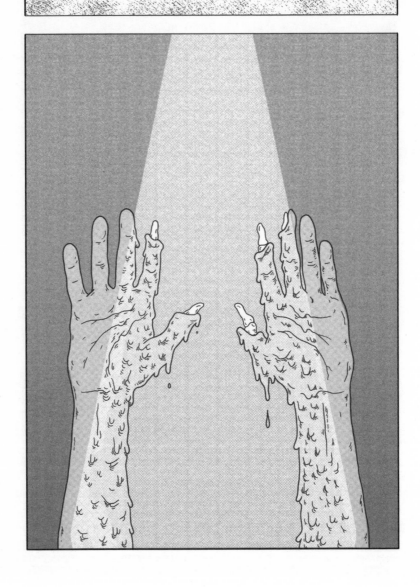

YOU KNOW THAT LIGHT THAT SOMETIMES SHINES OUT OF CUPBOARDS AND BASEMENTS, A COLD LIGHT THAT SEARS YOUR FLESH WITH ITS COLDNESS? THE LIGHT THAT COMES ON ALL AT ONCE AND MAKES YOU FEEL EMPTY, THAT GOES OUT ALL AT ONCE AND HAS NO SOURCE?

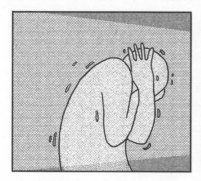 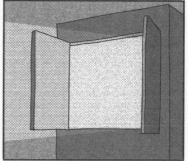

THAT IS THE LIGHT OF THE SMILING GOD. ALREADY YOU SEE PROOF OF ITS POWER. *WHAT A BLESSING!*

IF YOU ACCEPT THE SMILING GOD INTO YOUR HEART, AND ACCEPT AS MUCH OF ITS LIGHT AS YOU CAN STAND WITHOUT YOUR SKIN BLISTERING OR SLOUGHING OFF, THEN IT WILL TAKE YOUR WORRIES AND YOUR PROBLEMS AND IT WILL RISE UP AND CONSUME THEM.

BUT WHAT DOES THIS HAVE TO DO WITH ME?

ALL OF US, EVERY SINGLE ONE, HAS THE OPPORTUNITY AND THE RESPONSIBILITY TO GIVE OURSELVES TO THE SMILING GOD.

WE DO THIS THROUGH FAITH, WORSHIP, AN ANNUAL SEQUENCE OF BLOOD-LETTING, AND, OF COURSE, BY HELPING THOSE AROUND US FIND ITS LOVE AS WELL.

YOUR SINS? **IT WILL DEVOUR THEM.** YOUR UNWANTED DESIRES? **IT WILL DEVOUR THEM.** YOUR REGRETS AND YOUR WORST MEMORIES, THE THINGS YOU WISH YOU DID AND DIDN'T, AND THE THINGS YOU WISH YOU DIDN'T AND DID, **IT WILL DEVOUR ALL OF THEM.** IT DOES THIS FOR YOU, AND ITS SMILE NEVER WAVERS. **IT WILL DEVOUR.** IT WILL DO SO WITH GREAT JOY. A BLESSING TO ALL OF US.

WE ARE BLESSED BY ITS HUNGER. BY ITS SMILE. LET US LIVE IN THE LOVE OF THE SMILING GOD.

IF YOU WOULD LIKE TO START YOUR JOURNEY TO HAVING ALL THE WORST PARTS OF YOUR LIFE DEVOURED BY THE SMILING GOD, THEN PLEASE CALL THE JOYOUS CONGREGATION OF THE SMILING GOD.

THIS INFORMATIONAL PAMPHLET WAS COMMISSIONED FOR YOUR SALVATION BY PASTOR MUNN AND PREPARED BY THE WORDSMITH.

7

For the second time that day, Nilanjana had come across this person known as the Wordsmith. This solidified it for her. The strongest hypothesis for this situation was active malice, rather than a coincidence of natural events. Someone wanted to stop Carlos's work, and that person was the Wordsmith, or had employed the Wordsmith. And apparently the Wordsmith worked with the Joyous Congregation of the Smiling God.

She hadn't found anything useful in her samples from the pit. Her definitely-not-a-computer box with blinking lights had come back with no definite results. The only concrete piece of evidence she had pointed to this Joyous Congregation. And so that was where she would go next.

The helicopter lingered in the sky as she packed her car.

"Well," Nilanjana shouted at it. "It was good seeing you. Have a nice rest of your day."

"You too, Nilanjana," the bullhorn called. "I'm not a religious person myself, so maybe this is lack of familiarity breeding fear, but there's something cultlike about that church."

"Yeah," Nilanjana said. Not really *said*. It was more of a sound her mouth made. She moved to get into her car. "Well, good seeing—"

"You know, *cultlike* is unfair," the bullhorn continued. "I mean that brochure—hope you didn't mind me reading over your shoulder a bit—mostly focuses on good things, so maybe . . ."

The bullhorn carried on. Nilanjana had one foot in the car and a hand on top of the open driver side door. She maintained eye contact with the helicopter as far as eye contact could be made with a large flying machine, but tried not to show any interest or say anything that would encourage conversation.

". . . never went to church or temple or anything like that, although I had friends in high school who liked singing religious songs and playing guitars," the bullhorn said.

"Hey, how much fuel does that helicopter have in it?" Nilanjana changed the subject.

"These things don't take fuel."

"What? Really? How are you fly——"

"THIS INFORMATION IS FORBIDDEN. WHY ARE YOU ASKING?"

"No reason. Science." She waved. "Thanks for keeping me company. I gotta go."

"Okay. Hope to see you again soon." The bullhorn returned to its softer voice. "It gets pretty lonely this far off the ground."

She had never considered that the pilots of the government helicopters would get lonely doing their jobs, but then, on a larger scale, she had considered only a tiny portion of true things in a world that is made almost entirely of them.

Nilanjana took off back toward town, toward the church of the Joyous Congregation of the Smiling God. She didn't know much about their religion. She didn't care to. Gods and beliefs and all that were fine for some, she supposed, but Nilanjana much preferred line graphs.

After several years of practicing out of storefront churches in half-empty strip malls, the Central Church of the Joyous Congregation in Night Vale had been completed earlier that year. It was a few miles off Route 800, but its tall silver steeple was visible from the highway. As Nilanjana pulled into the main parking lot, she saw the church's sign. It had the full name of the church in backlit yellow plexiglass. Below that was a board with movable type that said:

THE SMILING GOD IS NEAR.
BE DEVOURED.

Nilanjana laughed. She loved church signs. They always had either clever idioms or funny misspellings. Like this sign. Obviously they meant "Be Devoted." Although the word *devour* reminded her of Larry's missing house. Of swallowing, consuming. The sign became less funny the more she looked at it.

The building was modern, stucco, businesslike. Half office park, half church. A church designed to be driven to on the way to other places. From the back of the church, the tall, modern steeple rose. Reflecting the glare of the cloudless noon sun, the steeple was a beacon to passing cars and the building's only architectural indication of the spiritual practice within. The other decorative features were the front doors, which were wooden and made to look old, like they belonged to a historic church. The handles of the doors were large iron rings. Protruding from each iron ring, along the inside curves, were tiny spines. It hurt a bit to grab the door handles because of these spines. Looking closer, she realized that the spines were supposed to be legs. The rings were sculptures of many-legged insects.

The faux history of the doors indicated a dedication to appearing like a much older religion. It was branding, pure and simple. If they could look like an old institution, then their newish religion would feel more trustworthy to the people of Night Vale.

Corporations and chains do this. Like Medieval Times. All of their establishments have a fake castle look to them. Or Olive Garden. All of their restaurants are shaped like olive trees, and restaurant patrons get a taste of Tuscan dining traditions as they take an elevator up through the "trunk" of the "tree," where they are put into oblong green sacks and hung from "branches" like leaves as waiters bring them giant olives to eat, each olive half the size of most diners' bodies. But these were chain restaurants. Architectural branding at a church felt phony, manipulative.

She glanced back down at the pamphlet. "Wordsmith," it reminded her. Someone from this church had been trying to turn the City Council against Carlos. Why?

"What are you up to in here?" she muttered to herself, tugging on the wrought-iron insect handle of the front door. The doors had no give. She was fairly certain they were entirely for show. She went around the side and found a modest double glass door that was unlocked. Like the rest of the building, other than the wooden doors, it felt like it belonged in a suburban office building.

She shivered in the full blast of AC as she entered. The church followed the baffling belief, common in warmer states, that if it's way too hot outside, then it should be way too cold inside to balance things out. The lobby was as businesslike as the exterior: beige carpet, low pile with stray strands spiraling up like sprouts in a garden; beige walls with brush marks still visible, paintwork uneven; a drinking fountain; and the usual six bathroom doors (Men, Women, No, Unsure, Angels, and This Too Too Solid Flesh). Towering over all of this, those ridiculous doors, even less convincing from the inside. Near the entrance was a kiosk marked "Visitors' Center," full of brochures and information about the church. She grabbed one and flipped through it. It was also credited to "Wordsmith."

There was the tremolo hum of an electric organ, like the sound of a loose wire sculpted barely into music. It was coming from the congregation room. Through the half-open door, she could see a stack of folding chairs behind a low stage with a small projector screen, torn at the edges.

She turned away from the sound to a half-open door revealing a long hallway that seemed to contain offices.

If Wordsmith is writing pamphlets for the church, they probably work here. If they work here, they probably have an office. She touched the half-open door. The lights in the hallway flickered under a faulty fluorescent tube. The electric organ squealed off key through the crackling speakers and stopped.

"You don't want to go back there," said a voice behind her.

8

"Yeah, that's just offices," Darryl said from the doorway of the congregation room. "Sorry about the noise. I was testing out the sound system for tonight with one of my favorite worship albums. *Ten Instrumental Odes to a Smiling God,* by Bono."

"It's no problem, I was only, it's . . ." Nilanjana said, trying to find the heartbeat she had misplaced. "You startled me."

"Wow, Nilanjana. You came to our church! So cool."

Darryl grinned. It was stiff and practiced, yet he looked like a person you could tell things to. He looked like a person who would understand and do whatever he could to assist you.

Hypothesis: She could trust him.

He stood upright and casually. He did not keep his hands in his pockets or folded under his arms. His chin pressed outward, like he were getting a portrait made. He did not break eye contact. That odd smile though: His lips were pulled back and apart, exposing several bright teeth.

Alternate hypothesis: He's a psychopathic cult member who knows how to manipulate people.

"There are no public services today. We have Senior Praise tonight at eight, but there's a Young Professionals Mixer tomorrow night for prospective members," he said. "That would be perfect for you. I'll be there, too. There are so many great things about the Joyous Congregation, but the most important thing is the people. The people are what make this church work. Jeez.

I'm just so excited you came. It's really hard these days to convince people to join a religion, especially one that—"

"Darryl." Nilanjana took a step toward him, one hand up.

Alternate alternate hypothesis: He's a nervous dork.

"I'm just having a look around. Could I get a tour?"

"Oh sure," he said, sounding sarcastic.

"You don't have to."

"No, I want to," he said, hearing his tone and trying to adopt a more friendly demeanor. "But let's start with the congregation room, not the church offices."

"Are the offices off-limits?"

"They're just boring. Who wants to look at offices?"

He stepped back and opened his arms.

"This is obviously the lobby. Nothing too interesting," he said, and he was right. "Although we got this new attendance board."

There was a wood sign on the wall that she hadn't noticed when she came in. It read, REGISTER OF ATTENDANCE AND OFFERING. Below that was a series of changeable numbers in wood slots:

ATTENDANCE LAST WEEK 171
ATTENDANCE TODAY 175
NOT IN ATTENDANCE 7,853,875,811

"That's cute. The world population joke."

"That's the number of souls we plan to win over," he said.

"Ah."

She still couldn't tell if it was a joke. She was reminded of the sign out in front of the church, the one she had found funny until it had stopped seeming funny at all.

He led her through the open double doors into the congregation room. As she entered, she was surprised at how tall it was. There were stained-glass columns every few feet along the walls, including a large glass mural behind the makeshift stage at the front.

"Each of these stained-glass murals depicts one of the Eleven Stages of Human Education," Darryl said. "We believe it is the Smiling God's mission to find what it is that makes each of us good, to draw that out of us."

"Sounds like a good plan."

"The best plan! Here on the left are the first five stages. It starts with Birth."

In the first column of stained glass, Nilanjana saw the moon against a deep violet sky, scattered with stars. In the center of the moon was a small tree.

"Earthly Nourishment."

The next column showed a small fox devouring a rat.

"Divine Nourishment."

The third column showed a slightly larger fox devouring itself.

"Friendship."

Nilanjana could not discern whether the fourth column showed a fire or autumn shrubbery, but above it all was an airplane dropping either water or chemicals.

"Love."

There were soldered seams in the glass forming some kind of image on the fifth column, but the glass was entirely clear. As best she could tell, the image was of several birds, likely doves, flying in a formation of interlocking triangles. But with the colorless glass, she mostly saw the parking lot.

"On the other side of the room, we have Passion."

A fox stabbing a bear with a sword.

"Awareness."

A sobbing fox standing over a headstone that had a large paw print on it.

"Family."

On the eighth panel, the fox was lying flat on its belly, surrounded by a bunch of smaller foxes. Each was digging into the main fox's back. The main fox was grimacing.

"Enlightenment."

The ninth panel was a fox sleeping near a hearth. It was a comforting image—the first of the bunch Nilanjana felt some positive connection to. A furry animal curled up near a warm fire. In the background were books on shelves, and in the middle of the image was an open window and a night sky. In the upper right corner of the window, a thin crescent moon, waning. She guessed the moon represented the later stages of earthly life. And then some yellow stars. But not many. She noticed only two stars, near the bottom of the nighttime window. They were jaundiced and almond-shaped, just above the sill. They weren't stars. They were eyes.

She hurried with Darryl to the next window, trying not to look back.

"Community."

This was the same scene as Enlightenment, although there were now half a dozen sleeping foxes. Nilanjana thought they were sleeping. A few were lying on their backs, their legs crooked. One had a reddish shard of glass along his orange body. The fox from the Enlightenment mural had a toothy smile—or possible snarl?—in this one.

"I love the Community mural," Darryl said, "because it is the story of the church. All of the other windows show solo moments or revelations. But here, our central figure has invited those around him to share the warmth of Divine love and grace."

"It kind of looks like that fox killed those others?"

"That's a theory held by some church scholars."

"They look really dead."

"Even so, it's still a beautiful story: warming your dead by the fire."

Nilanjana cringed.

"Metaphorically sharing Divine warmth even with those you have lost."

Nilanjana nodded without conviction. Darryl moved them on to the final window, above the projection screen.

"And finally the eleventh stage of human education: the Devouring."

In the central mural, which ran all the way up to the ceiling and about half the width of the wall, Nilanjana saw the stars against the dark purple void at the top. Below that the sun. Below that the thinnest wisp of a moon. Below that a layer of blue sky. Below that tall white clouds. Below that, flat gray clouds. Below that, rain. Below that trees. And in the center of the trees was a dark gray mound, with two jagged lines sticking out of its rounded top. The base of the mound extended like a tube, ending at a wooden door. Through the door, around the tube, there was a desert scene, with sand dunes and cacti.

Nilanjana stepped closer, studying the image. The mound and the long tube were a body, lined with two spiny rows of legs. It was like the iron insect handles on the church's front door. A centipede. The window was a huge ornate image of a centipede.

"That's the embodiment of the Smiling God. The Devouring is

the Joyous Congregation's parable for how, once our souls and our purposes are fully realized, the Smiling God will emerge from Heaven, where it lives, and devour our earthly bodies."

"It's so violent."

"It's a beautiful story," Darryl said simultaneously. "Oh, sorry. I spoke over you. Did you say something?"

"It's a beautiful story," she agreed.

"The most beautiful story ever told," a cheerful voice boomed behind them. They turned to see a firm handshake of a man striding down the aisle.

"Nilanjana, this is Gordon."

"Please," he said, "call me Gordo."

"Hello, . . . Gordo," she said. His smile was broad and unhinged, but his eyes were flat. She found herself afraid of the man. "Are you the pastor here?"

He boomed a laugh directly into her face.

"Me? Oh no. I'm the assistant pastor. Pastor Munn is much too busy to deal with day-to-day details, so she sends me around to take care of them."

"Do you think I could meet the pastor?"

Gordon frowned, and Darryl blanched.

"I'm afraid she's much too busy," Gordon said. "No, she doesn't even have time to talk to members of the Congregation without an appointment made well in advance."

"But that's why there's people like me to show you around," Darryl offered quickly, trying to change the mood. "Which, I should keep doing. Next are the classrooms."

Gordon held up his hand, and Darryl stopped talking.

"If the pastor needs a message delivered," Gordon said quietly, "she sends me to deliver it. Likewise, if she has a question, she sends me to ask it. She knows what needs to be done. And then I make sure that it happens. And Pastor Munn has a question for you."

"Absolutely, I have nothing to hide," Nilanjana said, trying to hide the fact that she did.

"What, precisely, is your interest in our Congregation? We don't get a lot of scientists around here."

"What makes you think I'm a scientist?"

"You're wearing a lab coat."

Gordon was right. Like all scientists, all of her outfits were lab coats.

"Generally we find that your kind doesn't have much interest in what we have to offer," he said.

"That's true," said Nilanjana. "But . . . science isn't everything, you know?" It is, she thought. Science is literally everything. "I felt like I needed more in my life. There was some kind of meaning missing." If there was anything missing, it wouldn't be found in your fairy tales, she thought.

Exactly, Darryl thought. She totally gets why what we do is so important.

Gordon nodded, expressionless, and then his smile reappeared a few moments later, like someone arriving late to a meeting.

"Fantastic," he said without conviction. "Just fantastic. Well, I'm confident our Darryl will take good care of you. Darryl, I'll let the pastor know what a great job you're doing."

"Uh, thanks, Gordon," Darryl said, frowning at the mention of the pastor, then remembering himself and turning it into a toothy smile.

"Please, it's Gordo," Gordon said, his eyes narrow and smug.

"Sorry. Habit from when I was a kid."

"Nice to meet you," Nilanjana started, but Darryl was already pulling her through a side door into the children's room. Gordon watched them go, his smile unchanged.

If Gordon acted as Pastor Munn's mouthpiece in casual conversation with members of her own congregation, Nilanjana wondered, what other kind of communication did he perform in service of this church?

Hypothesis: Gordon was hiding something. A lot of things, probably.

Evidence: Everything about him.

The children's room consisted mostly of toys and a few books. Things like wooden dolls with human faces painted on them, wooden cars with human faces painted on them, and candles. Lots of candles. Little kids love candles, and this church knew it. Most of the books seemed to be religious in nature: *Felicia Finds an Obelisk* and *Smiley the Centipede Accidentally Swallows the Earth*. There was a dry-erase board that read "What Is Divine Pain?," which was clearly from their last prekindergarten-level class.

"You seemed a bit freaked out when you were talking about the pastor," Nilanjana said.

"Oh, it's nothing," Darryl said, with a voice full of false cheer that implied the opposite of whatever he was saying. "She's a very important person. It intimidates me a bit, you know?"

Nilanjana thought again about the window showing "The Devouring." She thought about the entrance to Heaven that the Smiling God was emerging from. There had been an odd detail to it that just then struck her.

"So Heaven . . ." she said. "It's a desert?"

"Yes!" said Darryl, perking up at a question about the church's beliefs. "You see, our prophet Kevin found an old oak door, and, when he went through it, he was in the desert of Heaven, and—"

"Hey there." A friendly looking woman poked her head out from one of the classrooms. "I thought I heard your voice."

"Jamillah! Oh, this is Nilanjana. Nilanjana, Jamillah."

Jamillah switched the power drill to her left hand and extended her right hand to shake.

"Nice to meet you," she said.

"And behind her, that's Stephanie," Darryl said. "She teaches classes and conducts some sermons. We've been friends since we were kids. Hi, Stephanie!"

Nilanjana could see a young woman, holding up a large-screen television. She was clearly straining. She did not wave back so much as wiggle a couple of fingers.

"Yeah, I gotta do this," Jamillah said, running back to Stephanie, who looked both relieved and irritated.

"We finally got licenses from the city to legally use computers here," Darryl beamed. "Jamillah's volunteering to set up our servers and monitors so we can show movies and presentations. It's really exciting."

Jamillah's drill went off as Darryl spoke.

"Stephanie's great," he shouted over the noise. "She's getting her degree in theology. She hopes to become a Church Elder at the Central Church of the Joyous Congregation someday."

He looked at Stephanie with a relaxed, happy expression, and Nilanjana noted the difference between that and the forced, customer service friendliness he directed at her. It made sense. The two of them were part of the same community, and had known each other for years. He would of course prefer to be around someone he knew over an outsider, who lived in

Night Vale but would never truly belong there. Not that any of that mattered. Darryl could prefer whomever he wanted. She was only being a good scientist, noticing small details and adding them to the data available to her. Nothing more.

Stephanie was busy keeping the large monitor stable as Jamillah bolted it into the wall. Nilanjana could see sweat on Stephanie's brow, her hair pulled tightly back, her arm twitching a bit from the sustained weight of the screen. Stephanie's eyes shifted to meet Nilanjana's. Her eyes were not kind.

"You thinking of attending services?" Stephanie asked.

"I . . ." Nilanjana hesitated.

"Nilanjana was interested in learning more about the church." Darryl jumped in, covering her awkward silence. "No need to rush her into anything else."

There was one last roar of the drill. Jamillah patted her hands: "Ta-da!" Stephanie let go with a relieved groan.

Darryl tilted his head. "Oh, nice. Just a thought. What if it was like six inches to the left?"

"Darryl!" Jamillah snapped.

"I was just saying what if, not that you have to do it. Like if it's a big deal, then fine. I'm only saying."

Jamillah rolled her eyes and walked out of the room, taking her power drill with her.

Darryl touched Nilanjana's shoulder.

"Stephanie has a lot of important work for the church to do. We should leave her to it."

"Hope you enjoyed the tour," said Stephanie, with the same flat eyes and lack of conviction that Gordon had, only without the smile. "Darryl's a good recruiter."

"Oh, I did," Nilanjana said, matching Stephanie's tone. "And Darryl's been really welcoming."

She placed her hand gently and unconsciously on Darryl's arm. She quickly removed it as she became aware of the possessiveness of the gesture.

"Great!" Darryl said, looking at the part of his arm where her hand had been. He led Nilanjana back to the lobby. "Maybe I'll see you at the Young Professionals Mixer?"

He didn't seem like Nervous Dork now. She was back to the hypothesis of either Trustworthy and Sincere or Manipulative Psychopath.

Nilanjana imagined for a moment herself going to the Young Professionals Mixer. It would be some step toward getting to know others in her community. She hung out with Mark, of course, and Luisa and Carlos. They talked all the time. At the lab anyway. They made each other laugh, challenged each other. They had lunch together and worked on experiments together. But they didn't go to concerts or fairs. They didn't invite each other over for dinner or to watch big television events like the Oscars or the Oscars Preshow Commentary or the Next Morning Oscar Parties Roundup. And they were all outsiders, like her, scientists who had come to Night Vale in order to study it.

What was she thinking? She wasn't here to become close with people in this congregation. She was here to find the Wordsmith, and she had some suspects: Stephanie, unfriendly, and deeply involved in the work of the church; the mysterious Pastor Munn, who communicated through intermediaries; and, then, there was . . .

"Absolutely, Nilanjana," Gordon said. "Come to the mixer."

He stood in the doorway to the offices, staring at her with the same strange smile he'd had before. He was hiding something huge, she decided.

"I'd love to, really, Gordon, but I've gotta work." The friends she had were just fine.

"It's Gordo," he said, face unchanged.

"Sorry, I'm running some experiments out in the desert all day tomorrow. Thanks for your help," she said to Darryl. "I'll let you know if I have any more questions."

"You can ask me anything," said Darryl.

His lips were pulled back, exposing those teeth again. Then he did that fist-circling gesture in the air.

Hypothesis: Yep. Psychopath.

9

The helicopter didn't arrive until 11:00 A.M.

"Glad you could make it to work today," Nilanjana teased.

"Hush," the bullhorn boomed.

She was investigating some of the other sites where the rumbling had been detected. They were pits, similar to the first one she had seen, but scattered out in the desert, far from any buildings. She stared off at the distant mountains. She knew people didn't believe in mountains, and that seemed a bit strange to her, but not entirely unreasonable.

We see things all the time that we can't explain, and we take them for granted. Like clouds. There are some scientists who will say that clouds are water droplets that rise into the sky forming these white or gray puffs. Unless you're a cloud scientist, you'll never have a chance to test that information. You just have to take what people tell you as truth.

But given what happened with the lunar landing in 1969, why would anyone do that? For years the government told its people that they had sent men to the moon, and in 1976, when the people figured out that it was all a lie, the government came clean and admitted that it was all staged. They had faked the photos, and they had hired famed Hollywood director Stanley Kubrick to film the moon landing scenes. Then in 1985, under pressure from the Screen Actors Guild and the CIA, Kubrick admitted publicly that he never shot that footage because he was a hologram invented in NASA labs. At the end of that press conference from his home in St. Albans, England, he vanished from sight, and several entertainment reporters began asking one another what they were all doing there. The estate they had been in front of was gone. They were all in an open field, with only scratches of notes about someone named Kubrick and a moon landing. Later the government revealed that they had indeed landed men on the moon, but they had lied about it because they didn't want everyone to know that they had failed their core mission: to destroy the moon with explosives. The bombs never ignited. Perhaps they will someday, but in 1969 they failed. We failed, the government said, slumping over. We failed America, the government sobbed.

There, there. The important thing is you tried, America said, patting its government on the back, but knowing it could never trust anything the government said ever again.

Nilanjana knew most people would never set foot on a mountain, and without that living proof and a chance to affirm a theory, it would be hard for them to ever believe anything was true. Science is fact-based, but those facts have to come from hypotheses, and hypotheses come from inferences from what one sees, or wants to see.

For instance, hypothesis: Gordon was the Wordsmith.

In Nilanjana's memory, Gordon bared his teeth with an off-puttingly wide smile. He acted as the messenger for the pastor, delivering her thoughts to the outside world. He was, in that way, a kind of wordsmith for her. He had gone to the City Council and told them . . . what? What message had Gordon delivered to the council on behalf of the church that had so totally set the city against Carlos and science?

And then there had been Darryl's description of the church's idea of heaven. Entering through an old oak door into another world, which is a desert. Had the church made contact with the same desert otherworld Carlos had encountered? If so, what had they found there? What did they believe would be emerging from that otherworld during the "Devouring"?

From the pit she was standing near, she could see two other pits in the distance. None of them had been anywhere near town. It seemed most likely that the city was the one carrying out these attacks, since they had many more resources and much more power than a church. But why had the city gone from harmless pits in the desert to the murder of Larry Leroy? Or, if their intent was to strike terror, to threaten Carlos, then why had they bothered with creating pits out where no one would find them? Tests maybe? For a system that was now perfected?

The din of the helicopter rotors overhead drowned out the sound of Darryl's car. Nilanjana didn't notice him until the slam of his door.

Data gathering: She was alone in the desert with a possible murderous cult member.

Hypothesis: shit.

"I brought you a sandwich," Darryl said, waving the foil-wrapped object over his head. "I stopped by the Moonlite All-Nite Diner. It's falafel. Wasn't sure if you ate meat or not."

"I don't. Thanks for thinking of that." Nilanjana stared at the sandwich, wondering if there was a way to *see* if something was poisoned. She smelled it. It smelled the way any falafel smelled: like chocolate.

"I eat meat occasionally," Darryl said, leaning on Nilanjana's car, taking a bite of his own sandwich. "But not much lately. Hard to tell what kind of stuff they put in meat these days.

Hey," he added, seeming to realize that there might be something unusual about showing up in the middle of nowhere to give a new acquaintance a sandwich, "hope you don't mind me joining you out here. You mentioned you were going to be out in the desert so I went to where the surveillance helicopter was. Figured if it was all the way out here it was probably watching you."

"Oh," she said, not opening her sandwich.

"Yeah, it's just that you're the first person I've had show a lot of interest in the church since I started doing this. I wanted to follow up. No pressure or anything. We don't even have to talk about that. I just . . . I brought you a sandwich."

"Factory farms use a lot of antibiotics and hormones," Nilanjana said, as a way of changing the conversation's course.

"Absolutely, factory farming is an issue. But my real problem with meat manufacturing is the marketing materials. I found a fifty-cents-off coupon from American Airlines in a top round roast a few years ago. And during Thanksgiving, we found an AOL CD inside the turkey breast."

"The meat industry really sold out."

"It's silly. I'm much happier with vegetables."

Nilanjana picked at the corner of the sandwich wrapper.

"What were you looking for from the church, Nilanjana?" Darryl said, violating his promise to steer clear of the topic. "You don't seem like a person seeking religion."

"Why do I need a reason to want a tour?"

"I'm just curious. People don't often respond to our tracts. Not people your age. Definitely not scientists. And when they do, they usually come to a mixer, not to the church during off-hours."

"I wasn't snooping."

"Whoa." Darryl looked at her suspiciously for the first time. "I wasn't even thinking you were snooping. Were you snooping?"

"No." She peeled open the foil and took a large bite from her sandwich. There was no pita. It was just falafel balls, vegetables, maple syrup, and tahini. Wheat and wheat by-products were still banned in Night Vale because of the incident back in 2012 when all wheat and wheat by-products turned into snakes. There had been many injuries, but the greatest injury was the burden the subsequent ban put on people who loved bread.

"I wanted to give you my number at the coffee shop the other day. I didn't want to be forward, so I gave you the tract instead. I was just shocked it brought you to me. Do you want to go on a date?"

Nilanjana had a mouthful of sandwich, so all she said was "Mmmmp."

"Okay, I didn't land that question well. Not a date. Maybe, like, catching up. I remember you now. You're the one that was talking to me about time back when I worked at the watch store. That conversation really made me think for a while. We didn't agree, but I had fun. I thought we could go somewhere, talk some more. I guess that's kind of a date. I'm just going to own it. Do you want to go on a date?"

Nilanjana swallowed some, still chewing.

He continued to fill the silence. "Anyway, my attempt to not be forward turned into me being incredibly forward. I'm sorry about that. Also about following you to work. This must seem creepy."

"Also you bought me a sandwich," Nilanjana said, her mouth finally free. "It's a pretty creepy sandwich."

"I didn't even buy that for you. I was out picking up sandwiches for me and Stephanie."

"This was supposed to be for Stephanie?"

"I'll get her another one on my way back."

"Oh," she said. Of course the sandwich was an afterthought from his interest in Stephanie. She shouldn't have interpreted it as anything more.

"That *is* pretty creepy," the helicopter bullhorn announced.

"Sorry, sorry. Let's start over. You're interested in something at the church. Is it me? I don't know. You don't have to answer. Wait, is it me?" Darryl said.

"Dude," the helicopter said.

Nilanjana quickly took a giant bite of the sandwich and then pointed at her mouth and rolled her head back and forth, as if to say, "Caught me with my mouth full. Can't talk. Gimme a minute."

"Not trying to be weird. But I am being weird. I'm sorry. I have this thing where I try to convey one thing, and people think I'm conveying something else. Like I'll be sincere and people will think I'm sarcastic. I just—" The box with blinking lights that Nilanjana had set at the edge of the pit started beeping, interrupting him.

"Mmmmp," Nilanjana said, an index finger up in a gesture of "hang on." She wrote down the order of the blinking lights. She counted each one and made tick marks on her paper. She would have to take the data back to the lab to decipher it. She would love to get a license to own a computer. It would make her work way easier.

"Let's go out sometime," she said once she was done. This wasn't a good idea, seeing someone related to her investigation on a casual basis. But wasn't she entitled to some fun? And, she justified to herself, maybe she could gather more useful data this way. "I'm not much into dating, I don't think, so let's just . . . go out. Eat. Talk. Is that a phrase people use?"

"Yes. 'Go out. Eat. Talk.' is how people say that. Yes."

"Great. And maybe we can talk a bit about my interest in the church. But let's not make that the focus. Tomorrow night, okay?"

"Tomorrow's great. Do you think we're up to bad things at the church?" he blurted.

"I don't know, Darryl," she said cautiously. "Are you up to bad things?"

"No, of course not," he said. "It's just everyone else thought you were there investigating us or something."

He looked so genuinely worried that she almost asked him about the Wordsmith. But it was better for no one at the church to know she was following that lead, no matter how harmless they seemed. She wanted him to leave now, to go eat, to talk with him some other time, and not let him in on too much of her work or life.

"Let me get your number, okay?" she said instead. "I'll see you tomorrow."

They exchanged texts.

"I better go get Stephanie another sandwich," Darryl said, getting back in his car. "How was the falafel?"

"The least poisoned sandwich I ever had," she joked, and also hoped.

As she watched his car leave Nilanjana adjusted her hypothesis. Not a psychopath. A nervous dork, but maybe in kind of a cute way.

But that wasn't why she had come out here. She turned back to the pits. These powerful attacks that were, for some reason, done out in the middle of the desert. Another possibility for the lack of apparent logic behind the pits' placement was that they were created by a creature, following instinct rather than logic. She thought again of words like *swallow* and *devour*. She thought of the enormous stained-glass windows in the church. What kind of creature would create pits like this? And how big would it have to be to make the earth shake all the way back in town? Was it possible there was a monster hiding out here in the desert?

She scanned the horizon, but all she could see were the mountains. Most people would choose to not even see that.

After looking at the evidence, all Nilanjana had was a hunch that there was a living creature creating these pits, and a hunch wasn't scientific at all.

She was exhausted, ready to end her day, but first she wanted to see how Carlos had fared on his side of the investigation. She pulled her car back into the parking lot that Carlos's lab shared with Big Rico's Pizza, the last pizza place left in town, thanks to the passionate cooking and arson expertise of Big Rico himself.

Luisa and Mark were hanging out in the break area of the lab, eating pizza on paper plates. (Because of the whole wheat and its by-products thing, Rico's slices were just globs of cheese and sauce.) Having the lab next door to the pizza place was a real blessing. But sometimes, as she got out of bed in the morning, Nilanjana's sour stomach would remind her that there were downsides to that kind of constant temptation too.

"Where did you disappear to yesterday?" Luisa asked, in her usual tone of gentle disappointment. "It's unlike you to ignore your experiment like that. You'll never win awards for ignoring experiments. They just don't give awards for that."

"Roger Arliner Young won a Nobel for her studies on ignoring whale sharks," Mark countered, "which was incredibly brave given how insistent whale sharks can be."

"But still," Luisa said.

"A new project came up," Nilanjana said. "I had to get some readings. It took longer than I thought."

"A new project?" said Mark. His face went slack, like a child who didn't get the present he wanted on Bloodstone Day. "How come you didn't talk to us about it? I'm real sick of trying to get this machine to work. A new project would have been great. Is taking on new projects a thing famous scientists do? Maybe I should try that."

"Yeah, I'm sorry I didn't mention it. There wasn't time. Mmm, that pizza looks great, though. I'll be right back to talk to you all about it. I just need to check with Carlos real quick. Sorry!"

She rushed past them into Carlos's office. He had entrusted this problem to her, and she wanted to be the one to solve it. She didn't need anyone's company or help to do that. As she shut the door behind her, she could hear Mark say, "That project sounds secret and fun," and Luisa sigh, "I bet she wins an award."

"Everything okay?" Carlos said. "I was worried when you didn't come back yesterday."

"I'm fine," she said, touched. Carlos cared deeply about science, but he cared most of all about the people around him. "Find anything new?"

He showed her the dials, which were set to his favorite numbers. He had a pad of paper where he had written down all the numbers with a smiley face next to each one. He was an excellent scientist.

"I think I was too obvious about my experiments the last few times. I set up the lasers earlier today in discreet places around the house, and can run them all remotely from this machine. Hopefully, the city, or whoever is sabotaging me, won't notice."

"Can I ask you something?"

"Of course. You have the human perception of free will, same as the rest of us."

"What was the otherworld like?"

Carlos searched for an explanation but found only ache. He had never even told Cecil the full truth of his time in that place, and he couldn't start now.

"Endless," he said, "but also limited. That sounds like a contradiction, but think of our world. You could keep going in any direction for your entire life, an endless journey, but you would be going over the same limited space again and again. It was like that."

"A globe?"

"Not a globe. More like a bowl, all curved down to the center, and at the center was a mountain. No matter how much you walked, you circled the mountain. Being that distant from everyone I loved . . . some mornings right after I wake up I worry that I'm still there, still circling that mountain."

He shivered.

"My going there and coming back means other things can cross. And they shouldn't. No one here should go there. And if there is anything there, we don't want it coming here. The City Council doesn't understand that we need science to protect us from that otherworld."

"Whatever they learned from the person called Wordsmith has them spooked," she said.

"We don't have time for more talking. I want to run another experiment, and it's getting late." He looked at his wrist.

"You're not wearing a watch."

He nodded.

"Watches don't work here anyway. Time is weird."

"It definitely is."

She went over to the panel and checked all the dials, set to his favorite numbers. One dial was colors, and had been set to red. She didn't like red much, preferring green. She turned it to green.

"Good catch," he said. "All right, on my count."

They put their fingers on buttons that would activate the machine.

"If this works, the information should be instantaneous, right?" she said.

He shrugged.

"Things work strangely with that house. Even laser readings might take a while. No one has tried shooting lasers into alternate universes since the Civil War. Okay. One, two, three."

The machine started up, whirring away.

"That should do it," he said. "Hopefully we'll have something soon, without the city running interference on it. This is, well, it's quite neat."

"Sure," she said. "Neat." Nilanjana had never described anything as neat on her own, but it was one of Carlos's favorite words.

There was a heavy knock on the door, which turned into a banging, which turned into the door bursting open.

On the other side was Pamela Winchell. Pamela used to be mayor of Night Vale, but she stepped down before the end of her term. Most suspected it was because she never wanted to govern a city. She just liked delivering emergency press conferences—sometimes during an emergency, sometimes during an impromptu rant in a department store. Whatever the situation, she loved the power of shouting orders and decrees, calling for citywide restrictions, and locking down citizens and services, even if the emergency was just that she was feeling sad.

The current mayor, Dana Cardinal, on taking office, had

appointed Pamela to the new position of Director of Emergency Press Conferences. Pamela relished her role as a fiery spokesperson. She spent most of her time plotting with the City Council to create emergencies she could hold press conferences about.

She looked around the office. She was holding one of Luisa's potatoes, eating it raw and crisp like an apple. Luisa was in the doorway, looking disappointed that Pamela would do such a thing.

"There was no need to prepare anything fancy for me," Pamela said. "And I see you did not prepare anything fancy for me. Not even balloons or streamers or flutes of champagne. Basic courtesy."

Carlos stepped back, hoping his human frame could impossibly hide the massive machinery behind him. Nilanjana hoped they could distract Pamela long enough for a useful reading to result.

"Mmm," she said, putting down the potato and exchanging it for a notebook on Carlos's desk. She said this through a mic connected to a portable amp she always carried in case an emergency press conference came up. She looked through page after page of Carlos's favorite numbers. "Mmm," she said again, loud and breathy into the mic.

"Always a pleasant surprise, a visit from you, Pamela," said Carlos. "But I'm afraid today is quite busy, so . . ."

Pamela raised an eyebrow. Then she sneezed. The sound of it was distorted through the portable amp.

"Dammit. I think a raised eyebrow is so effective, but it also makes me sneeze. Every time."

"It was still pretty effective," Nilanjana offered.

"Don't patronize me. Now, I am here on behalf of your

mayor and your City Council. You were ordered to ignore certain things and to stop doing other things. It seems you have continued to do things and pay attention to stuff. That will not stand."

"It's not within City Council's purview———" Nilanjana started.

"PURVIEW!" Pamela shouted. She didn't sound angry, just loud. "Such a fancy word. Did you know that it comes from the Greek *purvien,* which means 'a sow at half term'?"

"No, I didn't, that's fascina———"

"Of course you didn't. Because I just made it up." She sneered at Carlos's whiteboard, covered in equations. "That's what we do. We make things up, and then everything we've made up is true as long as no one looks at it too closely. I've been having foot cramps. Are there certain foods that cause foot cramps?"

"Yes!" Carlos said, excited. "I was just studying this, let me get the resul———"

"Don't interrupt. That was a rhetorical question. It might have also been a metaphor. I'm not confident what a metaphor is and I refuse to let anyone tell me."

A light on Carlos's machine started blinking (this was a light that detected if there was science going on), and Pamela frowned at it.

"You have ignored our warnings. That makes me unhappy."

The ground began to vibrate a little.

"When I get unhappy, any number of events can result. I once got unhappy at a Burger King. Do you know what happened to that Burger King?"

"No, Pamela, what happened?" Carlos said.

"I cried in it. I cried in that Burger King. Deep, gulping sobs, until the muscles in my chest ached from the tensing and untensing of them. Everyone in that Burger King was made to feel deeply uncomfortable. That's what happened. And then later I got unhappy at a Best Buy. Do you know what happened there?"

She didn't wait for an answer. The vibration in the ground had turned into definite shaking. The floor was unreasonably warm.

"I imprisoned every employee in the abandoned mine shaft outside of town and hired a crew to turn the Best Buy into a large, impractical house. I live in that Best Buy now. I call it Best By, a small and meaningless piece of wordplay, which is also a by-product of my unhappiness."

The shaking was now a strong rolling. Carlos and Nilanjana edged toward the door out of concern.

"If you continue to make me unhappy, who knows what could happen? Who could say what the consequences will be for you all?"

The walls groaned with the force of the shaking. The floor was almost unbearably hot now.

"Even I couldn't say," she said. "And I can say almost anything. Like: My feet are extremely hot, which is painful, but is helping alleviate my foot cramps."

There was a pop, or a sizzle, or a tear. A horribly loud, unwelcome sound from outside the lab. The shaking stopped with the sound. Then, moments later, a second sound. Mark screaming.

Carlos and Nilanjana hurried out of the office, across the lab, which was strewn with what had been shaken off the shelves and tables, and out into the parking lot, where Mark and Luisa were staring at something. Luisa looked more disappointed than usual, so disappointed that it verged on sorrow. Mark had his hand over his mouth, and his face was flushed.

Nilanjana followed their horror, and saw. Big Rico's Pizza was gone. In its place was a deep pit surrounded by shattered pavement.

11

"What did they do?" was all Nilanjana could think to say, looking at the deep pit before her. Her fingers were at her mouth. She could only inhale over and over.

Tragedy is so usually witnessed now through a screen, prerecorded, ready for playback whenever convenient. Seeing it here before her, playing out in real time, she still felt as though she were watching it through a screen, that at any moment she could pause to get herself together, or rewind to check on a detail she hadn't caught the first time.

Where there had once been a busy pizza restaurant there was now only the sinkhole. The pavement drooped down toward where the restaurant had been, like slowly dripping fudge, and beyond that it spiderwebbed out into a shattered ring.

"How could they have done this?" Carlos said, and Nilanjana didn't know whether he meant practically or morally. Probably a little of each.

Pamela stood behind them, impassively watching others scrambling to look for survivors.

"It is interesting what can happen in this world," Pamela said. "Even thunderstorms, if you think about it. Or trees. Trees are a surprise too."

Carlos turned to her, and Nilanjana was startled to see disgust on his face. He was a man who rarely showed anger or rage, mostly restricting his visible emotions to kindness, concern, worry, and scientific intrigue (which was the same as his face for sheer joy). But now he wrinkled his face as though smelling a dumpster left in the sun.

"Pamela, you've gone too far."

She smiled.

"I have no idea what you're talking about. Generally, I have no idea what anyone is talking about, because I never care enough to find out. Remember what the council has told you today, Carlos. I hope we don't have to tell you again. Now, please excuse me. I need to call an emergency press conference."

She nodded at the hole in the ground as though it were an acquaintance she was greeting from across the street, and then she placed her portable amp carefully in her passenger seat and drove away.

Carlos sputtered at her car as she left.

"Unimaginable," he said. "It's a . . . well . . . I can't believe that anyone, let alone Pamela . . ."

He slumped, and Nilanjana touched his back. He flinched. He didn't like people touching him. She removed her hand.

"Forget about her," she said. "We should see if there's anything we can do to help. And after everyone's safe, let's do our best to learn from this site while it's still . . ."

The word was *fresh*, but that seemed abhorrent given the tragedy of what had happened, so instead she waggled her hand toward the smoking pit.

"Right," he said. He pulled himself together, a curious scientist once more. "Let's see what we can learn to prevent this from ever happening again."

Mark, Luisa, Carlos, and Nilanjana tended to bystanders with burns and cuts. They called ambulances for those with deeper injuries. But injuries were few. Anyone who was in Big

Rico's when it disappeared was just gone. Like Larry Leroy. No bodies, no rubble. Swallowed, she tried not to think.

The Sheriff's Secret Police arrived and prepared to rope off the area, so Nilanjana and Carlos studied what they could before being forced out of the crime scene.

The pit looked much like the one Nilanjana had initially investigated in the desert. Nearly vertical sides, and a bottom that was flat and damp. Smoke rose from the dirt. Nilanjana saw one difference. The bottom of this pit was squirming with earthworms, dipping in and out of the soil. There seemed to be thousands. The dirt was alive with them.

"Worms don't naturally exist in that kind of density," she said.

"No," Carlos said. "Another problem to consider. A related problem?" He shrugged. "Correlation does not indicate causation."

"But correlation suggests the possibility of causation. Did you see that?"

She pointed. There was light from the pit. And movement. It was difficult to reconcile with the rest of what they were looking at. It was like a movie was being projected on the wriggling mass of worms. No specific images. Shapes, colors, light. She could smell, within the harsh smoke and the melted soil, a dry and ancient smell, like a creature that had been mummified in a desert tomb.

Hypothesis: The worms and the moving lights were an illusion caused by a traumatic experience.

Evidence: She'd just had a traumatic experience.

She wasn't alone in that.

The bystanders who had seen the disaster at Big Rico's told others. The cumulative terror of what had been happening in town began to weigh on its citizens. First Larry Leroy, now Big

Rico. Both vanished along with entire buildings. Any citizen of Night Vale could be next. The Secret Police interviewed witnesses, asking them questions like "You didn't see anything, did you?" and *"Did you?"* and "Would you like to shut up and go home now?"

Basimah Bishara hadn't seen either of the pits herself, but she heard a lot about them through friends. She was a high school senior, mostly worried about whether she should attend Night Vale Community College or risk leaving town for college, knowing that many who manage to leave Night Vale never find their way home. Perhaps it was this anxiety that amplified the fear for her. Or the fact that her father had left to fight in a distant war when she was little, and would never come home.

Either way, the disappearances, and the terrible gaps they left in the earth, became something of an obsession for her. She would lie in bed at night and doubt the stability of the earth, the reliability of gravity. Even air seemed like it might be a temporary construct. Every breath she took could be the one that drew in nothing and left her choking.

"Mom," she said one day. "Tell me everything you remember about Dad."

And her mom told her, without asking why. It was an act of kindness on the part of her mother, and an act of cruelty on the part of Basimah, making her mother go back through the memories of the person they had both lost.

During the day, Basimah would walk the perimeter of her house, each loop laying down more footprints she could follow. She would feel the solid packed earth beneath her bare feet, and she would doubt it. She would circle her house, and wait, each loop, for the house to be gone before her next step.

After weeks of this, she decided she would attend a school in California. If she couldn't find her way back, she couldn't find her way back. There was no safety anywhere. Houses could disappear. Fathers could disappear. If she disappeared too, so what? And in making that decision, her fear left her, and she slept soundly again, in a house that was no different than it had been the night before, but felt solid and safe once more.

Mab, unlike Basimah, had witnessed the disaster firsthand. She had been on her way to lunch at Big Rico's between routes. Mab was a long-distance bus driver, who drove round trips that usually took her all over the region, leaving Night Vale as the sun was a band of light blue on the horizon, and pulling back into the bus station as the last pink was fading out from the other horizon.

That day she had been scheduled for two shorter runs, over to Pine Cliff and back, twice. She hadn't made it to either of those destinations, as it's incredibly difficult to leave Night Vale, but people bought bus tickets, and it's important as a bus driver to at least attempt your route. It didn't matter much to Mab anyway. Those weren't her normal routes. She had been covering for a colleague who had come down with a mild case of throat spiders and needed to take a few days off for all of the eggs to clear.

Usually Mab ate whatever was available at the gas stations or fast-food restaurants where the bus stopped for bathroom breaks, but today she had the unbelievable luxury of being in her hometown at lunchtime and decided to celebrate with pizza made the way no one but Big Rico could make without their pizza restaurant mysteriously burning down. She had been almost to the restaurant's door when she realized she had left her wallet in the vehicle and had to go back to get it. If it hadn't been for that lapse in memory, she would have been in the store when, well, when whatever happened happened.

As it was, she had just shut the passenger side door and was turning, shoving the wallet into her pocket with one hand, when the restaurant had gone. There was a strange light that stung her skin. The place didn't collapse, but instead seemed to be lowered, as though on a high-speed elevator. She had frozen, hand still in her pocket, and then turned, got into her car, and started driving. She didn't feel panic. She felt fine. It wasn't until she was back on her bus attempting to reach Pine Cliff for the second time that day that she realized she had never eaten lunch.

There was a movement in the driver's side mirror of the bus. Some jerk trying to pass her. She glanced out of the window. Nothing there. Must have been a bird or a ghost or something innocuous and common like that. Another flicker in the mirror. What was that?

She was fine, there was simply a terrible driver endangering her bus by trying to pass her. Except there was no car there. The road toward Pine Cliff was empty that day. She could see that. But every time she looked forward, she would see movement in her mirrors. Someone endangering her and her passengers. She wasn't safe. She didn't feel safe. Her hands were taut and pale on the steering wheel. Eventually, she and her Pine Cliff–bound passengers would arrive back in Night Vale, wondering how anyone got anywhere at all.

Terry Williams also saw the restaurant disappear. He was only seven, and didn't understand what he had seen. He understood little. His brain was still forming out the model of what a world is, and how a world works.

The disappearance, and all that would come after it, didn't have much of an immediate effect on him. He played with his friends. He made paper airplanes but didn't throw them, instead whooshing them around the backyard in his hand. He wanted to be a pilot. He didn't even consciously remember the day that Big Rico's Pizza had slipped into the waiting earth, like something snatched by a thief.

He did become a pilot. This was after high school, after college. Like Basimah, he decided to leave Night Vale to go to college, to get some experience of the world. It took him more than a dozen attempts, but he was finally able to leave the city. He even spent a European semester abroad in Svitz, where the legal age for talking about clouds was eighteen. He spent many long nights, more than he should have, staying up till dawn discussing clouds, thrilled at the taboo of it. It was only when he returned to the United States that he had some regret, that he didn't truly understand Svitz as a country or a culture, and had missed his chance to really experience it, because he had wasted his time reveling in a place where he could legally talk about clouds.

He never did leave the country again, even after becoming a commercial pilot. Domestic routes only, and he was okay with it. Not everyone gets to do everything, and he knew that.

Mostly, he had forgotten Night Vale. It was a strange place to grow up, but many people have strange childhoods, and he had no way of comparing if his had been more or less strange than others. He definitely didn't remember the day that a building had disappeared, just like that, before his eyes.

But on his fortieth birthday, heading to a local pizza and

beer joint to meet some friends, he found that his hands were shaking. He stood in the parking lot, by himself, his friends waiting inside at a table, ready to celebrate with him, and his hands wouldn't stop shaking. And then he was crying, and on his knees, and a puddle in the parking lot ruined one leg of his pants. And he didn't know why he was crying or shaking, but for some reason, looking at the pizza place where he would celebrate his birthday, he felt all at once the absolute tenuous nature of his life. He felt it all slipping away from him. He sat on his knees, remembering without remembering, crying without knowing why, a man who had been taught a lesson thirty-three years earlier that he was only now starting to learn.

12

They had spent several hours going over what they had collected from the pit. The soil was soil, although the composition of it was unusual, with some of it perfectly dry, some of it melted, and the rest wet and muddy. How dry dirt had ended up mixing in with wet soil without soaking up any water they hadn't been able to figure out. The worms were just earthworms, notable only in their unusual quantity.

Nilanjana needed to approach the problem from a different angle, a human one. Pamela had threatened them. And then Big Rico's had gone.

Hypothesis: Pamela and the City Council had done this.

Nilanjana thought back to the sign in front of the church, and the word *Devoured*. She thought back to the Wordsmith meeting with the City Council and "warning them," whatever that meant. She thought about the stained-glass image of a centipede rising up and devouring.

Hypothesis: The church is also involved somehow. Helping the city. Or the city is helping them.

Either way, what they had here was likely not a natural phenomenon, but a crime. And when investigating a crime, it was helpful to look for a motive.

The first and most obvious motive would be an attempt to stop Carlos from researching further into the desert otherworld. But why, instead of directly going after him or the lab, were they instead swallowing entire buildings with innocents inside who had nothing to do with his research?

To find a motive that matched the crime, Nilanjana told Carlos she needed to look at the victims who had been targeted, Big Rico and Larry Leroy, and see if there was any particular reason why the city or the church or whoever was doing this would go after them.

"That sounds like journalism, not science," said Carlos.

"They might lead me to more information about what or who is causing these buildings to completely vanish into pits."

"Fine, you go have conversations. I'll be here doing science."

She drove back out to where Larry Leroy's home had been. The first thing she confirmed was that this pit had no worms in it. No signs of life anywhere in or around it. Only garbage. Past-due electric bills. Empty cereal boxes. A lot of empty cereal boxes, with shapes missing from them. She examined a box of Flakey O's, and traced the outline of an arm and head that had been cut out of it. Interesting. There was a larger cardboard box nearby, and she checked to see what shapes had been made from it, but there were no cuts. Instead, flipping the box over, she found she was looking into a little world. It was a diorama depicting the famous ending of *The Wizard of Oz*, in which a crying Dorothy floated over Kansas in a war balloon, firebombing it into a sterile wasteland. It was one of the most famous scenes in children's literature, and this diorama brought out the natural drama of it. Here was Auntie Em, fleeing from the inferno, carting an unconscious Uncle Henry on her back. Here was Dorothy, head bowed, lips just parted. Nilanjana could almost hear her whispering her famous line: "There's no longer a place like home. There's no longer a place like home."

It was a stunning work of art, and made from the most simple of materials. She hadn't thought much of Larry Leroy, except that he was a man who disappeared into a pit, but the revelation that within his quiet life he was incubating a work with as much technique and power as this stunned her. There are moments in life in which it is made clear to us how vastly we have misunderstood.

She combed the surrounding area, but couldn't find any more works of art. Instead she found torn envelopes, all of them addressed to Larry Leroy, Out on the Edge of Town, with a return address of City Hall. She couldn't find any of the letters that had once been in them. What was Larry's correspondence with city government?

As she wondered this, she realized she was being watched. Not by the Secret Police or its helicopters. Not by the black sedan with agents from some vague, yet menacing, government agency taking zoom-lens photos of her and writing down cryptic notes about her movements. Something far stranger than that. A tall, black being, with many eyes and almost as many wings, watching her from the yard of Old Woman Josie's house down the street.

It was an actual angel. This angel, like all angels, was named Erika, and they were staring directly at the sun.

"Does it seem different today?" they called out. Nilanjana walked toward them.

"The sun?"

"Yes."

Nilanjana squinted near it.

"Maybe a little brighter today?" she offered.

"Hm," said Erika. They turned their face down toward her. She smelled something like an enormous heap of pea shoots lit on fire. Green things and ash.

"Larry was a decent neighbor," the angel said. "He acknowledged my existence, which was nice. Most people won't say aloud that angels exist. It's a kind of assault, this constant insistence that we can't be publicly acknowledged. Sometimes an act as simple as a person recognizing you, your bulk, the tangibility of your skin. That can mean everything."

"I can see that," Nilanjana said, although she couldn't really. She understood feeling like an outsider, that made total sense to her, but she couldn't feel what it was like to not have your bodily existence accounted for. She understood drowning, theoretically, but still she took each breath with thoughtless ease. "Do you know what happened to Larry?"

"What happens to us all? We disappear, eventually. Some of us disappear slowly. Larry disappeared quickly. The result is the same. It's a shame he couldn't leave behind his art."

"I found one of his dioramas. It's beautiful."

"The dioramas were only models for what he really wanted to do. Full-size sculptures throughout Night Vale. Commemorating great literature and important historic events. He spent years arguing with the city. But the City Council believes that art is dangerous to public health, since it might be seen or, even worse, understood. Imagine a child trying to look at or understand art. In this case I do side with the City Council. We need to protect people."

"Would the city have wanted to get rid of him?"

Erika studied her. They blinked several of their eyes in a slow, intentional rhythm, while maintaining an unblinking gaze with several of their other eyes. The effect was disconcerting.

"Not for making art. Maybe for acknowledging my existence. I don't know."

"What about the Joyous Congregation of the Smiling God? You're an . . . uh . . . you're an angel." Alarms went off around the neighborhood, letting the city know that someone had acknowledged an angel. "Do you know much about the church? Was Larry a member?"

Erika laughed. It sounded like a fistful of sand thrown at a hardwood floor. "Just because I'm an angel doesn't mean I have a religious studies degree. We don't have angel meetings to discuss who goes to what church. We're just angels."

"You're right. I'm sorry."

"He wasn't a member of any church," Erika said. "I don't think he ever talked to anyone from the congregation. Good luck on your inquiry, Nilanjana."

"Thanks."

"Hey," they said. "Do you have a few bucks? Just a few dollars?"

"Not on me right now."

"Dang," the angel said, and then vanished with a loud crack.

What a strange creature, thought Nilanjana. She put her hands in her pockets as she turned to leave, and realized she did have a loose five in her jacket that she had forgotten about.

She tracked down one of Big Rico's cashiers who hadn't been at work that day. Josh Crayton was a teenager, still in school, and worked a few evenings each week so he could afford things for himself, like clothes. He was a shape-shifter, and so his clothes budget was higher than most. In this particular moment, he was shaped like a meticulously carved rhinoceros horn with octopus tentacles at the bottom to provide movement.

"That's a cool look," she said, on sitting down with him.

"What? This?" he said, with a teenage mixture of deep insecurity draped in a fragile layer of nonchalance. "I've been practicing more creative looks. Trying not to get bogged down on categories like species or whatever."

"You liked working at Big Rico's?"

"There are worse jobs. I used to help my sister, Jackie, with her pawnshop, but she couldn't pay me much. My mom wouldn't let me be an intern at the radio station. She said none of those kids end up making anything of themselves. Mostly because the death rate there is high. The death rate at Big Rico's was really low, surprisingly, given what everyone always said about Rico. I mean, it used to be low. Now it's a lot higher, I guess."

He seemed sad about it, but it was hard to tell. Nilanjana had no way of reading emotions on a carved rhinoceros horn.

"It's sad," he said, aware of the problem this shape had with communicating emotion. "Those were my friends. The day one of the worms got onto a Hawaiian pizza and Sharon and I had to go through the rest of the pizzas to check that there weren't any other worms. We made jokes about that for weeks. I'm going to miss Sharon. It sucks."

He shrugged. Nilanjana had never seen a horn shrug before.

"Wait," she said. "Go back. There was a worm?"

"Huh?" he said. "Uh, yeah. Sometimes that happened."

"There were thousands of worms in the pit where Big Rico's disappeared. Do you know anything about them?"

"Nah," he said. "Listen, I don't want to talk about that. Big Rico always had a lot of secrets. Most of them we didn't know.

And given his reputation, the last thing any of us wanted to do was learn any of his secrets."

"Do you think Rico had enemies inside the city? Did you ever get a sense that the City Council, or the Secret Police, were—"

"I don't know that much. I'm sorry." He was a human boy now, with glasses. His bottom half was still octopus tentacles. "You should talk to Rico's brother."

"Rico had a brother?"

"Yeah, Arnie Goldblum. The mailman. He knows way more about Big Rico than anyone in town."

"I had no idea he and Rico were related."

Josh squinted up at her.

"I wish I could help you more. You seem like a nice lady with good intentions. But I don't want to get in any trouble. And I'm just a kid. I like to think I'm more than that, but sometimes I'm just a kid. I'm sorry."

"You've done great," she said. She patted his shoulder, and he lightly touched her wrist with a tentacle.

It's hard to catch a mailman. That's the common wisdom anyway. They're sneaky and quick, and if you want to get your mail you need to either set a trap or hide in the bushes and have quick reflexes.

But there is another, easier way. Nilanjana decided to wait for Arnie to get off work, and then she followed his SUV back to his house.

He opened the door on her second knock, beer bottle in hand, already changed from his postal uniform into a Hawaiian shirt and khaki shorts, still sweating from evading people trying to catch him and force him to deliver their mail.

"Can I help you?" he said.

"Possibly," she said. "May I come in?"

"I don't keep the mail with me once I'm off work. Catching me here won't count."

"It's not about the mail."

He took a swig of beer, the bottle sweating in the late-afternoon heat almost as much as he was. He shrugged and wandered away from the door.

"Make yourself at home then."

"I wanted to talk about your brother," she said, a few minutes, one refused offer for a beer, vague but not particularly hopeful flirting on Arnie's part, and some polite small talk, later.

Arnie let out a long breath.

"Tough time for that. Richie meant a lot to me."

"Richie?"

"Or Rico. Sure. Changed his name. No one would buy pizza from a guy named Richie Goldblum. But Rich always had a knack at pizza. And arson. Those two combined, he had it in him to be the pizza king of Night Vale. So he changed his name. Big Rico. That was kind of a private joke. We always had this thing in our family that he was the runt, even though he and I were basically the same size."

Arnie squinted out the window, looking not at the outside world but inward, to a distant, younger version of himself. He took a long swig of beer.

"Wasn't a cruel thing. He was in on the joke. Called himself the runt more than anyone else did. We used to play football in the backyard, I was fifteen, he was thirteen. He would tackle me and then say, 'How do you like getting tackled by the runt?' Had a sense of humor about himself. But I think he also had a lot of issues with who he was. Two nerdy Jewish kids living in a town not exactly brimming with Jews. We're born outsiders.

It's in our culture. But Richie didn't want to be an outsider. He wanted to be the center of his community. So Richie was dead, and Big Rico was born."

Arnie's eyes welled, but his voice had a laconic steadiness.

"Can you tell me why there were so many worms under Big Rico's Pizza?" Nilanjana said, as gently as she could.

"Ha! The worms." He shook his head. "Big Rico was all about secrets. Tons of secrets, most of them useless. Most of them misdirection to keep people from noticing the biggest secret of all, himself. His own body, his culture, his personality, those were his real secrets, and so he created a cloud of conspiracies around him to distract from what people were staring literally in the face."

"The worms were misdirection?"

"Beats me, honestly," Arnie said. "He always kept thousands of worms in the basement. Would never tell anyone why. Not even me. Maybe it was another distraction. Or maybe he really was doing something with them. With Rico, it could have gone either way. He was a complicated guy."

"I know he was Jewish, but did Rico have any connections with the Joyous Congregation?"

"I don't know what that is, but as long as they didn't owe him money or weren't a rival pizza place, he probably got on great with them. He didn't have an enemy in town. Or at least any enemies that lasted."

Arnie rummaged around next to his easy chair and came up with a pile of envelopes.

"Ms. Sikdar, you seem like a nice person. I was lying before. I do keep the mail with me. Here's your mail for the last few weeks. I'll try to slow down when I'm coming by your place. Make it easier for you to catch me."

"That's kind of you," she said. "I'm sorry to make you go over all this stuff about your brother, right after . . ."

"Nah," he said. "It's good. Good to know someone is looking into all this. I loved my brother." His voice finally broke. She took his hand and he held it without meeting her eyes. "I'm going to miss him. No one made pizza like that runt Big Rico."

Nilanjana left Arnie's house feeling like Night Vale was a deeper, sadder town than she had given it credit for. But with all that she had learned about Larry and Big Rico, the fact remained: As far as she could tell, the victims had no connections. Which suggested that the victims were randomly chosen.

Hypothesis: There was no motive, because there was no sentience behind the attacks.

Or, far more terrifying,

Hypothesis: There was a sentient being behind the attacks, but it had no logical or consistent motive.

13

Tourniquet was the hippest foodie hot spot in Night Vale. It was neither particularly hip nor culinarily groundbreaking, but it used enough of the terms and techniques to make everyone feel gratifyingly annoyed as they tried to just order some god-damn food. Which is to say that it was the perfect date spot.

Not that this was a date. This is not a date, Nilanjana sternly reminded herself, as she entered the small reception area, where the host was required to keep his back to you, humming and pretending he didn't notice you for a full five minutes before turning around, screaming in surprise, and running away. It was the classy details like that that made Tourniquet different. Better.

But if this wasn't a date, then it was meeting someone for a drink, and she couldn't remember the last time she had done that. It had been difficult, after moving, to feel comfortable in Night Vale's dating scene, even though apps like Lurk and Void were quite popular. She had gone on a few Lurk dates, but had never been able to stumble on where they were hiding, and had found the whole process exhausting when she really wanted to get back to her experiments. A little part of her, though, felt sad that those dates didn't work out.

So it wasn't solely a desire for information about the church that led her to these drinks with Darryl. She liked hanging out with him. He seemed, god help her, like a cool guy, whatever that meant. But even as she kind of hated the concept, it felt true to her and she went with it.

Darryl was already at the bar, kicking his legs into the crushed red velvet paneling, and so she brushed past the host, who was still pretending she wasn't there, and sat next to him. He did his fist in the air, circle it around thing. He had that stiff, toothy smile, which was somehow endearing on him.

"Hey. I've never been here. I hope it's good. It looks good?" she said, unsure of what makes a restaurant look good.

"Yeah," he said. He wasn't sure, either. "Their cocktail menu is really something."

The bartender came by. He was dressed in cool vintage clothes; a Snuggie and mesh trucker hat, just like a Prohibition-era barkeep.

"Let me know if you have any questions you need answering," the bartender said. "About anything. They gave me near-infinite knowledge of the universe and it is shattering my mind. I'm barely hanging on."

He gave a thin-lipped smile and went back to carving a large piece of ice into a perfect sphere using his front teeth.

"Wow, yeah, these are really fancy," Nilanjana said.

There was some back-and-forth about what are you having, no what are you having, I was thinking this, oh I was thinking that too, well if you're going to have that then maybe I'll have something else, you can try mine, oh good good.

"Have you made up your minds?" said the bartender. "Also, here's something I know: The nearest alien civilization died a million years before humans existed. There is a planet of golden obelisks. Every few centuries, an obelisk gives and falls. It is beautiful, a forest of metal none of us will ever see."

"Right," she said, "I'll have the Mulch Mojito and Darryl . . ."

"I'll have the Sangria Manhattan. Sounds fun."

"It is, definitely, very fun, sir," said the bartender. "Cats hate us. They hate us so much. But they also need us. They need us more than they hate us. I'll have those drinks right up."

"So you've been in the church since you were a kid?" Nilanjana asked, once the bartender had left. It must have been at least five minutes since she had come in because the host screamed in surprise and ran away from nothing.

"Yeah, you know some of my earliest memories are in the Joyous Congregation. I feel like I was half raised by the church. My parents were good people, but good people aren't always good parents. They were busy. Away a lot. Then when they passed, I—" He paused, staring into his folded hands. "I remember when Gordon came by the house to tell me, uh, what had happened. I wasn't sad immediately. Sad wouldn't come until a lot later. What I remember feeling was that there was no way to reverse this. That I had crossed a threshold and there was no way to cross back out. It was the worst feeling in the world. That was when I learned how much the community of the church matters. Someone at the church is always there for you. It's a family. Sounds so pat, but it's true."

"I get it," she said. "You have to find that thing that makes you feel at home. That's how I came to Night Vale, wanting to be a scientist, studying scientifically interesting things. I started working for Carlos, and no one else had ever nurtured what I did so completely. He loved science and discovery even more than I did. My dad was an immigrant, he wanted me to find a stable profession that would establish our family in this country. My mom loved that I was into science, but not that I didn't want to stay in Indiana. It was hard to explain moving to Night Vale to them. I only told them that I needed to move for new opportunities, just like my dad did at my age."

Behind the bar were shelves and shelves of liquor. She scanned the bottles, wondering how many of them were ever poured. Were there really people ordering Goldfrapp? Or Pine-Sol?

"I remember," she said, "when I was ten, my mom took me to this astronomy convention. Sounds silly, but I had so much fun. It was when the Mars Rover landed, and they had a live feed on a big screen. The first images from Mars came back and this whole room of people started cheering. My mom and I held hands. When she was a kid, that kind of thing was still in the pages of pulp novels, and now it was actually happening, and she got to share it with her daughter." Nilanjana smiled at the memory, and then took Darryl's hand. "I get what you're saying about the threshold. If I lost my parents . . . when I lose my parents, I'll spend my life thinking of that memory, trying to understand how that moment could be right there, but always impossible for me to go back to. I'm really sorry your parents died."

"It's okay," he said, squeezing her hand. "It's been a while. It's okay."

"You grew up around here?" she said, trying to lighten the tone.

"Sort of. I grew up in the neighboring town of Desert Bluffs, but I think of Night Vale as home now. You?"

"I don't think of home as a place. It's more the ritual of my life. The work I do every day, and the things I like to eat, and where I like to eat them. That kind of thing. And that ritual exists here, so this is, I guess, home, but . . ."

"Yeah. Sometimes where you live is just a place, no matter how long you live there."

"Right," Nilanjana agreed, a bit surprised no one at the bar had shouted "Interloper" at her yet. "I feel like Indiana is more my home than Night Vale, even after a few years."

"Here are your drinks," the bartender said, having hovered over them listening intently to what they were saying for most of the conversation. Bartenders are good listeners, which is part of the appeal of bars, and also why the government started paying bartenders to report the content of these private conversations.

Darryl's manhattan came with an ice cube engraved with his social security number. The presentation for Nilanjana's mojito was far less flashy, although she thought it was a nice touch when the bartender sprinkled some mulch on the bartop around them. They both took sips of their drinks.

"Interesting," she said.

"What . . . fascinating flavors," he said.

"That would be the splash of Pine-Sol," said the bartender. "Let me know if you need anything else." He slipped into the back room to radio what he had heard to his government handlers.

"It tastes, like, a little sweet and little bit like fruit, right?" Nilanjana said, once he was gone.

"Right. Just kind of like fruit," Darryl said. They sipped their disappointing drinks again, and then left them alone.

"That's why I was so stubborn about time when you came by the store a couple years ago," he said. "I just think, if time is weird, then my parents' death isn't irreversible. Nothing is. We could go backward on anything. And that's not the case. Time moves on, whether we want it to or not."

"I get that, but time being weird doesn't mean anything is possible. Only that more things are."

"Like better drinks?"

She laughed.

"Thanks again for showing me around the church. It was more enjoyable than I thought it would be. You're a good tour guide."

"Oh yeah, no worries, it's nice to have someone show an interest in that, you know? Most people act like we have some kind of disease they might catch. Or like we're going to hold you at gunpoint and make you recite our sacred scriptures. And we only do that once a year, on Gun Day, so."

"I don't get religion, if I'm honest."

"You sound like you're honest."

"I mean for my own life. It doesn't make sense for me, but watching you talk about it. You get so excited, and it's easy to understand why you believe it, even if I can't."

He frowned. He had been pushing the church thing too hard. "You don't have to join the Congregation, Nilanjana. I'm not trying to convince you to—"

"I'm sorry. I'm bad at this. What I'm trying to say is your positivity is attractive. You're attractive. You looked attractive just now when you were smiling and talking. Is what I'm saying."

"Oh, I, thanks," he stammered. Then it occurred to him how to respond: "You are also attractive."

His tone made it sound like false flattery, but she was starting to understand that he was sincere even when he didn't sound it. She grinned, not at his compliment but at his sudden awkwardness. It put them on an equal plane.

"Listen," she said, and she pulled out a PIN pad. This was a bold and sexy move.

"Oh, wow," he said. "Um, yeah, okay." He pulled a stack of forms out of his bag. "I don't want you to think I was expecting anything, but I thought I'd bring these in case."

Sex in Night Vale, like most things in Night Vale, is heavily regulated. But that doesn't mean that people can't have fun with it. There is something intensely flirty and erotic about the process of filling out forms in triplicate, providing a medical history, and entering one's individual Sex PIN to verify one's identity and interest in the forthcoming activity.

It took them a while to get all of the paperwork done, and there wasn't much chance to talk, what with having to work through the sometimes complicated and often contradictory questions on the forms. When they were done, and the bartender, who moonlighted as a notary public, had stamped everything, they took a moment and looked at each other.

"So, yeah," he said.

"I'm sorry, this wasn't too soon? I don't know how it works with your beliefs."

"No, it's okay. For some people, worship of the Smiling God is all about some imagined purity, but that's never what it's been about for me. Shall we?"

"Go to the doctor and have the blood tests done? Let's get it over with."

A couple hours later, having received all the necessary results, they were back at Nilanjana's apartment. She hadn't cleaned it before going on the date, as part of a half-baked plan to not invite him home when she really wanted to. The plan hadn't gone well, and now she could only apologetically kick aside laundry and research papers. Being a neat person, she was annoyed at herself about the mess she had left. All he noticed about her apartment was her.

"This is a nice place, I like the, uh—" he said, and she kissed him before he could say anything else.

Sex in Night Vale has a lot more steps leading up to it than it does in many other places, but once it actually happens, it works like it does anywhere else. In this case, it worked wonderfully.

There was a moment, right in the middle, when she saw his face close to hers, sweaty, a few stray hairs from his sideburns sticking out, and she thought, How strange we are, how strange this is, but how nice, how good, but how strange.

Their bodies formed a crescent on the bed, her bed, which was pushed up against the wall in her bedroom, which was just off the living room—slash—kitchen combination of an apartment on the second floor of the Homely Prospector Apartment Complex. The complex was not within the crime-ridden science district, but near it, because Nilanjana didn't want to have to walk home too far at night. From her window, if either of them had been looking, they could have seen the blinking light of the broadcast tower off in the desert. From the tower, theoretically, a person could see her window, but it would just be a light among many lights. Easily lost in a universe that was full of light, and a lot of other things too.

14

The light on the tower still blinked the next morning, but it seemed feeble against the blue-white brightness of the sky. It did not have the strange divinity that it had in the darkness, blinking out from distance and from nothing. Instead, just metal struts and beams, and the dirt service road leading to the highway, leading in turn to the center of Night Vale. And near the center of Night Vale, the Moonlite All-Nite Diner, a twenty-four-hour place for food and drink and a reminder that other people are alive and exist, even in the most quiet and lonely hours of the night. Framed by the window, among the morning crowd, were a couple of people scanning the room for an open table. Not a couple by any definition except quantity, a pair with no specific affiliation except the pleasurable memory they both shared of the night before.

"Take any table you want," said Laura, bustling by with two cups of coffee on a tray, the cups no more a couple than the people she was speaking to. Long branches sprouted from Laura, although in this season they had no leaves. For a few weeks in November she would shed leaves all over the dining room, apologizing and raking them up when she had the time.

"By the window, do you think?" Darryl said, right when Nilanjana said, "Just at the bar?" and then they both agreed with each other, and then switched back again, and after some confusion settled on a booth by the window. As they started for it, Jackie Fierro, owner of the local pawnshop came in.

"Hey, Nilanjana," she said. "Hey . . ."

"Darryl," he said.

"Hey, Darryl. So, breakfast, you two?" The only thing subtle about Jackie was that she didn't give a giant wink and elbow nudge.

"Yes," Nilanjana said, answering the implication.

"Cool, man, cool." Jackie genuinely seemed to find it cool. "I've been going on some dates myself. Never went on dates before, you know?"

"Oh, we're not," said Darryl.

"Or whatever it is. Relax. It's breakfast time. I find breakfast highly relaxing. Anyway, now that I'm twenty-five, I feel like dating is maybe long past due."

"You're twenty-five already?" said Nilanjana.

Jackie had been nineteen for a long time, decades maybe, and had recently started to age again. Time doesn't work in Night Vale, Nilanjana thought, resisting opening that argument with Darryl again.

"Right, yeah, I skipped a few years. Felt like I had some catching up to do, and I was ready to be twenty-five."

Darryl had no response to this contradiction to his belief that time isn't weird. He was used to a world that contradicted his beliefs, and was comfortable operating on faith.

"That's brave of you," Nilanjana said. "I mean, you can't go back, so jumping forward like that . . ."

"Can I not go back?" Jackie frowned for a moment and then shrugged. "Who wants to go back? It's like my mom says, 'You can't change the past without creating a cascading series of un-intended consequences.' She says that every morning and cries."

"Wise woman, your mom," said Nilanjana.

"Right? I've been dating a particular someone. They have a job high up in city government, so we're keeping it pretty quiet. You know how it is with any small-town government official, their life is a complex network of secrets and lies. But they're really nice, once you get past what people think about them and anyone else that works in government."

"That's so wonderful," Darryl said. "Well, we'll leave you to breakfast." He liked Jackie, but he was hungry enough that he liked food more in that moment.

"Sure thing," she said. She held up her left hand for a high five and he was starting to do his rotating fist thing, but adjusted to meet her hand. She held it up for Nilanjana. "You too, dude." Nilanjana gave it a solid slap. "All right. Well, talk to you all later."

Jackie took a seat at the counter, and Nilanjana and Darryl sat themselves in a booth.

"I hope it's okay I said that we're not dating," Darryl said. "I don't want to make it like I'm definitely not interested. I mean we did go on a date, right?"

"Oh yeah," Nilanjana said. "But way too early to put labels on things. Or, I guess, like in my day-to-day job I love putting labels on things. Labeling bottles, labeling beakers, my favorite thing to do is organizing and labeling. But when it comes to this, labeling is different. I mean."

She knew they weren't dating, and she was fine with that. In her own head she agreed fully with Darryl's not-dating stance. They'd had drinks at a nice bar and later slept together. That's not dating. But his saying it aloud drew attention to it.

It was like being overweight. Nilanjana was fine carrying extra weight and did not feel uncomfortable about her body for that, but when others drew attention to it, she felt like she should be different, and she was made uncomfortable.

Hypothesis: There was no need to put a label on what she and Darryl were doing.

Evidence: She felt fine.

She placed her hand on his, to show how fine she was, but also to touch his hand again. He lightly squeezed her hand. His palm was warm and dry. His eyes were on hers, not needy or searching, just glad.

Any reprise of physical longing was put on pause with a sweep of Laura's long, bare branches. Nilanjana had to duck to avoid getting conked.

"What can I get you?" Laura asked.

"Omelet," Darryl said, decisively. Nilanjana hadn't even looked at the menu yet.

"Uh, do you have some sort of smoothie or something?" she said.

"We have waffles," said Laura.

"That's not much like a smoothie though," Nilanjana said.

"No, I suppose not," said Laura. She waited expectantly, her pen over a pad.

"I'll have the waffles then, I guess," Nilanjana said.

"Great." Laura carefully worked her branches between the eating customers back toward the kitchen.

The momentum of their conversation disrupted, Darryl and Nilanjana sat across from each other in friendly silence. He nodded. She tapped a rhythm with her knuckles on the tabletop.

Across the room, Laura filled Jackie's coffee cup and winked at her.

"I've been hearing some whispers about you and a certain Sam," Laura said.

"Don't believe everything that ruffles your leaves," said Jackie, winking back, but Laura looked devastated.

"Jackie, that's so offensive. At this time of year?" She gestured to her bare branches.

"Shit, I'm sorry, man. I wasn't thinking. That was my bad. Yeah, me and Sam have been seeing how things are. Sorry again."

Laura shrugged curtly and whisked her branches expertly past the stacked dishes behind the counter without bumping a single one.

"If I can ask," Darryl said, just as Nilanjana was saying, "I don't think I even like waffles," and then they both said, "Oh, sorry, you go," and then both stopped.

"No, really, please ask whatever question it was," she said, laughing a bit at their conversational stumble. "I was just putting out words to fill up the space."

"Okay. These last couple days have been nice. Last night was especially nice."

She smiled out of reflex. Maybe she did want to date someone. He had kind eyes, said kind things, touched her in kind ways.

"But I was curious," he continued. "If you definitely aren't interested in joining the Congregation, which is fine, can you tell me more about what brought you by the church that day? I would like to be of help, if I can."

She considered Darryl, the way his face looked in the morning light through the window, the way he threw one arm up on the back of the booth next to him, the way he crossed his legs. He seemed like a man at ease, a man not hiding any other version of himself. Simply a man who was the man he was in the moment he was it.

But what did she know about him really? He belonged to

an organization that she believed might be involved in terrible things, and was, a possibility she hadn't eliminated yet, trying to keep Carlos from properly studying the nature of the other desert world, and the strange house that served as a gateway to it. And here he was in the jittery afterglow of their first night together bringing up her visit to the church.

Darryl was likable. But there is a difference between likable and good. In many ways, Nilanjana felt like one of the most important parts of growing up, and of approaching the world as an adult, was understanding the difference between likable and good, and recognizing that one often had no effect on the other.

She had no way of knowing what he wanted from her, and so the question here was how much of her life did she want to live with the comfort of trust, and how much did she want to live with the painful necessity of suspicion? This balance, she felt, was the rest of what it meant to be a grown-up. And she decided that the kind of adult she wanted to be was one that lived openly as much as possible, even if that occasionally meant being open to pain.

"It's hard to explain," she said.

"Reasons for coming to church often are."

"Right, sure. I'm sure, but not like that. See it started with a laser."

He laughed.

"Okay, you got me. That is the first time a reason for interest in our religion started that way."

"Well, not a laser, I guess, but more a house. Wait. Let me start over."

And she told him most everything that had led to this point. The house that doesn't exist but looks like it exists. The desert otherworld, an empty place that could be reached through the house. Carlos trying to study this otherworld, and how an unknown force or group or groups was trying to prevent him. How something was destroying Night Vale, great pits opening up in the earth, swallowing buildings, people, entire lives, whole. How that something was maybe the same thing that was trying to stop Carlos from discovering more about the desert otherworld.

"The whole situation's a blur from our vantage," she said. "We're too close. We can see colors, maybe the outline of a shape. But we need to find a way to get farther out, try to see this thing as a whole. That's the only way we'll understand what's going on."

"Huh," Darryl said. "But what does the Joyous Congregation have to do with all of this?"

His tone was confusion, but also suspicion. Just what are you accusing us of? was the question under the question.

"Waffle," said Laura, dropping the plate in front of Nilanjana. Both Darryl and Nilanjana had been so absorbed in the moment that they hadn't heard her coming, and Darryl grunted in surprise, and then smiled to hide his embarrassment about the grunt. "And omelet."

Grateful for the distraction, Nilanjana dug into her waffle, which had been cooked to a perfect medium rare.

Darryl watched her eat. He had been hungry before, but now he wasn't touching his omelet. He wanted to hear what she had to say first. She reconsidered her thoughts on dating and was now glad they were not. This was why dating and friendships were so difficult. People want to confront you about differences of opinion, question you about what you're doing, be always present in your life. She liked the measurability of numbers and nature.

"No, I don't think your church is doing anything in particular," she said, around a mouthful of food, wishing now that she hadn't started eating. "Well, your description of heaven sounds a lot like the desert otherworld, which is interesting. And then, your pamphlet."

"What about it?"

"It said it was written by someone named Wordsmith."

His face was unreadable.

"And why was that interesting?" he asked, in a careful and flat voice.

"Well," she said. Oh, what the hell. She had already told him this much. Maybe he would be willing to help her. "City Council said that the Wordsmith had told them about the otherworld, had warned them about what was out there. It seems like whatever conspiracy is trying to keep us from understanding the desert otherworld, the Wordsmith is at the heart of it. Maybe even collaborating with the city to stop Carlos's research. Who knows? And then, in the pamphlet: Wordsmith. So this person has something to do with your church. And that's why I was there."

Darryl nodded, and finally took a bite of his food. She watched him chew, waiting for some kind of response.

"So? What do you think? Do you know who the Wordsmith is, and what they're planning? Could you help me find them?"

Darryl laughed, quickly and without humor.

"Yes. I can help you find him."

He held out his hand, like a prospective employee meeting his interviewer.

"It's nice to meet you. I'm the Wordsmith."

15

"You little shit . . ."

. . . was a phrase she could have said.

SLAP

. . . was an action she could have done to his face.

[stands up; leaves without saying a word]

. . . was a stage direction she could have performed.

"Oh . . ."

. . . was the actual sound she made.

"I'm not so good at verbal communication," Darryl said. "Maybe you've noticed. So when I need to get a message across, I write a note. I got really good at writing because of that. Friends in college started calling me the Wordsmith and it stuck."

It sounded like bragging. He was unaware of that.

"Do you have a nickname you wish people had called you? Like, in middle school, I tried to get my friends to call me D-Day, because my name starts with *D*, and that sounded tough. Plus I'm a big history buff, and, of course, D-Day is short for Dog Day, which happened during World War II, when we defeated the Germans by not letting them come over to pet our dogs anymore."

I don't know if you have a way with words, but you certainly have a lot of words, Nilanjana thought as she dabbed her face with the napkin and placed it on the table.

"Are you mad at me?" Darryl lowered his voice.

"Of course not. I'm just thinking about a lot of work I need to get done today. No. No. I'm not mad at you," she said, not exactly meaning it.

"Okay," he said, not exactly believing her.

"The church asks you to write stuff for them? Because you're so good at it?"

"I write pamphlets and flyers and stuff. Did you see the illustrations that Jamillah made? She's great at those. Has to do them one-handed because she never puts down the drill."

"Did you ever talk to the City Council?" Nilanjana worried about asking, about making so clear the direction of her investigation, but her instincts as a scientist drove her forward.

"Yeah! That was a cool day. I decided to try to convert the City Council. Everyone else told me not to. That the council is dangerous. But I wanted to try anyway. I mean, I was afraid I was going to die the whole time, but it was . . . It felt important. A chance to have our say in front of beings who mattered. I gave them a pamphlet and talked them through it. They got excited when they learned about the Smiling God. Thanked me for 'informing them of this matter.' I half expected them at services the next week but it never happened. At least maybe they won't be so quick to crack down on the Congregation. I felt good about that."

"What exactly did you tell them about the smiling god and the house that doesn't exist?"

"How would I tell them about the house when you just now told me about it? And I gave them the basic story of the Smiling God. What is this about anyway? Why are you so upset?"

There was silence. It was awkward. It was less awkward than

his talking, so it was fine. The City Council had said the Wordsmith had warned them. Either he had lied to her, or the City Council had found information in his pamphlet that he hadn't realized was in there. Now she needed to make him think that she didn't suspect him anymore.

"I didn't realize you were the Wordsmith, and so now I know that my investigation into that was a dead end," she explained carefully. "It just made me realize how misguided I was to keep pursuing anything with the Joyous Congregation. You were so nice to show me around and welcome me in. Your friends and church were lovely. Then you brought me a sandwich, and we went out last night and had a lot of . . ."

Darryl coughed.

"Fun. *Fun* I was going to say."

He laughed.

Nilanjana did not laugh at first. And then she laughed but it was too late. A poor acting choice.

[stands up; leaves without saying a word] . . . would have been a better acting choice, she thought.

"I'm not trying to recruit you or anything," he said. "It's not like that. I just. I just like you, Nilanjana."

"I'm not worried about your church, Darryl. And I'm not worried about you." Lies. "You're not a dangerous person." Not a lie necessarily, but certainly not her current working hypothesis.

Darryl did not react.

"A delightful person, in fact," she said.

He smiled his usual wide, forced smile. He did not intend for it to come off as forced, but it did.

"You're delightful too."

"I'm going to be late to work."

They split the bill and she drove him back to his car. Nilan-jana wished it had been in awkward silence, but he told a long story about how Stephanie was such a good volleyball player that they started a church volleyball team. One time, during a game, she spiked a ball so hard that it broke the crystal pyramid at the top of the oaken tower. No one knew what the purpose of the pyramid on every volleyball court was, and no one had ever seen one get broken before.

Everyone was cursed for days after. It was terrible. A few people lost pets. Someone else was falsely imprisoned by the Secret Police. Darryl's car was broken into. Once the pyramid's curse had been lifted, they all had a good laugh about it as they buried all their volleyballs and nets and made Stephanie prom-ise to never play the game again.

"She's so awesome," Darryl said.

"Sounds like," said Nilanjana. His adoration of Stephanie didn't bother Nilanjana. And so she ignored the fact that it did. She did as many scientists do against the precepts of their own profession: She was selective about which facts she allowed into her data set.

They were next to his vehicle. "Let's do this again," he said.

"Sure," she said. She didn't mean it, she adamantly told herself.

Darryl watched as she left. He texted Jamillah about what had happened and she texted back the cry-laughing emoji, fol-lowed by the orange tree on fire emoji, followed by the child walking through the contemporary sculpture wing of the art museum emoji.

"Wonderful, you're back," Carlos called out as Nilanjana car-ried her field notes into his office and laid them out in neat rows on his table. "It's all been quiet here, but I've been afraid to start any experiments until I heard from you."

"Some developments on our search for who Wordsmith is and what they are planning," she said. "I slept . . . I had sex with him."

"Huh," said Carlos. He didn't seem upset, but then he preferred to express himself through words or actions rather than emotive gestures.

"I thought he was someone else. I thought he was a nice guy with . . . I don't know . . . a body I guess. Someone to have a drink with. And it's not clear to me that he is definitely part of any conspiracy. He claims he only went to convert the City Council. That is, if you believe him."

She slumped into a chair and sighed into her palms.

"This isn't going well," she said.

"Based on last night, it sounds like it's going great."

"You're cute."

He frowned.

"Of course I am. I'm a scientist. All scientists are cute."

Even his frown was cute.

"No, you're *being* cute."

Carlos took off his glasses and rubbed his eyes. He looked tired but also perfect. His perfection was only emphasized by the small human details of exhaustion and stress.

"Let me tell you a story, Nils. When I first came here, I was frightened of this town. I was confused by it. Time didn't work. The City Council were creatures I had never seen before. There were angels, actual angels, wandering around, and they were all named Erika. But the strangest part of it was that everyone here treated it as normal. No one was a bit surprised at the form that City Council took, or that UFOs are a regular part of the night sky. I would listen to Cecil on the radio, calmly describing the day's events, and I would try to call him, to get him to understand that everything was all wrong, that time didn't work here. But it wasn't that he didn't see the things that I saw, he just interpreted them differently. I was afraid of him and all the people of Night Vale because of that.

"But as I spent more time talking to him, explaining science to him, I realized that even though I didn't understand his worldview, I liked talking to him. And even though he didn't understand my worldview, he liked talking to me. And we liked being with each other. And that like turned to love. Sometimes still he'll calmly report something on the radio that I know is impossible by all current scientific knowledge, but that same day he'll squint up from bed with a pillow-wrinkled face as I bring him coffee, and he smiles like it's the first time he's ever seen me, and he says, 'How did I end up this lucky?'

"I see my younger self in you, and I'm glad you're helping me with my research. You and I are both outsiders. We always will be, but it gets less as we accept more of the town's strangeness. And I know that's hard. It was hard for me too. Still sometimes is. Everyone in this town is frightening and friendly and kind and awful. But everyone everywhere is."

As he talked, Nilanjana glanced down at her findings next to Carlos's findings, and something caught her eye. She scanned the data as Carlos continued with his lecture.

"People are complicated. This Wordsmith of yours, maybe he is working with the city, maybe he isn't. But he isn't necessarily bad. Of course, he could also be bad. You can only trust someone based on what you experience with them. People are complex. You can't reduce them to charts and equations. I've tried. I've tried so hard. But it's not possible yet."

She finished looking through the combined data and pounded her fist on the table.

"Okay, I'm sorry," he said. "You're upset. I'll drop it."

"There's something big happening, Carlos."

"Nilanjana, I'm sorry if I offended you. Sometimes I can't tell—"

"No, in the desert. Look."

She pointed at the chart. Then at the graph below it.

"We've been assuming that agents from City Hall have been causing these events. But look at this."

The first few events had happened several days apart, each one minor but larger than the last. They were scattered all over the map. Then the next few happened a day or two apart, increasing in magnitude, but still with no pattern to their placement. The most recent events were even larger, more frequent, dotting all over town and culminating in the vanishings of Larry Leroy and Big Rico.

"Most result in the disappearance of material and people," she said, "and leave behind those pits. And they correspond with every time you try to study the house or any other aspect of the otherworld. This supports the idea that it is the City Council, trying to stop your work."

"Pamela nearly said as much," Carlos agreed.

"But there are also these."

She indicated smaller events, with a different set of data. Short localized tremors. Sketching a series of triangles in the desert outside of Night Vale, out toward the mountains if you believe in that sort of thing.

"This movement doesn't correspond with your experiments at all. I've gone out to look at these pits, and there's nothing anywhere near them. It looks like the random movement of an animal."

Carlos traced the triangles with his finger.

"I've seen something like this before," he said, "but I can't remember where."

"Let's say it's possible that a living thing is causing this, then what kind of creature moves like this?" she said. "The incidents don't connect linearly. How does it appear, destroy, and then appear somewhere completely different?"

"Perhaps it is moving underground, and we only see it when it pops up from below?"

She thought about that. And she thought about a stained-glass image of a gigantic creature emerging from an old oak door. An old oak door that leads to "heaven," which is a desert.

"Or," she said, "when it pops up from another world."

16

If there was anything moving out in the desert, the helicopters would see it. And she knew of one helicopter that had shown a particular interest in her. So Nilanjana went back out to the desert, to a quiet place in the scrublands, and waited. She didn't have to wait for long.

"How's it going up there?" she called to the helicopter when it arrived.

No response.

"I'm just hanging out here looking at this cactus. Kinda boring," Nilanjana said. "Thought some conversation would be nice."

The helicopter hovered noisily and wordlessly. Whap-whap-whap.

"Do you mind if I use a pen and paper? To take some notes. I know writing utensils are illegal, but, like, everyone uses them, right?"

"WRITING UTENSILS ARE BANNED FROM NIGHT VALE CITY LIMITS, CITIZEN," the helicopter loudspeakers boomed.

"Okay." Nilanjana took out her phone and typed her notes into the screen. "How's this?"

No response.

She decided to try a more direct approach. She held up the graphs and charts from Carlos's notebook.

"I'm looking for something big out here in the desert. Have you seen anything? Anything like the movement these charts are showing?"

Whap-whap-whap.

"Ah, sorry," Nilanjana muttered, putting the papers down. "There's no way you can see tiny charts from that far up."

"I can see the charts perfectly. My vision is excellent," the loudspeaker said. "And don't be so hard on yourself."

"Oh! Thanks." She held the charts back up.

"That data indicates wild seismic stuff all over town. Fascinating," the loudspeaker said. "Are you taking into account air pressure and humidity levels? Also are you checking those with the City Earthquake schedule?"

"Yes and yes."

"And those movements out in the desert. Those are interesting. They suggest something moving underground maybe?"

"What makes you say that?" Nilanjana asked.

"I'm a big fan of Stephen R. Covey's *Seven Habitats of Highly Effective Beings*. Number two is Beneath the Earth's Surface. It used to be the lizard people lived down there, but they all returned to space decades ago."

"And these events are too random to be the work of the lizard people," Nilanjana pointed out. "So you're up there, it seems, all the time? Have you seen any of these events actually happen?"

Whap of the blades. The loudspeaker crackled.

"Can you hear me?" she said.

"Duh."

"Well?"

"DATA RECORDED BY SECRET POLICE IS CLASSIFIED." The loudspeaker volume had increased quite a lot.

"Wait. Not classified. IT DOESN'T EXIST. FORGET I SAID CLASSIFIED. I'M JUST FLYING A HELICOPTER HERE. No, wait. I'm not. YOU DON'T SEE THIS HELICOPTER. LEAVE THE AREA."

Nilanjana sighed and put her stuff back into her car. The Secret Police recorded everything in town: conversations, people walking to work, financial activity, people sleeping, people playing with their cats and dogs. It wasn't uncommon to see Secret Police standing outside a person's window taping cats playing with catnip-stuffed toys. They loved that garbage. She knew that the helicopter had to have taken video of this area, showing some kind of moving thing, or at least a visual on how the pits had formed. She stood at the open door of her car for a few seconds, trying to figure out what to say that would change the pilot's mind. But what did she know about how the helicopters thought? After all, this wasn't her town. She hadn't grown up with them.

"That guy that was out here with me last week. Darryl," she tried. "He works with the Joyous Congregation of the Smiling God. He's nice. I think he's nice. But I also think the church is maybe doing awful stuff. We had a date last night. Like it went well, but I didn't realize how far up in the church he was until this morning, and it made me feel awful.

"I think something terrible is happening, something related to the church. Or maybe it's the City Council, in which case I don't expect you'll tell me. Larry Leroy is dead. So is everyone at Big Rico's. There are these pits out in the desert. And rumbling under the earth. And I don't want to become part of a police investigation or get arrested. But I think that if I could see some kind of footage, that would help."

Whap whap whap.

"Why am I talking to you? You're probably recording all of this and are going to report me. I'm going to have to go down to the Secret Police station and turn this data over. You know what? Let's just pretend I didn't say anything. Are we cool? Can I go?"

No response.

"Damn it. Damn it. Damn it," she said.

She stared at the ground and realized that maybe the helicopter was giving her a silent opportunity to leave. Go! Get out of there, her mind shouted at her.

She jumped into the driver's seat, said, "Glad we're all cool. Seeya!" and slammed the door. She started the engine and turned the car toward the main road.

"HALT, NILANJANA SIKDAR! HALT YOUR VEHICLE."

Her engine cut out, stopped remotely by the helicopter. Most car problems in Night Vale turn out to be caused by the sabotage of government or city agents. Auto mechanics regularly end up arrested for tampering with government operations. As the engine stopped, her stomach fell. So did her head. Her forehead bumped in frustration against the steering wheel.

She got out of the car and raised her hands.

"Put your hands down," the loudspeaker said.

She did. There was a pause. She didn't know what to do with her hands now that they were down.

"Last week my boyfriend left me," the helicopter said. "'You fly around in that helicopter all the time,' he told me. And I said, 'Not all the time. Don't use superlatives, Nate. You're always using superlatives.' But he wanted to go to Aaliyah Seance Night at Dark Owl Records. Aaliyah does occasional concerts via a medium at the record store and they're nearly impossible to get tickets to, because the owner of that place doesn't want anything to get too popular, so she only makes three tickets available to the public."

"Aaliyah was so great."

"Still is. Anyway, I couldn't go because I was out here doing this. And I love hovering in place and staring at all the sand, but Nate's right, I do this all the time, and it's hard to find someone who is nice and understanding and brings you falafel on your lunch break. How was the Moonlite's falafel by the way? I've been meaning to try that."

"Fine. A bit dry, but the paraffin wax chips and butterscotch marmalade were tasty."

"Good, good. Darryl's a nice guy. I looked up some stuff on him. And that church is weird, no doubt. But I don't know. I'm not telling you you have to be in a relationship. But finding a person to have cocktails with. Ooh, how was the Mulch Mojito at Tourniquet? My bartender friend Arjun told me that you ordered that drink."

"Not good. Darryl's manhattan was better but the texture was too crunchy."

"Too bad."

"Listen, no offense, but I think I'd rather be arrested than have a helicopter cop explain the importance of dating to me. Is this what you do now, seminars? I'm sorry to hear Nate left you. That's very sad. I'm sure you're nice too, like Darryl, but also like Darryl, you work for a pretty terrifying organization. I don't think the city has my best interests in mind here. I just want to find out what we're up against. That's all I want."

A minute of silent hovering in which Nilanjana was too scared to move, and then a huffing sound from the loudspeaker. It sounded like sniffling.

"Are you crying?" she said.

"Yes."

"Oh, I'm sorry. I'm sorry. I wasn't trying to make you feel bad."

"No, I'm being an asshole to you. It's just this is my job, and I love my job. And you, you're nice. I like it when you're in the desert. I don't feel so alone."

"Me too. I like it when you're here."

"And your needs and my job . . . They kind of conflict, I guess. And"—more huffing until they recovered their words—"I miss Nate. I miss him. I can't sleep. I miss him."

"Come here. Come here."

The helicopter lowered to the ground. The wind whipped sand into Nilanjana's shirt and hair, and she had to turn her head and squint. She walked sideways toward the cockpit. The windows were heavily tinted and she couldn't see anything through them.

"I'm going to give you a hug, okay?" Nilanjana offered.

"I'M NOT ALLOWED TO EXIT THE CRAFT. IT'S A SE-CRET POLICE VEHICLE AND THERE ARE SECRET PO-LICE THINGS IN HERE. PLUS I'M SHY."

The loudspeaker was painfully loud from this short a distance. Nilanjana stepped up on one of the skids and drew her arms wide, placing her palms flat against the sides of the door. "Ssshhh . . ." she said, as she gently patted the door.

Sobs roared out of the loudspeaker. Her ears would be ringing the rest of the day.

"IT'S SO STUPID."

"It's not. Sssh," Nilanjana said, rubbing her hand back and forth along the helicopter.

A minute or so passed.

"I. I SHOULD GO. THANK YOU. I DIDN'T REALIZE HOW MUCH I NEEDED THAT."

Nilanjana's ears burned, not just from the volume but also from being pressed against the hot metal door. She let the helicopter go, and retreated to a safe distance.

"You're welcome. I hope to see you again soon."

"YOU TOO." The helicopter began its ascent.

"Hey, are you going to report this? I just need to know, so I'm not worrying about it for the rest of my life."

"You're good. Also, check your phone."

"Check my phone?"

"The government has more, but they'll never let you see. This was all I could send without being noticed. Good-bye, Nilanjana Sikdar." The helicopter returned to its spot 150 feet in the air.

"Thanks! Bye!" She waved.

No response.

Nilanjana returned to her car. It had been an unproductive day, but at least it hadn't been counterproductive. She grabbed her phone. No emails or messages. She opened up her files and found one that hadn't been there before, labeled "Sorry the Mulch Mojito Wasn't Good."

She clicked the file and gasped as she realized what she was looking at.

17

The desert from a helicopter's point of view. Mountains separating blue sky and beige sand. For several seconds, nothing but that.

Then something moving in the sand. Possibly an error in video replay, but it looked like bumps of earth rising and then falling, one after the other, in a line. And then, some huge shape coming out of the sand, arcing through the air, and disappearing back into the sand. Then again. The resolution wasn't good, so the only thing certain about it was the movement.

She watched the video again and again. But the more she watched it, the less certain she became about what she was seeing. It was proof that there was something there, but didn't give her any information about what it was. The pilot had mentioned that this was all he could save from the city. Which meant the city had more. She would need to get it from the Hall of Public Records downtown, one of the most secure and private locations in Night Vale.

The archivists who ran the Hall of Public Records did not like lots of things. They didn't like journalists. They didn't like ancestry research. They didn't like questions. They despised Capricorns. Loathed them. They certainly didn't like scientists. They kept the archives behind thick vault doors and used an elaborate security system.

Nilanjana had been thrown out of the Hall of Public Records

once for trying to get a copy of her car registration. She had lost the original. Back in Indiana, something like that wouldn't be a problem, and it hadn't occurred to her that this would be different in her new town. She filled out Form 11-AU-RF and paid the thirty-five-dollar fee. The clerk stamped the form and the back of her check, then stapled them together, placed them into a manila file folder, took out a cigarette lighter, and burned the whole thing. They tossed the flaming paperwork into a metal trash can and then stomped it out with their boot. Nilanjana filled out the form again and wrote another check, got back in line, hoping for a different clerk. She got a different clerk, but when she handed the money and form to them, they gnawed the paper to shreds with their teeth. She asked what she could do to ensure that they would accept her form and payment, but this had been the wrong approach. The clerk pressed a button below their countertop and an alarm rang out. An LED screen above her began flashing the word TREASON. The others in line, who had previously been pointing at her and shouting "Interloper!" changed from that friendly greeting into a malevolent scream of "Fifth columnist! Fifth columnist!" She didn't even know what *fifth columnist* meant. She looked it up later, but the definition in the dictionary had been redacted. Then she went to the public library to look it up, and was nearly bitten in half by a librarian that had broken loose from its shackles. The learning process of moving to a new area can be exhausting, and even the most basic errands can feel like a struggle.

Now she knew she couldn't just walk up to the Hall of Public Records registrar's desk and ask for files on strange subterranean activities in the desert. So instead she walked up to the registrar's desk and asked where the restroom was, hoping to then sneak off and find the records.

The clerk glared at her for a long moment. So did the line of people she cut in front of to ask her question. Several of them grumbled "Interloper." Several others nodded and agreed: "Interloper."

The clerk looked the part of an archetypical government employee: elderly, at least seven feet tall, uneven shoulders, and wearing a visor, plastic vampire teeth, and orange peels for earrings. The clerk wore a name tag that said, CITY OF NIGHT VALE HALL OF PUBLIC RECORDS and then underneath was an etching of a spike-tipped cudgel.

Nilanjana tried again: "I'm sorry to interrupt . . . um, is that a mace or a club? I'm not sure I know how to pronounce your name."

The clerk hissed.

Nilanjana hissed back.

The clerk nodded and pointed toward an unmarked wooden door in the corner of the waiting area.

"Knock four times. Wait ninety seconds and then scratch down the center of it," the clerk said.

"Thank you."

Hiss.

"Interloper," said Charlie Bair, behind her in line. He was there to apply for a Haunting License, which would allow him to be a ghost after he died. The city only issued a few a year, because ghosts were cool and everyone wanted to be a ghost.

Nilanjana knocked on the door, then waited and scratched, as the clerk had said. A panel in the door slid open. It was dark behind the panel.

When nothing happened, she said, "Hello?"

Nothing continued to happen.

"Hellllooo?" She leaned into the hole but couldn't see anything.

"It's unlocked, just open it," the clerk shouted from across the room.

"Interloper," Charlie said again, but distractedly. He was worried he wouldn't get his license and would have to cease to exist after he died, which seemed boring to him.

Nilanjana turned the doorknob. It opened easily. She stepped into what felt like a hallway, but it was too dark to see. The door slipped from her fingers as she moved forward and it slammed shut behind her. She was in absolute blackness except for a single box of light on the floor from the panel in the door. The darkness felt heavy, and she imagined that there was someone just next to her. And then that imagination became a certainty. There was someone just next to her in the dark hallway. Frantically, she tried to open the door, but there was no knob or handle on the inside. Whatever was in the hallway with her was reaching for her, she knew. She knew that it was about to touch her with hands that would be cold and dry.

A face appeared on the other side of the panel. Two white eyes in the shadow of a backlit head. Nothing touched her.

Nilanjana stifled a scream. "You scared me."

"Everything should scare you," the face said. "Everything and everybody is scary."

It was not the voice of the clerk. She had no idea who this was.

"The bathroom is down this hall," the voice said. "Hang a left. Then another left. Then pass two hallways, then another left. Then take the stairs up two flights. Turn right. Go down one flight, and it will be four doors down on your right."

"Is there a light switch in this hallway?"

The panel slammed shut. It was completely dark. Any second now a cold, dry hand. She wasn't alone in here. She wasn't alone in here.

Stop it, she told herself. This wasn't rational. This was just fear. She needed to look at the data and make a hypothesis.

Hypothesis: The hallway was empty when I entered it, so it's still empty now. The feeling of not being alone is just my body's response to the dark.

She hoped that the data would continue to support this hypothesis.

She felt along the walls looking for a light switch, or even a door. Feeling in the dark, she found a bend to the left in the path. After more cautious blind walking, she found another bend to the left. She came to another apparent turn, but upon feeling the area out, she realized it was a four-way intersection. She decided to go right, against the voice's directions. After all, she wasn't actually looking for a bathroom, and with the way things were going, she wouldn't want to use any bathroom they had anyway.

She rummaged in her bag and found her cell phone. She activated the flashlight app on it and used its weak light to examine her surroundings. There was door after door, down the hallway as far as the beam of light went. Many of them were unhelpful, with markings that said things like ROOM 16-UX-9: SUPPLIES (which was confusingly right next to Room 2783: Commissary) or ROOM 12.4Z: THIS DOOR LEADS NOWHERE (which was completely accurate; the door opened onto a wall). She backtracked a couple of times looking for any kind of room with a label like ECOLOGY STUDIES or LAND MANAGE-MENT or even TOP SECRET SHIT IN THE DESERT. She laughed. That'd be convenient, she thought.

Failing to find anything spelled out, she tried the next door she came to (ROOM MMMM-459-P: PUBLIC PIANO REGISTRY) just to see what was inside. The door opened into a room that was as dark as the hallway. Her flashlight wavered over a high-ceilinged space, covered wall to wall with shelves full of document boxes. Then her beam found the face of a woman and Nilanjana yelped. The woman yelped back. She was sitting at a desk in the middle of the completely dark room. By her were stacks of boxes. Every single one of the boxes, except for the one nearest to the door, was labeled PIANO DECLINED. The one by the door said, PIANO DECLINATION—PENDING.

"Interloper!" the woman shouted.

"Hi. Sorry. Wrong room." Nilanjana backed out of the doorway and turned her light down the hall. She saw what looked like a figure at the end of the hall. "Who's there?" she said. She took a few more steps forward, and the figure became clear. It was the woman from the desk.

"You aren't supposed to be here, Interloper," the woman said.

"You are trespassing," the same woman shouted, but from the other direction. Nilanjana turned her light. The woman was still at the desk. Her skin was like rice paper, with pulsing blue veins underneath. She looked like a cave fish.

"I don't like trespassers," the woman said from the hallway. When Nilanjana turned the light back to her, the woman was much closer.

"Do you know what I do with trespassers?" the woman said from the desk. Now she was standing.

"I eat them," the woman said from the hallway. She was inches away. Her breath was hot against Nilanjana's face. It smelled like old cooking oil. In the upturned light from the phone, her face was a moonscape of shadows.

"Yes, I eat them," the same woman said from the doorway, her breath hot against Nilanjana's ear.

"I'm just looking for some records," Nilanjana managed.

"I ate the records," the woman said, with both of her bodies and both of her voices, slightly out of time with each other.

Nilanjana had no scientific model to understand what was happening at this moment, and so she listened to her instinct to run. As she stumbled backward, she swung the light between the two versions of the woman, catching the stop-motion movement of the woman's bodies jerking in strange postures toward her. "I," the woman said. There was only one of her now. She was a few feet away. "Ate." Inches away. "Them." A cold, dry hand around Nilanjana's neck.

"That's enough, Claire."

The voice was loud, amplified through a PA system. Fluorescent lights snapped on up and down the hall. There was no hand around Nilanjana's neck. Claire was leaning against the wall, pouting. Pamela Winchell walked forward, holding her portable amp and microphone. Behind Pamela were two Secret Police officers, wearing balaclavas and capes, like any member of a secret police force would.

"Arrest her," Pamela said into the microphone.

"Wait. Why? I'm just looking for the bathroom."

"Aren't we all, metaphorically, just looking for the bathroom?"

"I'm hungry," said Claire.

"Beat it," said Pamela. Claire growled and ran away on all fours.

"Why am I being arrested?" said Nilanjana.

"We know what's in that otherworld. We know what your boss's meddling could bring upon us all. We know what you are up to and we know what that church is up to."

"Who says we're up to anything? I'm just trying to find the bathroom."

"Who cares what anyone says?" said Pamela. "Let me tell you what I say. Somewhere in this galaxy is a moon. And it is filled with holes, that moon, and inside those holes are microbes. Life. A wisp of life, but life nonetheless. And the microbes do not know we exist. They do not know anything because they are uncomplex. They consume water molecules and other microbes, and then they expel air molecules and divide into new microbes. They do all of that without knowing why, without knowing that we are here in the same galaxy as them, and without even knowing that they are there. They don't even know about themselves."

"What does that have to do with anything?"

Pamela smiled.

"If you find out, please let me know." She winked and snapped her fingers to the officers behind her. The handcuffs were cold and dry.

"What do you know, Pamela?" Nilanjana raised her voice as the Secret Police carried her through an exit, outside to the cruiser.

The car door closed. Pamela stood unmoving in the doorway, her face placid.

"What do you know is in the otherworld?" But Nilanjana's words were lost in soundproof glass as the officers drove her away.

Charlie Bair left City Hall with the Haunting License clutched to his chest. He had been so anxious about whether he would get one. There had been a tightness in his chest when he tried to sleep. And then he was worried he was having a heart attack, and that worry made the tightness get worse. This cycle had left him terrified that he would die without the ability to become a ghost, and his years of journaling cool ideas for hauntings would have gone to waste. He walked with the license to his job as weekday shift manager at the Ralphs supermarket downtown. He was late, because the wait at City Hall had been way longer than he expected. But who could care about something as insignificant as scheduled work times when he had gotten something as significant as his license? The door hissed open for him, and he entered a world of filtered air, and pyramids of oranges, and a boss who had just about had it with him, but it was a world that was, unlike him, temporary. He would feel a fluttery elation for the next two days, until the floor got hot, and the ground opened up, and one of the mysterious pits appeared in the dairy section, taking out an entire case of lactose-free milk along with Charlie, who, looking up at a constellation of milk cartons in free fall above him, thought, At least I get to be a ghost now, but who was totally wrong about that.

18

Darryl looked at the fox, with its toothy smile. The other foxes sprawled around it. This was his favorite window in the church. Community. That said it all for him.

He smiled back at the fox, separating his lips and showing as much of his teeth as was possible. Smiling was an important part of worship and praise, and so teachers at church school would take everyone through the steps on a weekly basis, a fun way of starting the class.

"Step one: Separate your lips," Ms. French, his church school teacher would say.

"Step two: Use facial muscles to pull back the corners of your mouth," they would all chant together. "Step three: Expose as much of your teeth as possible. Step four: Widen your eyes."

"And that is . . ." she would finish.

"That is how to be happy!" they would all shout, showing each other their teeth and feeling happy, in the simple way children can and adults spend years and much of their money trying to recapture even a moment of.

Here, as an adult, he showed his teeth to the window, and felt somewhat happy, in a complicated grown-up way. There was a lot on his mind, worries and, Smiling God help him, even doubts. And so he returned to this image of community, and he smiled at it, in order to try to quiet something that was happening inside him.

"Hey, Darryl," said a voice. Gordon was behind him, with his teeth showing and the corners of his mouth pulled way back, in order to demonstrate how happy he was to be talking to Darryl. "Pastor Munn wants to see you."

All the calm of his meditation on community slipped away from Darryl. Pastor Munn rarely had time to speak to individual members of the community. That's what Gordon and the junior pastors were for. Being asked to talk to Munn was, well, Darryl had never heard of it happening before. Short of waving fists and saying "Believe in a Smiling God" at each other after services, he'd never had a conversation with her.

He hid his nervousness by showing even more teeth.

"Sure thing," he said. "Lead the way."

Pastor Munn's office was one of the largest rooms in the church besides the worship hall. Darryl had only been in the office once, during an orientation meeting for church volunteers. They had sat in the front sitting area and the pastor had not even been present. Now he was ushered past this area to the intimidating desk, made from repurposed old oak. He marveled at the art on the pastor's wall: original concept paintings for the stained glass, and a framed needlework piece stretching nearly the length of the office that said JOYFULLY IT DEVOURS! in old-timey script.

The pastor sat behind the desk. Her huge square yellow hat covered much of her face, but she was wearing her day clothes instead of the robes she wore at services.

"Darryl," she said, with the same warm voice she delivered her sermons in. A voice that made the sermons feel like they were directed individually to each member of the congregation, rather than collectively to them all. "We don't get to talk with one another often, do we?"

"No, Pastor."

"You're busy. I'm busy. We both love our work in the church so much. We sometimes forget the people who make the church what it is. Thanks for coming in for this chat."

"We appreciate it," Gordon said. He stood behind the pastor. His smile hadn't changed a bit since he had approached Darryl outside.

"No problem," Darryl said. "I just want to say how much this means to me. I mean, the Congregation is my family."

He paused. Pastor Munn was looking right at him but somehow beyond him, several thoughts ahead.

"I mean," he continued, "thanks for, well, I don't know what this is about."

The pastor smiled, not the step-by-step smile of the church, but a fluid, natural smile. She removed her hat and handed it to Gordon, who carefully placed it on a hook on the wall.

"This doesn't have to be about anything," she said. "I like to check in with people occasionally. Make sure that their journey with the Smiling God is going smoothly and happily."

"She wants to check in with you," said Gordon.

"You're a shining example of the kindness and energy we like to see in the church, Darryl, but I hope your faith remains as strong as when I first welcomed you as an official member. Do you remember that day?"

He did. He was ten. His parents were still alive, but they traveled often. They themselves rarely went to church, using the Congregation and all of its various classes and groups to serve as a kind of babysitter for Darryl. It was during a youth class that he had met Stephanie. They became best friends. She and her family were devout practitioners of the faith, while Darryl really needed a place to be when his parents weren't home, which was often.

Stephanie got Darryl interested in the faith itself, all of the many blessings of the Smiling God and the way It could devour all of the pain of your life. It was a beautiful story, especially when it was told to you by someone you trusted and cared for. A story never stands on its own, but exists in the context of the storyteller.

Once a year, the church holds its Youth Culling, where children can choose to become full members of the church. Stephanie convinced Darryl to join her in becoming a member. He remembered Pastor Munn's boxy, yellow hat and flowing robes. He remembered her distant eyes as she waved her fist over his forehead. He remembered the entire Congregation singing the famous hymn:

Bring them in
Cull the children
Lead them toward the sacred Teeth
Cull them
Devour their minds clean
Ooooo Oooo
Bring them in.

"I remember it well, Pastor Munn," Darryl said.

"Wonderful. But I am concerned," said the pastor, frowning to demonstrate her concern. "We are all concerned. About whether you keep good company. About whether you do good things."

"It's concerning," said Gordon.

Darryl didn't say anything at first. He wasn't certain what they knew. Were they alarmed that a scientist came to investigate the church? Did they know he and the scientist were dating (or whatever unlabeled thing they were doing)? Did they know what his time with Nilanjana had led him to do?

Some deep, childlike part of him felt that they knew everything, but he was grown-up enough to know that even if the Smiling God could see into his heart, the pastor and Gordon were as human as he was.

"I'm sorry to have concerned you," he said carefully. "I definitely don't want to be concerning. Maybe if you could let me know what behavior it is that is causing the problem, I could correct it."

Pastor Munn cocked her head at him. Gordon, seeing this, cocked his head too, but by the time he had, the pastor had straightened up again, and he hurriedly followed along.

"I'm not mad. We're not mad. Certainly the Smiling God isn't mad. What does the Smiling God feel, Darryl?"

"Happiness," he said, the answer he had been taught since he was a child.

"And why is It happy?"

"Because It gets to devour our sins."

She nodded, as though pleased he was getting so many of the answers right.

"And what are your sins, Darryl?" she said.

So they knew. Darryl had been secretly reading up on the church's history, trying to understand if and how it was connected to this other desert world. Nilanjana's explanation of this otherworld had sounded a lot like what he knew of heaven, and he had started to wonder if heaven was a physical place, one that Carlos had apparently been trapped in. This had led to an investigation of his own. Looking into the church's history was intentionally difficult. There were few books about the church available to members, because it was important to

Pastor Munn that the traditions of the church be studied only by Elders and then shared orally, rather than allowing any literate person to interpret the religion independently.

"I just wanted to deepen my faith."

"Deepen your faith by doing what?" she said, her voice genuinely curious.

"By understanding where we came from. And what we have to do with the otherworld, the one on the other side of the house that doesn't exist. Is the otherworld heaven? Does the Smiling God live there?"

"That is not for you to ask!" Gordon shouted, and the pastor waved him down without looking. He crossed his arms and returned to his place behind her.

"Gordon's right," she said. "That is not for you to ask. An otherworld? A house that doesn't exist? Where have you been reading these things? Why have you been reading? Who have you been talking to?"

She didn't give him time to answer, demonstrating that she already knew.

"You exist to do what the Smiling God asks of you. No more or less. Isn't that wonderful? Having every responsibility taken care of by a being much greater than any of us?"

"Yes, but . . ." he said.

"Do you know the difference between faith and science?" the pastor said. "Here we believe. We believe in each other, and in our community. Ours is a way of trust, of loving honesty. In science, they are taught the opposite. They are taught to doubt. Every aspect of the world, a scientist must doubt it, and test it over and over, and even then they must doubt what they've learned. Each thought that enters their head, they must try to disprove. Can you imagine the distrust that creates? How can there be an honest community when the entire structure of their thought is based on disbelieving the inherent truth of everything they hear?"

She shook her head sadly at the plight of scientists. Darryl searched the office for anywhere to rest his eyes that wasn't her eyes. Bookshelves lined the walls. If only he were allowed to read some of these books, he might have the answers he was trying to find. The seven-volume *A Brief History of the Congregation of Joy,* which took up several feet of the bookshelf. The slim book entitled *The Aspects of the Smiling God, Enumerated and Explained, for the Lay and Expert Reader Alike.* There was even the controversial bestseller *What's with All the Stuff About Teeth?: The Joyous Congregation Exposed,* which Darryl was surprised to see, as a normal member of the Congregation would likely be excommunicated for owning such a libelous book.

Any of those books probably held the answers he sought, but it was like the pastor said. The answers were given by the church, and members of the Congregation did not need to go looking into books for more. To do so indicated doubt, and to indicate doubt was to be unfaithful to all that the Joyous Congregation had done for him. And they had done so much for him.

"I'm sorry," he said. "I just wanted to understand our history better. It seemed like maybe our Congregation might have made contact with this otherworld, and brought something back with us."

JOYFULLY IT DEVOURS! the framed needlework said, carefully hung, and centered on the wall.

The pastor laughed, a short, performative laugh. She held out her hand, and Gordon passed her the hat. She placed it, big and square, so that it shadowed her face.

"There is no otherworld, Darryl. There is only Heaven, and the will of the Smiling God. Can you follow that will?"

"Son, can you?" Gordon repeated.

"Of course," Darryl said.

"Wonderful!" the pastor said, her voice warm and intimate again. "I'm glad we had this chat. Please drop by anytime you need to talk."

"The pastor is busy." Gordon gestured him out the door.

Darryl's friends were waiting for him in the lobby.

"You spoke to the pastor? What was it like?" Jamillah said, still holding the power drill. She liked to always carry it, just in case she found herself in a situation where it would be useful. And when you always carry a power drill, almost every situation seems like a situation in which a drill would be useful.

He felt embarrassed, a little angry that his first one-on-one conversation with Pastor Munn was a reprimand. He loved his church and its people, and he understood that digging for information in banned books was bad behavior deserving of rebuke.

"It was nothing," said Darryl.

"How long have you known us?" said Stephanie. She had worked her whole life to become a Church Elder. It was important to her to learn how to help fellow members of her Congregation through personal difficulties. It was also important to her to make sure her friends weren't involved in anything that could hinder her goals. "Tell us what's going on. Are you in trouble?"

Darryl thought about Nilanjana, and her investigation into the church. If she continued doing what she was doing, she was a threat, even if her questions were well intentioned. Her vague theories were a threat to Darryl's faith in the church. She was a threat to his community. All because she believed that the church might be involved with something dangerous from the other desert world. And Darryl had believed her and wanted to help her because he liked her. A story never stands on its own, but exists in the context of the storyteller.

"I need your help," he told his friends. "There's a problem, and I need you to help me fix it."

19

They kept Nilanjana overnight in the abandoned mine shaft outside of town, where they keep people who drink too much in local bars and also people who vote incorrectly in municipal elections. The cell she spent the night lying down in (sleep never came) was not bad in comparison to the dark hallway she had been arrested in. At least no one was trying to eat her.

The next morning, a hood was pulled over her head and she was put into a car. The car drove for hours. Most of it, she felt, was in circles, but she couldn't tell for sure. When her hood was pulled off, she was in Old Town Night Vale, near the bus station. A man who wasn't short was in the driver's seat.

"Pamela wants you to know she'll be watching you," the man said.

A man who wasn't tall opened her door and pulled her out.

"Pamela wants you to know that you won't be leaving next time," the other man said. "She wants you to know that people have been in that abandoned mine shaft for a long time. She also wants you to know that the mine shaft has free HBO." The man shrugged. "In case you do end up there forever. Just so you know it's not completely terrible."

"Take care, Ms. Sikdar," the man who was not short said, as his partner got back in the car.

"That's Dr. Sikdar," she said, but he was already driving away. She took stock of where she was. She was outside of a fancy salad place (WE DUG YOUR LUNCH OUT OF THE GROUND! said the sign in the window). Across the street was the Last Bank of Night Vale (FREE CALENDAR OF THE END-TIMES WITH EVERY NEW CHECKING ACCOUNT!). Sitting on a bench outside the bank was a familiar person.

"Have some ice cream," Carlos said as she approached. He was holding two cones and offered her one.

"No thanks," she said.

"You had a rough night. You could use ice cream." He waggled the cone he was offering. She took the ice cream. It was her favorite, chocolate with just a little dried pasta mixed in to give it texture.

Hypothesis: Ice cream makes nothing better, but makes things feel like they're better.

"This is my fault," Carlos said, once she had sat next to him.

"It's no one's fault," she said. "It's not even a problem. This just means I'm getting closer to the truth."

"But I should be the one doing the investigating. Nils, I'm sorry I dragged you into my struggle with City Hall. I wrote Pamela a note explaining it was all a misunderstanding and that you thought you needed to prove yourself to me. And that I already had all the data I needed for my one hundred percent legal scientific learning. And that it won't happen again."

"But it wasn't. And you don't. And it will."

Carlos ate his mint ice cream in silence for a bit. A drop fell from the cone onto his lab coat, a single pastel stain on the otherwise impeccable white. Nilanjana winced, but it didn't seem to bother Carlos and so she said nothing. She tried not to look at that annoying smudge on his coat.

"Science is important," he said eventually. "Science is very important. But so are you. Never start thinking that science is more important than yourself. That's what Cecil taught me. Before I met him, I was like you. But his hand on my cheek, you know? When I come home and he's surprised me by cooking dinner? That's way more important than science."

He gestured for them to get up, and they started walking down the street, back to her car.

"I don't have a Cecil," she said. "And I don't belong to this town, I just live here. So the only thing I have right now is understanding. This isn't for you anymore. I need to understand this."

"And how will you do that?"

"I have strong evidence that it is some sort of creature making these attacks. I have a video of it."

"Yes, I know about that. Pamela sent me an email with that video attached and told me that you had gotten it somehow and you weren't supposed to have it and that you needed to forget it and that I also needed to forget it as soon as I was done watching it. Then she sent it to me four more times. I don't think she's great with computers."

"I was trying to get more evidence when I was caught," Nilanjana said. "But as she was arresting me, she let slip that the city believes we are working with the church to do something dangerous. The church is definitely involved in this. So my next step is to find out what the church is up to."

Carlos didn't look at her. He didn't have anything to say to that.

"Don't silently judge," she said at last.

"I've already spoken my concerns and you have spoken yours. We both argued our points well and we still disagree. I can't tie you to your desk. All I can do is judge."

He shrugged.

"But point taken. I will work on better acknowledging what you say. Like that. I just acknowledged something. How was that?"

"I acknowledge that it was pretty good," she said.

"Thanks," he said. "So assume the church is involved. What is your next step?"

Nilanjana thought about the church. "Joyfully It Devours," read their pamphlets. Also their T-shirts. Also their tapestries. Also their needlework crafts. Also probably several tattoos. The Smiling God devours the sins of its followers. The entire religion is predicated on this lore, and belief is the economy of religion. Fervor, its currency. Was it possible that they had created or called forth some monstrous creature to demonstrate their joyful devouring?

Consider the Glow Cloud. Night Vale had a glowing cloud, which caused anyone near it to chant fealty to its awesome size and power, and which continually rained dead animals down on the city. The Glow Cloud was the president of the Night Vale School Board and had been doing an efficient job, but this was mostly because the Glow Cloud could get the rest of the school board to do whatever it wanted using its mind control powers. Most of what it wanted was good for students and teachers, because the Glow Cloud had a child attending the high school. Once the young cloud graduated, things could be different. The off-track-betting sites had set the over/under for number of days after the young cloud's graduation until the Glow Cloud crushed every school building under dead animals at twenty-five days. People could also bet on which dead animals would be most abundant in the crushing. Cows were far and away the favorite at five-to-three odds. Hardly seemed worth the bet.

If the Glow Cloud was possible, anything was possible.

That of course was a leap in logic, Nilanjana corrected herself. Just because one bizarre thing exists doesn't mean all bizarre things exist. And who's to say a glow cloud is that extraordinary? For some reason tiny, hard specks we find on the inside of fruits can be put into dirt and then months later there's a damned tree with a bunch more of that same fruit on it, also filled with a bunch more of those tiny, hard specks.

The point is, Nilanjana focused her thoughts, that fruit trees and even the Glow Cloud can be scientifically explained. They have been studied by botanists and meteorologists quite extensively. But whatever was happening under the desert floor was leaving her little evidence to work with. She had insufficient data to come up with a useful hypothesis. Her only source for more data was the city, and that avenue of investigation, for now, was unavailable.

She would have to turn back to the church itself. They were involved somehow, she was more and more sure, but, to her great frustration, she couldn't say exactly why she was sure. This was not scientific, Nilanjana reminded herself, but then again it would be bad science to rule out anything she couldn't understand as simply impossible.

All the things we don't understand in the universe comprise religion. Diseases are curses. Animals are ancestral reincarnation. The stars are heavenly signals of the future. Science studied many of these things and found that there were complex but empirical and logical data for them, and thus they were removed from the domain of religion.

Diseases are not curses from the gods but simply viruses and bacteria which attack the human body, causing symptoms as innocuous as the sniffles and as ghastly as throat spiders.

Animals are their own living creatures. Some of them (deer) house real estate agents inside of them. Some of them (birds) are human-made animatronic cameras. And yes, some of them are reincarnated humans, but this is not because the human soul upon leaving its mortal body drifts into a newborn cub or calf. It is because that person registered with the zoo's reincarnation program. It isn't really reincarnation. It's just that for a sizable donation to the zoo's endowment, animal handlers will train an animal of your choice to behave like you after you die. They will teach it your physical mannerisms and vocal inflections, maybe play it some of your favorite songs. The program had only achieved middling results, but still a lot of the more wealthy citizens of Night Vale had signed up for it.

As for the stars, no one knows what those are. Some more fanciful scientists say they're continually exploding gas giants hundreds of millions of miles away, but that is more urban legend than scientific model.

"Nils," Carlos said. "I promise I'm always on your side. I will stick up for you no matter what. Just be careful and smart, okay?"

"I want to infiltrate the church."

"Okay," he said.

"You on my side?"

"I am. I just hope you know what you're doing. This is getting a long way from science as we understand it. There aren't any numbers written on chalkboards or anything."

"I don't know for certain that they're connected, but I want to see their rituals. I think it's possible that they are the ones who created or are controlling the attacks against us."

He shook his head.

"Religious rituals aren't science. Spying isn't science. Science is bubbling beakers and electrical devices that occasionally send a visible spark of electricity buzzing back and forth."

"Everything is science."

"I hear that you think that."

"Thanks for hearing me, Carlos."

He walked her to the parking lot by the Hall of Public Records, where Nilanjana's car still sat, a bright orange ticket on the windshield. She pulled it off and read it. She had no idea where she was going to get that amount of adult human hair, but she would worry about it later.

Nilanjana told him she'd be careful.

Carlos smiled. He could feel his face tighten. He tried to keep his eyes wide and caring, but he knew they were narrow and tired. Still, he forced the look.

"Thanks for picking me up," Nilanjana said, "and for listening." She started toward her car, and then stopped and came back to him. He wasn't fond of hugs, and so she just put her hand on his upper arm and squeezed it. He smiled.

"I wouldn't have lasted this long in Night Vale without you," she said. "You've never steered me wrong. But I hope you trust me on this."

"I trust you."

"Science is neat."

"You're neat," he said.

She got in her car and drove off. As she rounded the corner of the lot to the main road, the hot exhaust created a glistening, wavering mirage of a moving car. In the undulating waves of hot air, Nilanjana and her car looked like a dream scrawled across a visible reality.

20

Nilanjana sat at her kitchen counter, reading *What's with All the Stuff About Teeth?: The Joyous Congregation Exposed*. It wasn't the most scholarly place to start, but it was a quick, gripping read, and public information about the congregation was limited. Most of the books on the subject were bought up by the church, and so here she was with the one widely available book. She was pretty sure that a lot of it was made up, and that the author, Leann Hart, was writing more from a bias than from any attempt to understand. Nilanjana found it hard to believe the stuff about the vats of brain fluid that church clergy soaked in in order to stay young.

She was just getting to the chapter called "Don't Get Me Started on the Sex Scandals (Get Me Started on the Sex Scandals!)" when her phone buzzed. Probably Carlos checking on her, or Mark wanting to continue their debate about which scientists owned the tallest dogs (Mark had a blog on the subject). She didn't feel like she needed checking in on, and she didn't care how tall a dog was as long as it was the most adorable, best little boy ever. The good news is that almost every dog fits that criterion.

But it was neither Carlos nor Mark. It was Darryl.

u up?

What she wouldn't do for a good debate about tall dogs right now. She could always just ignore it. She would ignore it. She went back to the book, ready to read about some sex scandals. Her phone buzzed again.

we still friends?

Had they ever been friends? They had had lunch and then sex and then breakfast, but if that was all it took to become friends then the definition of friendship needed work. She decided it would be easier to answer the first question.

Yes, I'm up. What's going on?

She barely had opened the book again when the reply came.

mind if i come over?

It's late. I have work tomorrow. [emoji of a tired scientist causing a workplace accident]

k. feel like things were weird when we left the diner. everything ok?

Then, a moment later,

[emoji of a horse for some reason]

Then,

sorry, meant [emoji of a friendly but concerned face]

No, everything was not okay. People had died. There was possibly a huge and dangerous creature moving out in the desert, and the way the Joyous Congregation depicted and talked about their god made her suspect that that dangerous creature was the Smiling God, or whatever it was they mistook for a smiling god.

Darryl was a member of the church, and had apparently consulted with the City Council about that desert otherworld. He was absolutely the last person she should trust, it was clear. And yet.

When she inventoried herself, Nilanjana found that among the things she could definitely use, along with solid evidence of what was destroying Night Vale, and healthier food, and better sleep, was company. Nothing he had done had proved Darryl a bad person. He didn't hide his nickname. His explanation of his meeting with the city was borderline naïve. Their date had been nice. So had the sex. Even a gut check found that she felt okay about him. It was the church she didn't trust, but he and the church weren't necessarily the same.

Or she was looking for excuses, trying to make the data fit a hypothesis she wanted to be true. Science is designed to be an objective system of proof and disproof, but it is a system created by subjective people, so bias often enters into it in subtle, insidious ways.

We're fine. Do you want to come over?

Immediately:

yeah! on my way

She quickly added,

Just for a little bit. I do have work tomorrow.

He didn't reply. She tried to go back to reading, but Leann's insinuations and unfounded accusations just slid past her. Instead she decided to change out of her leisure lab coat, which had a few stains and was visibly fraying at the edges, into a newer, more stylish lab coat, a move she decided had nothing to do with who was coming over and everything to do with her newfound dedication to finally get rid of that old ratty lab coat.

Darryl knocked on the door, and she went to open it and then decided it would be better to just shout, "It's open." But since she had started to the door, she was standing weirdly in the hallway when he opened it. Then he went for a hug, but she was already turning to walk back to the living room, and so he started to retract the hug but she was turning back to receive the hug.

"I'm sorry," he said. "This is awkward."

Saying a moment is awkward has never made an awkward moment better, but it's a tactic that humans keep trying over and over.

"Do you want a drink? I have, well, I don't have much. Orange juice and tap water."

"Sounds great."

"Which one?"

"Oh. Orange juice and tap water. If you combine them, you get orangey water. It's fun."

That did not sound fun to Nilanjana, but she wasn't interested in arguing about the entertainment levels of beverages.

It wasn't until they were sitting down in the living room that she realized she had left the Joyous Congregation exposé out. This was carelessness, but it could come across as aggression. So much that comes across as aggression is carelessness, and vice versa.

"Sorry," she said, but he hadn't noticed the book yet, and so he said, "Huh?," and so she said, "About the book," and he still hadn't noticed it and so he said, "Okay," and then he did notice the book and said nothing.

"I was doing research," she said, as shorthand for a lack of available documentation on the church, and so her settling for any source of information, but this came across as flippant.

"That stuff is all made up, you know. Leann Hart never even went to the church. She didn't talk to any of us."

"I know. You should read some of the stuff she's written about the theory of gravity. She tries to use a few politically motivated fringe scientists to ignore the massive scientific consensus that gravity is real and causing hundreds of thousands of deaths and injuries a year."

"But don't you think it's worth hearing all sides on that? Gravity's just a theory, you know."

Oh god, what am I doing with this guy? she thought.

"Maybe you could tell me," she said, changing the subject, "what do you find in all this Joyous Congregation stuff? Like what does it do for you?"

"The Smiling God devours our sins. You must first accept—" he began.

"No," she interrupted. "What do *you* find in all of it? What does it do for *you*?"

He swirled his orangey water, looking in its murk for the right words.

"My friends there. I love them. I grew up with them. Community means a lot to me. The church gave me my family, my friends, my life. I don't know if I believe all of this stuff. Or no." He shook his head. "I definitely believe it all. I was just saying that to make you comfortable, but I'm going to try to be honest here. I believe in it because believing in it gave me Stephanie and Jamillah, my two best friends. Their families, among others in the church, let me stay in their homes when my parents died. They helped me buy school supplies and robes, and they fed me and prayed with me. Belief gave me the life that I am living now.

"Maybe it's not true. But what would finding that out give

me? What use is the truth in a world where we die either way? Isn't it better to live happy until that last moment, believing the story you are living, shoulder to shoulder with others who believe and live that same story? Why flounder in the void when there is no need to do so? The story ends the same way, no matter how you choose to perceive it. Why not choose to perceive it as meaningful?"

She thought about that. In some ways it made sense. But in most ways, it was absurd. To live in the world as it truly is, is the only way worth living in the world. That is objectively better than living in a fiction, right?

"That's sweet," she said. "But what if that belief leads to bad actions? What if a lot of people could get hurt because of what that belief leads people to do?"

"What are you trying to say?"

She still didn't trust him. But she chose to believe.

"I'm going to sneak into your church and try to figure out what they're planning. Will you help me?"

21

The sun rose quietly for once. Nilanjana never bothered to set an alarm, because the racket of first light had her up early every morning. Some people—Carlos, for instance—slept right through it, but she was a light sleeper under the best of conditions.

This morning, though, she woke to find that the sunrise had been smooth and uneventful, or as smooth and uneventful as a million-mile-wide nuclear explosion seemingly emerging from the ground can be, and that the sun had been up for a couple hours. Even though it was still quite early, she felt as if she had slept in. That feeling came as a combination of luxury and guilt.

Darryl was still asleep. A sprawling, snoring slumber that made it tricky to share a full bed with him. She retrieved her legs from under his legs and got out of bed, intentionally shaking the mattress as she did, but he slept through it.

He wandered out an hour after she had had breakfast, poured himself a cup of cold coffee, and toasted her with it.

"Feeling ready?" he said.

"I feel determined. Is that anything like ready?"

"It's the closest most people get."

She nodded, offering him the box of Flakey O's, but he shook his head.

"You're supposed to fast before services," he said. "That way, your hunger will remind you of the hunger of the Smiling God."

"You don't think it's weird to follow a religious rule right before spying on your church?"

He sat across from her and bit his lip.

"I'm willing to help you prove that my church isn't actually up to anything. But the practices of my religion aren't a bunch of meaningless restrictions. Being hungry during the services as we talk about the Smiling God devouring our sins makes me feel connected to Its hunger. And that makes me feel connected to my fellow worshipers, and to the universe. The simple act of not eating for a few hours can make me feel close to the great, glowing coils of the universe. You know, Nilanjana, I still believe in this stuff, even if it turns out the people behind this organization are doing bad things. Which they aren't. But still. I don't expect you to understand."

"No. I think I get it." She didn't get it at all. "Let's go over the plan."

During services, the Joyous Congregation kept tight security, something that seemed completely normal to Darryl and deeply suspicious to Nilanjana. As a result, she wouldn't be able to walk through the front door that day without a lot of questions, and without being subjected to extra scrutiny that would make any snooping around impossible.

"You snooping around is impossible anyway," he said. "I'll be the one to go into the offices. I know what to look for. It's the same kind of stuff I was trying to find the other day."

"You were already investigating your church?" She was pleasantly surprised.

"I was being curious about a book or two. Anyway, I think you should see a service. It's special, and usually only church members are allowed to be a part of it. And you'll get to hear the pastor speak. She is an impressive and forceful person. I know how the offices are organized, so I'll search them for anything suspicious. During the service is the one time they're completely empty."

"Absolutely not. I'm not having anyone else do this. Especially, and I'm sorry, but especially not a member of the church."

She could have just said, "I don't trust you." It would have taken less time. He screwed up his face, and then relaxed his body, took a deep breath, and gentled his voice.

"Nilanjana, if you got caught back there, well, I don't know what would happen. Because no one has ever tried to sneak in before. But it would be bad. They could have you arrested for trespassing or, worse, deal with it internally. Me, if I'm caught, I can find an excuse. Worst thing that will happen is I'll get chewed out a bit. I've been chewed out before."

"I don't care about the risks. This is my research. I'm taking the risks."

"I understand. But I'm asking you to trust me. If there is something wrong with my church, then I have more at stake in finding out what it is than you do." He placed a hand on her cheek. It was condescending, but it was also soft and warm. His eyes were sincere and caring. She suppressed a deep urge to kiss his palm. She suppressed an equally deep urge to smack his hand away.

"Okay, I trust you," she said, not certain if she meant it or not. "Now what's this stuff?" indicating the bag he had gone home to get the night before.

"This is the robe and headpiece. It's how you'll take my place. Every part of us is covered during services, so no one will know you're you. I'll leave my seat, go let you in, and then you'll go sit down as me."

"We're . . . different sizes. I think they'll notice."

"You'd be surprised how bulky these things are. We get people confused all the time. We actually have a committee to address the problem next month, so this is good timing."

Looking at the bright yellow robe, Nilanjana thought of her lab table, with the petri dish of bacteria whose by-product was a pesticide with applications in industrial farming. That was the work she belonged to. This was so far from that. She missed her pesticide project, and the simplicity of wanting the bacteria to make symmetrical patterns.

"All right," she said. "If this is the plan, then it's the plan. Let's go."

She offered to carry the duffel on the way to the car, but he said it was no problem. His voice said that she was questioning his strength, and he needed to now prove it by carrying as much as possible. She rolled her eyes as he loaded himself up, looking ridiculous in order to prove a point that didn't matter and that no one in the world cared about. As he waddled his masculinity out to the car, she saw him flicking his thumb around. He was texting with one hand, glancing down occasionally and typing quickly.

She tried to glimpse what he was writing and to whom, but he had angled his body, hiding the phone from her. She decided that it wasn't her business, plus she didn't want to derail her chance to get inside the church by openly debating her trust in him again. Either he was on her side or not, and this seemed as good an opportunity as any to find out. Instead, she thanked him for carrying the bag and got in the car.

The parking lot was jammed at the Joyous Congregation. More people went there than she realized. This gave Darryl a perfect excuse to park in a residential neighborhood a few blocks away, so no one would see her getting out of his car.

They went separate ways to the church: his direct, saying hello to his friends and nodding to the security guard on the way in, hers roundabout, cutting across a pebble-and-cacti median and coming down a grass slope to the emergency exit in the back.

Then there was nothing for her to do but wait and trust.

She tapped her foot. The congregation robe, yellow and flowing, made her feel like a date stood up at a prom. She felt ridiculous. The hot breeze ruffled the grass, glistening with water stolen from wetter regions, and she tried to pretend that this was fine, that she was fine.

After several minutes she realized that Darryl wasn't going to open the door for her, that the whole thing was a cruel joke, that probably this robe wasn't even part of the Joyous Congregation but a silly outfit he had a bet to see if she would wear, that he and his friends were probably watching her on a closed-circuit camera and laughing, that she should cast the robe off, put on her lab coat, and walk right through the front door, tell them she wanted to know what the hell they were doing, interrupt the service if she had to, because if they were putting Night Vale in danger then she wasn't about to stand on niceties, how dare they think they could make a fool of her, and then Darryl opened the door and she exhaled.

He was wearing the same robe as hers, and had his headpiece under his arm. His face was sweaty.

"It's time," he said.

She put on the headpiece. It was muggy and hot. She was looking at the world through yellow mesh, and so everything was cast in sepia tones.

"Lead the way," she said.

This was the first time she had ever been to any kind of religious service. But a person doesn't need experience or knowledge of something to have opinions about it. It turns out all they need for that are opinions.

Her feeling toward religion had always been one of tolerant disapproval. She didn't think that the people who believed this kind of stuff were doing anything wrong—*wrong* as in *bad*—and she certainly felt like they should have the right to believe it if they wanted. But she also thought they were thinking something wrong, *wrong* as in *incorrect*.

She had a simple and rational view of the world. It is what it is, she thought. There are the stars and the moon and soil and dogs and hands and love and UFOs and secret government agencies and mole people, and there is nothing magical about that. Reality is what's real and nothing more. She had faith in the utility of an absence of faith. Her faith in this was powerful. So she entered the service with a combination of apprehension and pity.

The room was as she remembered it: simple, save for the eleven stained-glass columns, each beautiful on its own, but garish when inserted into plain, beige drywall paneling. People in robes filled the chairs, the spectrum of their gender and race and even body shape hidden by the unity of the robes and headpieces, and she could kind of see the beauty of that. Of coming together as a community while leaving aside all that makes a person different. Because all that makes a person different is all that person can and will be judged on. Removing those differences, even for a brief period, meant removing any foothold for judgment, forcing them to interact with each other on new terms.

Nilanjana stepped hesitantly into the room, her difference hidden but still sharply felt. It was a heightened sensation of the feeling she had lived with since moving to Night Vale: being the outsider.

Darryl, from behind the doorframe, urged her forward with a light squeeze on her arm and then was gone. Now she was him, as far as everyone in the room knew, and so she did her best to walk forward with unhurried confidence toward the empty chair he had indicated to her. No one seemed to give her much notice, although it was hard to tell with the headpieces. They were in the middle of a hymn, an upbeat song led by a robed figure playing an acoustic guitar. It was a simple, catchy melody, written in a modern, pop style. More early Beatles than Gregorian chanting.

What will It do
in the final hour?
It will take us in.
It will devour.

This refrain repeated several times, the congregation singing and clapping along. Then there was a key change upward and the guitar sped up a bit. Nilanjana found her seat and sat down.

"About time," said the voice of Stephanie from the headpiece of the person sitting next to her. Of course, Darryl had been sitting with his friends. "We're almost to the sermon. You feeling okay?"

Without seeing the speaker's face, she couldn't determine the tone of voice. It sounded sarcastic, knowing. Had Darryl alerted his friends to her presence? It reminded her of the documentary film *Carrie*, about a girl who was tricked into thinking she was popular (even being named prom queen, in a bully-rigged election), only to have pig's blood dumped on her head at the dance. Carrie responded by successfully suing the school and having the students responsible for the blood pouring arrested for assault.

Unable to answer the question with her voice, Nilanjana settled on shrugging, and then trying to clap along with an enthusiasm that wouldn't invite further conversation. Darryl had offered the night before to teach her some of the songs and basic choreography involved in the service, but they ended up doing other things instead. She didn't regret the other things, but she wished she had rehearsed.

Sunlight stuttered across her face, broken by the plastic blinds along the sliding glass door on one side of the room, hanging from cheap metal chains. The blinds clattered liquidly against each other, the sound of a rainstorm against a view of an arid sky.

And what will I do,
when It eats me whole?
I will feel cleansed,
right down to my soul.

The song came to an end and the rhythmic clapping scattered out into applause.

"Thank you, Gordon," said a woman without a headpiece over her face. Instead she wore a huge yellow hat. With three words she brought the congregation to a hushed focus. There was adoration in the air, but also fear. The absolute power she radiated was balanced by the cheerful lightness of her tone. "What a beautiful song of praise you've offered to us all this morning. Some of you might not know, but that song is an original composition by Gordon. I think it's just wonderful. I think it honors the Smiling God quite completely."

"I am only doing the work It demands," said Gordon. "All praise is due to It."

"Of course," said the pastor. "But take a compliment. Okay. Today I'd like to preach to you all on the subject of Purity. It is a great goal, Purity, but it is not one we can achieve ourselves. Only by allowing the Smiling God to devour us do we achieve the Purity that It demands from us."

She clicked a remote and the projector bulb flipped on, shining a blank square of light against the screen.

"Oh, dang it, hold on," she said. "It always takes a moment to warm up. You would think one of these days I would figure that out!"

The congregation laughed just long enough to acknowledge the joke, but not so long that the laughter became about her troubles with the projector. It was a finely tuned laugh, based on years of respect and awe.

A strange illustration appeared on the screen, along with the caption "Skin is a necessary evil."

"There we go," said the pastor. "Now, Purity."

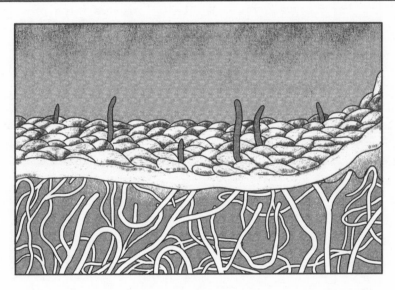

22

Skin is a necessary evil.

Purity is not a state of mind. It is not a physical state. It is not even a spiritual state. There are no elements to it. You cannot piece together purity. Purity is a state of entire existence. It is an unbroken thing, and cannot be received in fractions. We must be made pure in one big gulp, swallowed whole. Joyfully, it devours.

Change is constant and final. There is no reversal. We must give ourselves over to change, the way that we give ourselves to the Smiling God. Both will devour us. The process may not be pleasant, but pleasant isn't everything. A life that was merely pleasant would be a failure of a life. After all, you have been condemned to death. Your crime is birth. There is no appeal possible.

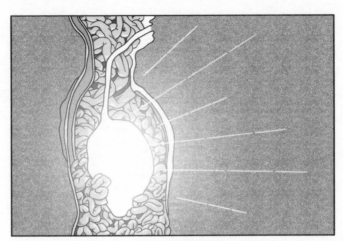

Everything you eat is sunlight made physical.
You are radiant and forever.

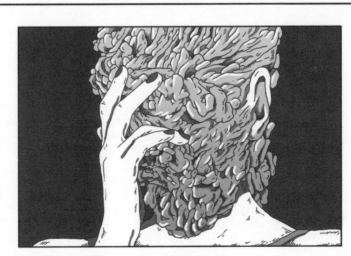

Try to remember what you look like.

Hope is the most powerful force in the universe, besides time, tectonic shifts, volcanoes, acid, and certain sharks. Steel is also more powerful. It can hold up buildings. Can hope hold up buildings? Unfortunately no. Disease is also more powerful. No one was ever cured through hope. Despair is sometimes more powerful. That is entirely up to you. How much weight you give to hope and how much to despair cannot change much in the way of outcomes, but it will change your experience of those outcomes completely.

A scientific fact: Most things aren't. Most events haven't. When considering our place in the universe, we must recognize that by having this one position we are negating every other possible position we could have. There is no gain without loss. There is no stance we can take that isn't denying every other stance we could have taken. Every sunrise we see is a dream we miss. Every trip of a lifetime is that much less of a lifetime spent comfortably at home. Once we accept loss, we have the key to accepting everything else.

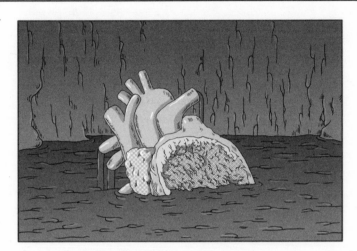

Your heartbeat is approximate.

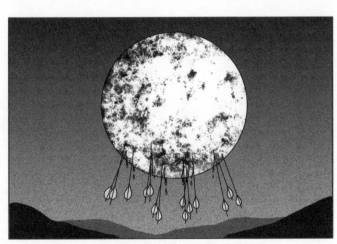

The moon is not our enemy, it is our friend. Please do
not attack or provoke the moon.

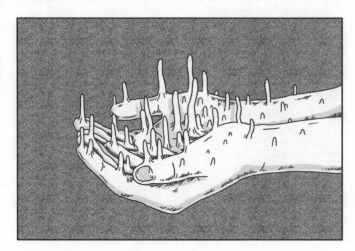

Make no mistake.

Do not seek purity. Wait for it. Accept it. You are not made holy by your actions but by your acceptance of the actions of the world. Once you are in tune with those, once you recognize the sacred plan in all that happens to you, you will be ready to enter into the plan of purity, of holiness. And in entering this, you will truly be joyous. And then you will truly be a member of the Joyous Congregation of the Smiling God.

The ceremony of the devouring will honor purity by calling the Smiling God from Its glorious home to our congregation and our world.

Out in the desert is a road, built by no one. Its blacktop is cracked; its paint faded. You will walk it one day. It goes nowhere.

23

"Amen," the pastor finished, recontextualizing everything she had said before this as a prayer.

"Amen," the Congregation responded, accepting this recontextualization.

"Now, Gordon, please lead us in another joyous song."

Gordon did, with an accordion this time.

Sing, sing, sing; give a joyous shout
For the ground below us is about to give out
And from deep underground comes a hungry mouth
Sing, sing, sing; give a joyous shout.

Hypothesis: The church plans to summon something from the otherworld.

Evidence: They basically said so in the sermon with the insinuation that there would be a ceremony of devouring. What Nilanjana didn't know was how they would achieve it, or even if a summoning was a real thing that could be carried out.

Stephanie nudged her, and she realized that she was the only one in the room not singing. No headpiece would hide a lack of participation. She did her best to hum along, but then decided that was bringing more attention to herself. And what would she do when the service started to wrap up? Surely there was small talk? Most situations that don't involve scripted actions involve small talk. She wasn't great at small talk in the best of situations, and pretending to be a man she barely knew was, if not the worst of situations, close to it.

SWALLOW SWALLOW SWALLOW SWALLOW
SWALLOW SWALLOW SWALLOW SWALLOW
GULP GULP GULP GULP GULP GULP GULP GULP
YEAH! SWALLOW SWALLOW SWALLOW. YEAH!

Gordon finished with an unnecessary flourish of the accordion, and the pastor forgave it with a beatific smile.

"And now," she said, "let's have some testimonials. Who will go first?"

This seemed to involve individual audience participation, and while there were a lot of people in the room, there weren't so many that Nilanjana could feel safely lost in the crowd.

"Let's hear from Martin first," the pastor said.

One of the interchangeable robed and headpieced figures hopped up enthusiastically and jogged to the podium.

"Hey, gang," he said. "I'm Martin McCaffry. As most of you know, I used to run TSA out at the Night Vale Airport. I wasn't happy with my career. The hours were long. The pay was unrewarding. I continuously made drawings of an elongated dark figure and I had no memory of making them. One day I had had enough, and I set traps all over my house to catch whatever demon or evil force was haunting my life. Sacrificed mice at tiny altars in order to gain protection. Built a complex machine that predicted the future by murdering wasps. The whole deal. I guess you could call it a midlife crisis.

"But was I happy? I was not. I only thought I was happy because of how many animal sacrifices I had made. It wasn't until

I ran into May over there (hi, May!) and she told me about the devouring mercy of the Smiling God that I saw the truth. I couldn't fight the demon on my own. I needed an even larger, more terrifying force on my side.

"It has been amazing getting to know all of you over the past couple years, and my new job overseeing the summer camp counselors is rewarding in a way that the airport thing never was. It pays way less though. Way less. Would love to talk about the compensation plan with someone. But other than that, it's perfect.

"Thanks to all of you, for being a community who supports each other. Thank you to Pastor Munn, for all that you give us. Thank you to May again. Wouldn't have gotten here without May. She's a real pal. And thank you to the Smiling God, for devouring our sins with Its great and holy Maw. Oh boy. Just love that Smiling God."

"Amen," said the pastor, now using the word as a signal that it was time for Martin to stop talking. He twirled his fist in the air, nodded at the pastor, and went back to his seat.

"What a wonderful testimony Martin gave us," the pastor said. "Thank you for giving us the gift of your experiences. Now, who would like to go next? Who can speak on the power of the Smiling God?"

Many hands went up. It seemed that all of them could speak on the power of the Smiling God. Nilanjana didn't know whether it would be better to put her hand up or stay as she was and risk being singled out as the only nonparticipant.

She settled on nodding enthusiastically, as though she totally agreed with how much everyone wanted to get up there and talk. Great job, everyone, her bouncing head said.

But it didn't matter. The pastor glanced at the room briefly before settling her eyes on Nilanjana. It felt as though she could see through the headpiece.

"Darryl," she said. "Or should I say the Wordsmith? Always so eloquent about the joy you find in this community. Please, share one or two of those wonderful words with all of us."

Nilanjana swore there was something mocking in the pastor's tone of voice, although no one else in the room seemed to notice. There was an enthusiastic cheer. Darryl was well liked here. Would that make it better or worse when they caught her? Her mouth was dry, and her stomach was making moves.

The figure on the other side of Stephanie stood up. "I would like to share a testimony." It was Jamillah. Nilanjana could see the tip of a power drill hanging down from one of the long sleeves of her robe.

"Sit down, Jamillah," the pastor snapped, and Jamillah immediately did. "Get up here, Darryl. Don't turn shy now. Speak from the teeth."

Pastor Munn knew. Everyone in the room was looking at what they thought was Darryl. Where was he? Even if he was watching, was there anything he could do to help her? Maybe she shouldn't have trusted him at all. Her stomach lurched, the back of her neck dripped sweat.

The pastor made a commanding gesture with her arm, and Stephanie pushed Nilanjana on the shoulder.

"What are you doing?" Stephanie whispered. "You can't ignore the pastor."

Nilanjana went through her options. One, of course, was to allow herself to be caught. After all, under Night Vale law, what could they do to her? She had not violated any civic code, federal law, or mandate of the secret world government. She'd have to check, but she was pretty sure that even the ancient laws of the lizard people who run all human government had nothing to say about sneaking into a religious service. On the other hand, it didn't seem like a great idea to be caught by a group that had just been singing about a god eating them.

She could run, of course. There were few situations in which one could not just start running, although the consequences of this action varied quite a bit, and in some situations could include exiting a moving car, being mauled by a bear, or falling off a tightrope. On top of that, the impulse when someone runs is to chase, and that was not an impulse she wanted to ignite in this group.

But she had to do something, and quite quickly, because the decision was about to be made for her. The moment she opened her mouth it would be over. The moment she opened her mouth.

She knew what she had to do. She swayed, dramatically. She put one hand on her stomach. And then she opened her mouth.

"Oh no," said Jamillah. The pastor's face radiated anger and disgust. Gordon pulled off his headpiece, revealing his sweaty and worried face.

"Darryl, are you okay, son?" he said.

Nilanjana stood with the vomit still dribbling down the yellow robe from underneath the yellow mesh mask. With the fear pulsing in her gut, it had been easy to intentionally retrieve her breakfast. She gave a loud moan, in the lowest tone she could muster, and then, hand still on stomach, she stumbled out of the room. In the lobby, she figured she had only seconds, and so she opened the door to one of the bathrooms, set the doorknob lock, slammed the door shut, and continued down the hall toward the church offices. Behind her she could hear Gordon's concerned voice.

"Darryl? Son, are you all right in there?"

Hopefully it would take them some time before their worry about Darryl outweighed their feelings about privacy.

She pulled off her mask and stuck her head in and out of empty office after office until she found Darryl in the pastor's office, at the bookshelves. His eyes went scared and wide on seeing her.

"What are you doing here?" he said. "Is the service over? Where do they think I am?"

"Um," she said.

"And what is that all over my robe?"

"I can explain all of that when we're not in a place where we might be caught. Are those books about what the church is planning?"

"No," he said. "It's just a history of the church. We're not allowed to read this stuff normally, so I couldn't resist."

More shouting from the lobby, more knocking on the bathroom door.

"I'm glad you're indulging your rebellious side. But we need to be looking for evidence of contact with the otherworld."

He held up a stack of papers.

"I found these. The service wasn't anywhere near done, so I thought I had time to check out the books."

She took the papers from him and looked them over. It was page after page of handwritten text, apparently notes taken while studying. The word INVOCATION occurred over and over, always in the same all-caps, thick-lined style.

"Invocation?" she said. "Is that the ceremony of devouring she mentioned in her sermon?"

The knocking got heavier, edging toward pounding. The

shouting sounded less worried, more angry. This was taking too long.

"I've never heard of the term, but it does look like it's some kind of ceremony. If I'm understanding these documents correctly, it seems like it will be happening in the next week or so, and uses something called *The Book of Devouring,* which I also haven't heard of and can't find anywhere on these shelves."

Darryl shook his head.

"None of this makes any sense to me. This isn't the religion I grew up with."

"They certainly were talking a lot about devouring during the service."

"But that's all metaphor and parable. This is . . . I don't know what this is. I want to help you figure it out."

Now the bathroom door was being rattled. They were trying to open it.

"I have to get out of here," Nilanjana said. "Give me the papers and take this robe. You're going to need the vomit on it. Also a good excuse for why you just puked and pretended to hide in the bathroom."

"Why I did what?"

"I'll meet you at the car."

She darted out of the pastor's office and deeper down the hall, assuming there would have to be some sort of exit back there. But she couldn't find one. Behind her the bathroom door banged open, and the shouting intensified. It would be ideal if she were not here anymore, but the world is rarely ideal.

Giving up on a door, she opened a window and awkwardly squeezed out of it onto the drought-resistant shrubs outside. Scraped from the branches, and finding a leaf in her hair, she jogged a ways into the parking lot before cutting back to the sidewalk and heading toward the car. As she was stepping into the street, a hand fell on her shoulder.

"We need to talk with you."

The hand belonged to a security guard from the Joyous Congregation. He squinted at her under the blaring sun and over a thick mustache.

"I'm on a public street. You can't just grab me. You have no right to make me go anywhere."

"And you," he said, snatching the bundle of INVOCATION papers out of her bag, "have no right to take church property. Come quietly. We don't need to call the Secret Police. The pastor only wants to talk."

24

The woman in the huge rectangular hat smiled at Nilanjana. Gordon, standing behind her, crossed his arms and bared his teeth while stretching his lips wide. It was not a smile at all. It was a grotesque and off-putting expression, and Nilanjana did not know what to make of it. She glanced at Darryl, but he was not looking at her, only at the pastor.

"My, what a lovely day this is," the pastor said. Her voice was gentle but insincere. Like the wolf dressed up as the grandmother in the fairy tale. All of the stagecraft of kindness, but nothing at the heart of it.

"A great day," said Gordon, his bizarre grimace even wider than before.

"And why is it a great day, Gordon?" the pastor said.

"It's great because, well . . . uh." His stretched lips faltered.

"It's great because we have a new visitor. Someone who doesn't know our faith. And she has come to learn from us. That's a blessing, isn't it, Gordon?"

"It is," he said, relieved to be on more certain ground.

"Isn't it, Darryl?" she said.

Darryl looked surprised to be addressed.

"Yes, Pastor," he said.

"We want to thank you, Darryl," the pastor said. "We as a community owe you gratitude. And I as an individual want you to know that I am thankful. For bringing this woman into our services. This curious, curious woman."

"Curiosity killed the cat," said Gordon.

Nilanjana glared at Darryl. He winked without smiling. Was that supposed to mean "I got you" as in he betrayed her, or "I got you" as in he was on her side?

"I know what you are doing," Nilanjana said, tired of the games the pastor was playing, and wanted to get this confrontation going. As a scientist, she did not have much interest in games. Except science games, like Is That Beaker Going to Explode? and Will This Catch on Fire if Exposed to Oxygen? (The answer to both questions was almost always yes.)

The pastor took off her hat. Underneath she looked like a normal person. A person wearing a yellow robe and a huge golden medallion in the shape of a sun with some horrible creature wrapped around it.

"I find that hard to believe, Ms. Sikdar. Because the fact of the matter is that you don't even know what *you* are doing. You are flailing in the dark and hoping you will simply run into the truth. Am I wrong or am I right?"

"Wrong or right, Interloper!" Gordon shouted. It had been a while since Nilanjana had felt the insulting force of that word. Like Carlos had said, she had started getting used to it as a friendly utterance around town by strangers or, at worst, a dismissive grumble. But Gordon put her back in her place as an outsider.

"Gordon, she doesn't need to answer me. Because I already know the answer. While you are in the dark, Nilanjana Sikdar, we in the Congregation live always in the light. In this situation, I am the one who knows things. You are the one who does not. Tell me I'm wrong."

"You're wrong."

Pastor Munn wasn't wrong. Nilanjana was just guessing. But her gut told her it was a pretty good guess.

"Your church started when you made contact with the desert otherworld," Nilanjana hazarded. "Your people found something there. A powerful creature. And you started worshiping it as a god."

These were unsupported hypotheses, baseless allegations. Carlos would be so disappointed. But perhaps saying them aloud might bring real evidence out in conversation.

"And now it's attacking Night Vale. Hurting people. Killing them," she continued. "Maybe you are helping it, or baiting it to come closer. Or maybe you are just trying to hinder anyone who wants to stop it. The effect is the same either way. You are to blame for what is happening. Tell me *I'm* wrong."

The pastor considered her. Gordon started to shout some variation on "how dare you," but the pastor held up a finger and he fell silent. Darryl waved to get Nilanjana's attention, but she kept her eyes on the pastor.

"The Smiling God," the pastor said, "is coming to swallow Night Vale. It will devour all of us."

Darryl waved again, and Nilanjana gave in and looked. He winked at her. She had no idea what that meant and wished he would stop winking.

"So you are admitting to everything I just said," she said.

"It will take all of us inside Its body," the pastor said. "We will enter the divine Mouth and be consumed."

Darryl winked again. Nilanjana couldn't understand what he was trying to convey. He didn't seem triumphant or devious. He just seemed like a guy who was winking for some reason.

"It's a metaphor, Nilanjana," Darryl interjected, realizing his winking wasn't being understood. "I know some of this de-vouring talk can sound scary to newcomers. Like we're trying to get everyone eaten by a monster. But it's a beautiful meta-phor, about how the Smiling God will devour us and, in doing so, take in everything that's bad about us. It's a story about the church accepting all people, no matter who they are."

"A metaphor?"

"Maybe a violent-sounding metaphor." Darryl shrugged apologetically. "But its meaning is nice, right?"

"A metaphor?" she asked again, this time to the pastor. The pastor was looking at Darryl with an expression that could have been pitiful benevolence or quiet disgust.

"No," the pastor said, her smile now a scowl.

"No?" said Darryl.

"Absolutely not," said Gordon. His face had gone red. "Why would we deal in metaphors? We are the faithful, in the house of the Smiling God. Darryl, I thought better of you."

"Wait," Darryl said. "But the entire faith is built around the story of the Smiling God devouring our sins, all of our failings, leaving us pure. It's not real in a historical sense, obviously, but it imbues real meaning into our lives."

"No, Darryl," the pastor said. She sounded sad. "I'm sorry that the church failed in its teaching. I'm sure your scientist friend would agree: Why would anyone want to live in fiction? Nilanjana surely understands. She lives a life of hard facts. We too believe in the concrete reality of our spiritual life. The Smil-ing God is a real, physical thing. It is coming to swallow all of Night Vale."

"What does that even mean?" Darryl said. "How can the Smiling God swallow anything?"

"Ah, that part is easy," the pastor said. "Gordon, tell him."

Gordon straightened with pride.

"Because," he shouted, "the Smiling God is a centipede."

"Yes, exactly," the pastor said. "It's a giant centipede. It lives in Heaven and It will soon swallow us all."

"What?" Darryl said.

"I knew it!" Nilanjana said.

"I'm sorry, I thought we were pretty clear about this. There's one right on our door. Also overlooking the worship hall. The purpose of the Joyous Congregation is to summon a giant centipede and have It eat the entire world."

"Why?" Nilanjana and Darryl asked, simultaneously.

"Why?" Gordon mocked.

"JOYFULLY IT DEVOURS!" the needlework on the wall said.

The pastor frowned.

"Did you sleep through my sermon? Or were you too busy plotting ways to fail to fool us? Purity. The world is an unjust and impure place. By devouring the rich and the poor, the sinful and the saint, by devouring without discrimination, the Smiling God will purify the world. This is not something we inflict on others. We the faithful will be the first to be eaten. Followed shortly by all other people."

Darryl stood up.

"I grew up in this church. And I went to all of the services and all of the classes. And you're telling me that all of that, every moment of every year, was to get a huge centipede to eat the town?"

Gordon stared him down.

"Young man," he said. "Please watch your tone when you are speaking to your Church Elders. We know what is best for you. What's best for you is that you get eaten by just a great big centipede."

"We are a community!" Darryl said.

"Of people who will be eaten by a giant bug, yes," the pastor said. "I'm getting tired of explaining this."

"Are you putting out bait?" Nilanjana asked, wanting to finally get hard facts for her research. "Or using some sort of broadcast frequencies to agitate it? How are you getting it to attack us?"

"We haven't done anything yet," the pastor said. "I don't know about any attacks. What the Smiling God does on Its own time is Its own divine business. No, soon we will do a ceremony. A great ceremony that will summon our Smiling God. It's all in the notes you tried to steal. You can't have them because they belong to me. But allow me to summarize for you: The Smiling God will be called to rise from the sand and eat everything It sees."

"Not if I stop you," said Nilanjana, a not-wise thing to say, but she wasn't wise, just brilliant.

Gordon laughed.

"Stop us," the pastor said. She held out her palms. "How would you stop us? We are what is supposed to happen. Do you stop rain? Do you stop earthquakes?"

"Yes," Nilanjana said. She did not personally do that, but of course all weather and earthquakes were now controlled by NASA, so she was speaking with the collective *we* of all scientists.

"Ah," the pastor said. "In that case, if you try to stop us, we will destroy you utterly. We will destroy you so completely that even the traces of the life you've lived thus far will be gone. Your own friends won't remember you, even as they breathe in microscopic dust that used to be your body."

She beamed.

"I do hope you have a blessed day. May the Smiling God be with you. Until It is actually with you, very soon.

"And, Darryl," she said, turning back to him. "We want to thank you."

"We do?" said Gordon. Then, regaining his utter confidence, "We do! Thank you, Darryl."

"We want to thank you for uncovering this possible plot against our church and bringing Ms. Sikdar to us. It's so nice to have this time to clear the air with you, Ms. Sikdar. We couldn't have done it without Darryl."

"And what exactly did he do?" Nilanjana asked, looking right at Darryl.

"What he's supposed to," said Gordon. "He is a good boy."

"Nilanjana, listen to me," said Darryl. "You know me. Everything I told you was true. I didn't know this would happen."

But did she know him? Of course she didn't. She knew what he presented to the world. She knew how his hands felt, what the sweat on his neck smelled like. But that wasn't knowing someone.

A hand on her shoulder again. The mustachioed guard. She cried out.

"Don't worry," said the pastor. "We won't harm you. The Smiling God will do that for us. But it is time for you to go."

"Nilanjana, please believe me!" Darryl said, but the pastor motioned him sharply down and he seemed unable to disobey her.

Nilanjana was pulled out of her chair and pushed roughly through a door, and then a hallway, and then another door. She felt the gradients of air-conditioning as she moved from deep inside the building toward the windows of the lobby, and then one last door and she was in the heat of the afternoon.

"You have a good day now," the guard said.

"Where is Darryl?" If he hadn't betrayed her, then he could be in danger from the church. Who knew what they would do to him? If he had betrayed her, she wanted to put him in danger herself.

The guard did the weird teeth thing, a child's accidentally terrifying drawing of a smile.

"He is where he is supposed to be. He is with the community that loves him. It is time for you to go."

She turned, starting the long walk back to her apartment. She was already thirsty, and she knew that this feeling would get worse every minute of walking in the searing heat.

"I'll be seeing you," said the guard. She would be seeing him too. For the next few minutes, every time she closed her eyes, she saw the ghost image of his teeth under his large, unkempt mustache projected in neon against the insides of her lids.

Back in the church, in one of the small classrooms, Martin McCaffry met with his summer camp planning committee. They brainstormed themes for next year's camp. ("This Mortal Soil," and "A Bug's Afterlife," and "Centipede Cotillion" were the front-runners.) He ate chicken salad with the group and wrote out a to-do list, which included calling to recruit potential volunteers. Later he would go home and reheat the soup he'd made the day before and watch television news. He didn't enjoy watching the news. He just didn't know how to turn his television off or to a different station.

He still saw elongated dark figures in the corners of his home and outside his windows. They lurked behind the news anchors on the television. When he reheated his soup, he saw one in the reflection of the microwave window reaching out a spindly arm. Each time, he would scream and clutch his chest. And each time he would forget seeing them a moment later.

Martin felt great stress without understanding why. He tried to calm himself by returning to his longtime passion of drawing and painting, but the figures showed up repeatedly in his work. The drawings disturbed him. He threw them away, disgusted by his own efforts.

One day, three years after the day he ate chicken salad and planned a summer camp, a year and a half after he left the church because it ultimately had failed to help him with his problem, he'd accidentally left one of these drawings on the table instead of throwing it away. When he encountered it again a few days later, he found it less disturbing, perhaps even aesthetically interesting. He hung it up, and intentionally made more. Elongated dark specters, covering the page. He hung them all up. He grew to like them, his walls papered in landscapes and bowl-of-fruit still lifes, all with long, humanlike forms in the backgrounds. He no longer felt the same stress. He no longer saw these lurking figures in his real life, although since he did not remember ever seeing them, he did not consciously recognize the change. He simply noticed feeling more energy, more joy in life. He attributed this change to exercise and a series of books on self-confidence he was reading, but the effect of those was incidental. He rarely left his home. In narrow hallways cluttered with horrifying drawings, Martin would feel as happy as he had ever felt.

25

Carlos would know what to do. And he would also have to admit that infiltrating the church had been the correct next move, no matter how unscientific it had been. He was attending Big Rico's Pizza's grand reopening, so Nilanjana left her apartment to meet him there. She changed out of her sweaty clothes, got in her car, and put the air-conditioning on full blast. Trying to get the strong possibility that Darryl had betrayed her out of her head, Nilanjana switched on her car radio.

Community radio was important in Night Vale. Cecil Palmer, regular radio host and, of course, handsome husband to Carlos, served as a voice of the community. Informing them, but also expressing their fears and grievances and joys so that everyone could share in them. He was in the middle of a news report when she turned the radio on ("City Hall announced plans to expand the rec center to include a secret survival bunker, a secondary even more secret bunker, two helipads for quick evacuations, and a children's playroom. Children will not be allowed in the playroom so that they will not block evacuation routes to the bunkers or helipads.") as well as a traffic report, which was a series of sonnets about a rhinoceros who liked kites. Just as she was arriving at the shopping center, Cecil got to the weather. The weather report was Sturgill Simpson's song "Turtles All the Way Down," which was a popular cover of the Canadian national anthem. The weather reports on the radio were never that informative about the weather, but they were superinformative about life.

She stepped into the rare afternoon rain, unpredicted by the radio's weather report, and walked toward the giant pit in the ground that once was Big Rico's Pizza. The remaining employees were standing around the top of the pit, working under the worried and watchful eye of Arnie Goldblum. Arnie was feeling a lot of pressure, trying to honor the legacy of his brother. Plus people kept thinking that this would be the perfect time to catch their mailman, and he had to explain over and over that he wasn't carrying the mail with him today.

The establishment had technically reopened, but none of the walls or counters had been rebuilt, and no new cooking equipment or appliances purchased. There were no tables or chairs or self-serve soft drink machines. Just a deep pit in the earth with dozens of people milling around the edge holding out their hands as if supporting plates. They were lifting their other hands to their mouths and chewing on nothing, saying things like "It's as good as it ever was" and "Delicious! So glad Rico's is back" and "Oooh, I burned my mouth eating this scrumptious pizza too quickly," and then fanning their empty mouths.

Nilanjana could not determine if they were pretending to eat pizza in order to make Arnie feel better or if Arnie had staged this scene with friends in order to drum up publicity, or if perhaps he was making invisible slices. The Moonlite All-Night Diner served invisible pie, so it seemed plausible that Arnie was getting in on the invisible food movement. It was a popular fad, because it required almost no preparation to take a photo for social media of your own home-cooked invisible food, and so these days everyone's time line was full of pictures of empty plates with proud captions like "Homemade invisible black bean chili! Healthy, delicious, and totally real!"

"Hey, Nils." Carlos stepped up beside her. He was holding out a nonexistent plate in one hand. His other hand was positioned like it was holding a slice of pizza. "This is way easier to eat than the old globs of cheese and sauce with no crust."

"Carlos, I have to talk to you," she said. "I learned what the church is . . . Are you actually eating an invisible pizza or just pretending?"

"I have no idea, but play along. Arnie's having a tough go right now."

A man in a flannel shirt came by and slapped Carlos on the back.

"Oh, howdy there, Carlos. This pizza sure is powerful tasty!" said the man. He nodded at Nilanjana. "Hi there, I'm John Peters. You know, the farmer?"

"I know," she said.

John Peters had been the one to start the invisible food movement. He had the unenviable position of acting as a farmer in a desert. This is a common plight. Many of the nation's crops are grown in corners of California that would be, without the steady flow of federal water, barren plains. Pour enough water on anything, and it'll deliver food eventually. The problem for John Peters was that Night Vale's relationship with the federal government was shaky at best, given that it mostly failed to appear on national maps or censuses, and that the reality of Night Vale and the reality of the rest of the country did not seem to line up exactly. This meant that John's requests for canals or water deliveries from the government were often treated as hoaxes or filing errors by the officials who received them. So John's land stayed dry and empty. Then he came up with his most inspired idea. He announced that he had planted "invisible corn" and invited fellow town members to come and look at his empty fields, which were where he said the invisible corn was coming up nicely. Soon he put up a farm stand, selling his invisible corn to excited foodies eager to try this new variety. The Moonlite All-Nite Diner started selling invisible corn muffins made from the invisible corn, and, when those did well, they added invisible pie to the menu. After that, invisible food was everywhere. Nilanjana had been part of the team that Carlos sent to investigate John's claims about his crops. Their conclusion, a common one in science, was that looking into it too deeply would spoil the fun.

"We've met," Nilanjana said.

"I don't think so. Anyway, I'd shake your hand, but mine is all covered with invisible pizza grease right now." John held up his perfectly clean hand and shrugged. "What's your name?"

"Nilanjana. We've met."

"Nice to meet you, Niljona."

He smiled in a distant way and walked on, cradling his invisible or imaginary slice in both hands.

"I've met him so many times," she said to Carlos. Maybe she should reopen their investigation into his invisible corn.

"Sometimes I wonder if he always reminds us he's a farmer because even he has trouble remembering," Carlos said.

"Can we go talk somewhere?" she said, but his gaze went over her shoulder and his face brightened.

"Oh, Abby, Steve, over here!"

Abby Palmer waved back and headed their way with her husband, Steve Carlsberg, and their teenage daughter, Janice. Abby was Cecil's sister, and Janice was Carlos's favorite (and only) niece.

"Uncle Carlos!" Janice said, wheeling her chair over toward him.

"How's my young scientist?" Carlos dropped to one knee.

Janice grimaced.

"I don't like science," she said. "I want to be a professional athlete."

"But athletics is science!" Carlos said. "All that movement is physics. And sports that involve test tubes, like golf or water polo, are especially scientific. Here, I have a chart."

The chart was a piece of paper that had a picture of a basketball and the words SPORTS = SCIENCE.

"The data is irrefutable," he said. She laughed and he smiled, happy to have gotten the laugh from her. "I heard your game on Friday went well."

"We crushed the Pine Cliff Lizard Monitors. I think we might make state if anyone can figure out where that is and how we would get there from Night Vale. Leaving Night Vale's hard."

It is. Nilanjana felt a pang of homesickness for her family back in Indiana. She still went and visited them when she could (which wasn't often, because, again, leaving Night Vale is difficult). It was also difficult to explain her job to people not from Night Vale. Any time she told them what was happening there, they thought she was making fun of them. And because time doesn't work in Night Vale, she was never certain at what point in their lives she would arrive. Once she came home for Diwali to find that her mother was six years old, and her father was nowhere to be found, since he didn't move to the United States until he was seventeen. She played with the little girl that was her mother, the little girl that would grow up to be a chemistry professor and the main driving force for Nilanjana's fascination with the wonder of science. She remembered her mother teaching her about negative numbers when Nilanjana was only six, and how proud she had been to learn mathematics that seemed to belong to older people. And so she asked her six-year-old mother about negative numbers and listened to her mother chatter away about everything she knew on the subject as they sat on a park bench under the drifting fall leaves. Then she went back to Night Vale, and the next time she visited her parents, they were, more or less, the correct age. She had never dared ask her mother if she remembered meeting a visitor in a park when she was six.

"You're lucky to have your family so close around you," Nilanjana said to Janice.

"I know." Janice beamed.

"Now I'm sorry, I just have to borrow your uncle for one moment, because I need to talk to him about something important . . ."

"I love her," Carlos said as Nilanjana led him away. "You never think about a spouse's family when you're looking for the right person. But especially being from out of town. None of my own family is anywhere nearby, and so they've become my family here. It makes a difference, having family around."

Nilanjana felt another pang but ignored it.

"I did what I told you I was going to do," she said. "I snuck into the church. And then I got caught. But it worked out. Long story."

Carlos widened his eyes at something over her shoulder.

"No, Carlos, listen. I know there's lots of people to say hello to here, but I need to talk to you about what the church is planning." Carlos pointed at whatever he was looking at. She sighed. "We can go chat with whoever it is as soon as we're done here. Just give me five minutes. The Smiling God is real.

It's real and it's . . ." She trailed off as she became aware of the hissing, like static from a badly tuned radio, but somehow the noise of it made a physical bubbling on her skin. It was awful. She started to turn and Carlos stopped her.

"Act natural. Look into my eyes," he said as he put on reflective sunglasses. "Don't turn around."

She saw the bronzy, warped mirror of her own face on each lens. She saw behind her a deep pit surrounded by people, each tiny and curved in the reflective lenses, each standing in silent horror. And she saw behind them the row of figures in long cloaks and hoods. There were no faces visible in the hoods.

People begin to run. Janice usually moved herself around, but Steve got behind her wheelchair and sprinted them away, Abby right after them.

The hooded figures were a common sight in Night Vale, but no one knew who they were. They mostly gathered around the Municipal Dog Park, which was forbidden to enter. No one knew if the Dog Park was off-limits because of the hooded figures, or if the hooded figures gathered there because it was off-limits. An intern from the radio station had entered the Dog Park a few years back and had walked and walked through its seemingly limitless interior until she had found herself in a vast desert surrounding a single mountain. Through this, Carlos learned that the Dog Park, like the house that doesn't exist, was a gateway to the other desert world. The hooded figures often made a sound like static. No one had ever seen their faces. If anyone was foolish enough to walk home alone at night, they were often tailed at a distance of one block by a hooded figure, who would stumble and lurch as though drunk, but would move with a directed purpose after their target. Most people made it home, and locked their doors, and stayed out of sight of windows for a while. Some did not make it home. Those who were caught by a hooded figure were never seen again, not by human eyes.

John Peters froze, feeling a terror hold his body in place. The hooded figures had become a problem for him after the "planting" of his invisible corn. (Or maybe just planting, no scare quotes. The entire invisible food movement had caught on so strongly that even he was unsure if the corn was real or not.) Soon after the announcement of that first crop, he started to find, after the sun went down, hooded figures wandering his property. They would walk slowly through the fields, moving their hands as though pushing aside stalks of corn. He refused to go outside after dark, and eventually to even be in the dark in his own home. He slept with the lights on, wearing a sleep mask so that he could approximate a normal sleep cycle, but the thin band of light where the mask met his nose reminded him of his fear, which reminded him of the strange figures stalking through crops that weren't there, which reminded him that he was only able to plant invisible crops, which reminded him of his failure as, you know, a farmer. He would lie wide-eyed and awake, staring into the fabric of his mask, until the light changed around his nose and he knew that it was dawn.

The figures formed a circle around the pit. Carlos and Nilanjana hurried after the crowd, slipping away from the pit through a gap in the circle. The static was deafening and painful. The figures' hoods billowed in the wind, but the darkness beneath them was complete and unchanging. John Peters finally tried to run, but all gaps were gone. He backed away until there was no more ground left, and then fell into the soft dirt below, still alive with worms. There was no way out of the pit. He was the only one left. There was a high-pitched sound, like a kitten's mewl, elongated and looped. The hooded figures stood cloak to cloak, so the world outside the pit was no longer visible. And then the figures begin to violently shake. They shook and shook. John Peters curled into a ball against the squirming soil and hoped, best-case scenario, that he would just be killed.

26

Nilanjana didn't like John Peters at all, but she wasn't going to stand by as a person got taken by the hooded figures. Carlos was pulling her away, intent on his mission of survival, but she shook away his grasp and ran back toward the pit.

"Nilanjana, what are you doing?"

Good question. There was no gap in the ring around the pit, so, without giving herself time to assess the data and come up with a plan, she charged headlong into one of the figures. A squeal of feedback. The static doubled in volume. But she felt no actual body inside the cloak. It collapsed as she pushed through it like a curtain between rooms. Hopping down into the pit, she put her arm around John Peters, who was oblivious to anything but his fear. She dragged his stiff, resistant body to the edge, pulled him up, and, with the help of a waiting Carlos, moved him back through the gap in the ring to the sun-hot blacktop. John Peters was curled into a ball, his eyes and mouth distended, his only sound a seemingly endless, tremulous exhale.

"It's illegal to interfere with the hooded figures," said a voice full of authority. Pamela Winchell stood over them, arms crossed.

"So arrest me."

Pamela narrowed her eyes, but made no move toward them. John Peters coughed, coming back to the world.

"Where am I? My god, what happened? I'm a farmer, in case anyone didn't know."

Nilanjana didn't have time for his shit, or Pamela's.

"You all right, John?" she asked, then, without waiting for an answer: "We good to leave?" she asked Pamela, then, without waiting for an answer: "Where's your car, Carlos?"

"I took the bus."

"Steve and Abby already got out of here," Nilanjana said. "Let me give you a ride home." And they left.

"Thanks, this time of day the city buses are covered in tarantulas," Carlos said on the way to her car. "They don't harass me or anything, but I'm always afraid of sitting on one, or accidentally bringing one home if it crawls into my bag. I feel bad. The poor thing just wanted to get home from a long day, next thing it knows it's in my living room and Cecil and I are screaming."

"Scared of tarantulas?"

"Oh. Not at all. Screaming 'You're adorable!' and 'What's your name, cutie?'"

She pulled out of the parking lot. Behind her, Pamela got into her official government-issue car, a chrome and purple PT Cruiser. As she followed, she spoke into her wrist, where she did not appear to have any sort of microphone or radio. Nilanjana was still put off by a lot of Night Vale's strangeness, but she had gotten used to being tailed by government agents, so she took the moment to fill Carlos in on her time at the church.

"And so the church believes it is an actual giant centipede that will one day lift itself through the earth and eat everyone," she finished.

"Fascinating. I hope it's true."

"Why would you hope that?"

"Because in most religions, the deities don't physically exist, or there is no proof of their existence. It makes it difficult to scientifically study these beings that claims are being made about. If this Joyous Congregation is worshiping a corporeal being, there is a chance that we could study their god."

"The giant centipede."

"Centipedes are extremely scientific."

"How about we kill it first and study it later?"

"No," Carlos said, his voice unusually hard and decisive. "Absolutely not. We can't kill a living thing just because we're afraid of it, or even because we want to study it. A dead thing has less data than a living thing even if that data is easier to access. We don't even know the first thing about the way it lives. Is it alone? Are there others?"

"Let's hope not."

"What does it eat?"

"According to the church, everything. The entire world."

"Doubtful. How does a beast, even a large one, devour everything in the world?"

"Very carefully."

Carlos nodded seriously. He had trouble understanding when something was a joke.

"It would have to be done carefully, yes."

"Carlos, if that thing's real, it's going to devour the whole town before you get done writing one page of observations. If we want to talk scientific value, let's talk about how it's way easier to do good research when you're alive and not inside an insect."

"Actually, an insect . . ."

". . . has only six legs. You know what I meant."

"Nilanjana, science isn't about danger. Unless the subject being studied is danger. Then that's what science is about. The hooded figures. This centipede. You've gotten quite an appetite for bravery."

"If there's something threatening my town, then I will do what I have to do."

My town? Where had that come from?

"I mean, this town," she said. "I mean any town. Forget it. Why were the hooded figures there?"

Carlos said "hmmm" in a voice far too loud for the small car and stroked his chin, which was his subtle way of indicating that he was thinking.

"The hooded figures are attracted to the Dog Park," he said, "which is a connection to the otherworld. It's possible they're attracted to areas that have been attacked because there's something about the otherworld in those pits."

"We know that the house that doesn't exist is connected to the otherworld. Let's see if there are hooded figures there too."

Carlos grimaced.

"The house that doesn't exist. Going inside it was such a mistake. I was trapped in that otherworld for a year. I didn't know if I would see anyone I loved ever again. I need to understand what happened to me, and whether it could happen to anyone else in Night Vale."

"Somehow that house is connected to the centipede, I think, and the city, and Pamela, and the church, and everyone connected with the church, even . . ."

She trailed off and checked her mirrors. Pamela still was following them. Behind Pamela was a black sedan driven by agents from a vague yet menacing agency. It wasn't unusual for any given car to be tailed by multiple spying cars. It was a common sight in Night Vale, long processions of cars all tailing each other. But there was another vehicle, behind the black sedan. A beat-up white van. At this distance she couldn't see who was driving, but it didn't look government-issued. Who was it and why were they following her?

"Could we go into the house?" she asked.

"No! Absolutely not, no. I know you've found some spirit of derring-do in yourself, but you would disappear into the desert otherworld and maybe never get back. I can't let anyone else get close to it. That's why I've been running remote experiments on it using my machine. Or trying to, if these attacks would stop sabotaging them. I improved my machine yesterday by adding a long, corrugated metal cone, which tapers up to a small red ball. When I turn it on, visible electrical waves form around it making sounds like ZZZZZT."

"What does the cone do?"

"I just explained what it does. Weren't you listening? What I said was—"

He stopped.

"Nils."

"What?"

"What's that van doing?"

The white van was pulling around the black sedan and Pamela's car. Pamela waved her fist at them, shouting about tortures so unimaginable no one had even thought to make them illegal, but they didn't seem to hear her. The van pulled up next to Nilanjana and honked its horn. Carlos looked straight ahead, trying not to acknowledge them. Nilanjana glared at the driver of the van. He had a huge, familiar mustache and a huge, familiar smile. The guard from the church. Next to him was Gordon, displaying his usual upsetting leer. The van accelerated away with a coughing roar.

"Who was that?"

"It doesn't matter," she said. It truly didn't. Let them spy on her. She wasn't afraid of them. "Look, we're almost there."

She turned onto the cul-de-sac and pulled up to the house that doesn't exist. If she looked right at it, it looked like there was a house there, just like every other house on the block, but at the same time it wasn't there.

"What would happen if I knocked on the door?"

"Don't," Carlos said. "You might not like what answers."

"Fine. Fine. I just needed to see the place for myself."

What did it mean that a house she could see and smell and hear and touch did not exist? What would happen if someone tried to buy the house and move in? It was like that old real estate mantra "Existence. Existence. Existence."

"There!" she shouted, pointing.

A hooded figure meandered across the white pebbles that made up the front yard. They could hear the static from where they sat.

"The hooded figures appear to be drifting toward entrances to the otherworld," Carlos said. "This means two probable things. One, the presence of the otherworld is especially strong now. The boundary between the two worlds is getting thinner. Our work in understanding it is more urgent than ever. And two—"

"Two," she said. "The pit at Big Rico's, and therefore all the other pits, are directly related to the otherworld."

"Yes," he said.

"Maybe it was like I thought," she said. "Maybe the pits are caused by the giant centipede, but it's not moving underground. It's moving from the otherworld."

"That is a possibility."

They were so caught up in their conversation that the loud

knocking on the passenger-side window was followed by a startled pulsing in their chests. It was Pamela, leaning over the car. Carlos rolled down his window.

"We were warned about you," Pamela said. "We were warned about the otherworld, and about that monster that lives there. The Wordsmith alerted us to all of this, weeks ago.

"And after we heard from him, we knew we had to do anything to stop you. So keep that in mind. We will do anything to stop you." She met both of their eyes, and behind her the static noise of the hooded figure grew louder. Two more hooded figures appeared, and then two more, drifting across the lawn.

"Anything," Pamela reiterated, then returned to her purple PT Cruiser and drove away.

Nilanjana clutched the steering wheel tightly, trying to stay aware of the hooded figures' movements without looking at them directly.

"Darryl said he just gave them a tract, that he was just trying to convert them," Nilanjana said quietly. "But he's been on the church's side this whole time."

"It would appear so," said Carlos. "I'm sorry. I know you liked him."

He didn't touch her, because he himself didn't like being touched, and so did not like to comfort people that way. But he leaned toward her and gave her a kind and concerned frown.

"It doesn't matter." She was fine. Darryl was probably somewhere with Stephanie right now, laughing about how easily he had undermined her and how excited they were to summon this monster from another world.

"I'm going to tell you something, something I've never told anyone," Carlos said. "Can I do that?"

"Absolutely."

"I've never told Cecil the whole truth about the otherworld because I love him, and I don't want him to experience more pain than he has to. He experienced a year without me, and that is enough. But that is not all I endured."

"Carlos," she said softly, meeting his eyes. "What happened?"

"From the point of view of Night Vale, I was in the other-world for a year. But time moves faster in the otherworld. From my point of view, it wasn't a year. It was ten years. I spent ten years, not eating or drinking, not aging, not truly existing, just waiting in stasis, alone, away from the people I love. It is a place that is empty and hollow. Ten years."

He shuddered, the first time she had seen him do that. His eyes were steady but distant.

"No one must ever go through what I experienced."

There was nothing she could say to make it better, not even a little bit, and so she just said, "Carlos, I'm so sorry."

Past the hooded figures, who now looked like bored, over-dressed security guards, Nilanjana saw a light in the front window of the house. It was daylight out, but she could tell the light was on because she could see a modest iron chandelier over a simple round wood dining table. On the table was a plain glass vase. A shadow moved across the back wall and then a woman. There was a woman in the house, a woman in her fifties, wearing a simple, flower print dress. The woman lifted the vase and placed some fresh flowers into it. She left the room and returned a moment later with a cup, with which she poured some water into the vase. She looked out the window for a moment, as if savoring the morning light. She stretched, and yawned, but the yawn didn't end. Her jaw swung wider, and her arms got longer. She looked like she was caught in a black hole, helplessly elongating. Her mouth was half her body.

Her arms bent backward as they pushed against the ceiling. Her eyes sank back into her skull. She was just a mouth, two empty eye sockets, and warped arms creeping along the ceiling like vines. And then the woman dissolved, all of her, mouth and eye sockets and arms, into dust, which fell out of sight onto the living room floor.

"Carlos. Are you seeing this?" Nilanjana moved to clutch his shoulder, and then, remembering, stopped herself. "Was all that real?"

He shrugged.

"It happened in a house that doesn't exist, so technically no, I suppose."

27

"The scientists want to study the Smiling God," said Pastor Munn. "They think there's something 'scientifically fascinating and absolutely terrifying' about a giant centipede."

She looked at Darryl from across her desk. Gordon, who had returned from his surveillance mission in the van and was back at his usual place, behind her, glowered along.

"Does that sound right to you?" she asked. He was uncertain if she meant correct or justified.

"In my experience," Darryl said, "scientists find everything scientifically fascinating. It's one of their best and worst habits. They're always shouting about how the entire universe is an extraordinary place, and that the vast sparkle of a nebula and the grinding burp of a broken blender are all part of a spectrum of things that exist and how that is so unlikely and beautiful." He sighed. "It gets tiring. Especially when you have been raised with the heady and inspiring stuff that is a Smiling God coming to devour us all."

The pastor narrowed her eyes above her friendly, natural smile, but it didn't have the effect she wanted because it was hidden by her huge hat. She removed her hat and narrowed her eyes again.

"And what do the rest of you think? Is Darryl telling me the truth? Can we trust him or has he betrayed his faith?"

Darryl was flanked by Stephanie and Jamillah, and each one of them put a hand on him, claiming him as one of their own.

"There's no one more invested in this community than our Wordsmith," said Stephanie. "No one has put in more volunteer hours, or tithed more to support our foreign missions to Venezuela and Mexico and Double Mexico."

"I wish you could have seen the tons of hours he spent teaching our missionaries Double Spanish," Jamillah added.

"It's the doubling of the vocal cords that's the tricky part," said Darryl. "Once you're past that, it gets a lot easier."

"Or if you don't believe him," said Stephanie, "believe me. You know that I want nothing more than to be a Church Elder. I wouldn't let anything get in the way of that goal. And I know that Darryl is loyal to the church."

"Mm." The pastor said nothing more. She tapped the tips of her fingers together thoughtfully.

Gordon coughed.

"Pastor," he said. "Ma'am. You know I always am behind you one hundred percent, no matter what. But, well, we've known Darryl since he was little. I taught several of his classes. He stayed with my wife and me for a few weeks right after the Ramirezes . . . after his folks . . . uh . . . passed. I have watched him grow into a joyous, faithful follower of our Smiling God."

The pastor did not change her neutral smile.

"If you don't believe him, though," Gordon continued, "I don't believe him. For sure. But if it was me, just me, on my own, I think I would believe him. He wrote our brochure, for teeth's sake."

"Thank you, Gordon," the pastor said, her tone gentle, but not inviting further feedback. "And you, Darryl, what do you say for yourself?"

Darryl paused and collected his thoughts. As good as he was at writing, he knew he could be deeply unconvincing when speaking. His sincerest thoughts sometimes seemed to convey ulterior motives or inappropriate tones. And now he needed to be as convincing as it was possible to be. He rode a slow breath in and out.

"To me, there is no separation between the bodies in this room and the belief in our hearts and jaws," he said. "I think that what we believe and what we are, those are inseparable and singular. Every time I move my finger, it is a prayer. Every time Stephanie makes a joke and Jamillah laughs, that is a prayer. Every song Gordon leads is a prayer. Every touch, every thought, every conflict, every moment of weakness, even, is a prayer. The Joyous Congregation is everything that our lives are made of. I couldn't deny my faith any more than I could deny my skeleton, couldn't leave it without leaving every minute that my friends and I have ever spent together. I love the people in this room. And with that same love, not the same level of love, but the same single impulse of love, I love the Joyous Congregation, I love the Smiling God, and I love each of you." He looked into Gordon's eyes, and then into Pastor Munn's. He touched Stephanie's fingers on his shoulder. He held Jamillah's non-power-drill hand. "I don't know if that answers your question."

Jamillah ran her power drill a little, she couldn't help it. Stephanie gave his shoulder a hard squeeze. Everyone but the pastor was crying. Pastor Munn was smiling.

"Darryl," she said, "I knew you were special. You have always been special to this church. Not many of us in this generation grew up with the faith. Most of us drifted into the Joyous Congregation out of lives of temptation and heresy and

Bloodstone Circles. But this faith raised you." She reached out a hand across the desk, and he took it. It was a long reach for both of them. It was a really big desk.

"The Smiling God does not know grudges. It does not understand transgression. It only knows hunger. It only devours. It is perfect that way. And you still have a place with all the rest of your siblings of the faith in the dark, acrid belly of the Smiling God. Will you join us there?"

"Yes," he said. "Pastor, absolutely yes."

She smiled at him. He widened his lips as far as they would go and showed his teeth. So did his friends, and Gordon. They all showed their teeth to each other, indicating how happy all of them were.

"I have something important to show you," Pastor Munn said. "But first, a blessing. Please, stand, bow your heads, and keep your eyes firmly closed. Gordon, will you lead the prayer?"

"Yes, uh, which prayer are we—"

"The one about the Mark," she snapped.

"Okay. You heard the pastor. Eyes closed, heads down. 'O Smiling God. Who, more than you, hungers? Who comes out of the sand, like you, and devours all It can see? Who has larger teeth? Who has more teeth? Who else is an enormous centipede? No one. Only You, our gracious Smiling God.'"

As they recited the prayer, the pastor gave Gordon a tin of thick black paste that smelled a little like moss and a little like urine. None of the others had any idea what the paste was made from (it was made from crushed centipedes), but he smeared it under each of their right ears, drawing three interlocking triangles.

"'So you are marked, may you be eaten,'" Gordon continued. "'So you are devout, may you be devoured. So you are together,

may you be together within the stomach of our Smiling God.'
To this we all say:"

They all said it. "Amen."

"Well great! Together, we are the devout, the devoured," Pastor Munn said. "That's super. You all can sit or whatever now. And hey! Now I can show you the book. I want to show you the book. It's all happening so fast. It's quite exciting."

Even Gordon seemed a bit wary at this. People in Night Vale are not comfortable with books in general, understanding that they are, in the best cases, wastes of time and, in the worst cases, traps left by the Secret Police to find out who the curious ones are so they can be removed from the population. Plus, Gordon was the only Elder in the room. He was the one who should get to see whatever exciting book she was going to bring out. Deep down, he hated and feared books and would prefer never to have to read them, but if anyone in this room deserved the right to get to read a book, it should be him.

The pastor's desk had been empty before the prayer began, but now there was a huge tome bound in a leather none of them recognized (it was centipede skin). There was an intricate design made from nails driven into the cover, connected by bits of wire.

"This is *The Book of Devouring*," she said, patting it proudly. Despite the vastness of her desk, the book seemed to take up a great deal of space. "With this, we will call upon our God. This is called the Invocation."

"Where did the Congregation get this book?" said Stephanie, interested as always in the academic side of things. She could not wait to become a Church Elder and be allowed to read the great histories, stories, and secrets of the church. "Have we always had it?"

"It was written by the prophet Kevin," the pastor said. Kevin was a great figure in the history of the church. He had once been a radio host in a town called Desert Bluffs until one day he had found an old oak door. He had gone through that door, and had entered heaven, where he had met the Smiling God. When he returned, it was with the message of the Smiling God, a message that he spread through his radio shows until he disappeared. It was said that he had returned to heaven, to join the Smiling God there. "Kevin loved the Smiling God more than anyone. And he was able to observe Its habits, and from that he wrote this book. And this book was passed down to me. I mean, not passed down for long. We're not an old religion."

"Really aren't," said Jamillah.

"Relatively recent," said Stephanie.

"But we are the first religion with the gratifying knowledge that we have found it. The true explanation for everything. Centuries of searching, and we hold the answer here in our hands."

"Joyfully," said Gordon, holding up his hands and closing his eyes.

"So joyfully!" said Stephanie.

Jamillah ran her power drill.

"Joyfully," said the pastor, placing both hands on the book in front of her.

Darryl stood. He was crying, and his smile was wider than it had ever been.

He looked to the needlework on the wall, hanging uncharacteristically crooked. He repeated its boisterous message.

"Joyfully," he said, "It devours!"

28

Nilanjana sat straight up in bed, panting, sweating. She was cold. It was bright out. She had slept through the sunrise somehow. She had had a terrible dream. Like most dreams, it was lasting and memorable, but only in the part of the brain that hides information. The part of the brain that takes drama and trauma and buries it like whatever those specks are that grow into things (she still didn't remember what they were called), where it can grow over time into something that takes on a larger, more distinct shape, unrecognizable from its original form. Darryl had been in the dream, but she couldn't remember what he had been doing. She only knew that she didn't trust him.

It was too late in the morning to even think about getting back to sleep. She was discombobulated from the nightmare, the components of which had dissolved so much, she could only assume it was a nightmare based on her body's current state: clammy arms and chest, sweat on her upper lip, the kind of headache that doesn't hurt but that makes your head feel like styrofoam, and a deep worry for something or somebody unknown.

She and Carlos had been up late last night going over the information they had. Hooded figures were attracted to entrances to the otherworld. They had been attracted to the pit at Big Rico's. So this pit had something to do with the otherworld. It was possible that the pits were being created by the movements of a giant, devouring centipede that was worshiped as a smiling god. If so, then this centipede was related to the otherworld. But what was the city's role? Why did Pamela keep showing up around these disasters? And what motive would a centipede have to disrupt Carlos's experiments? On a motive level, it was more likely that the city was behind these attacks. But then how was the centipede involved, if at all? Back and forth, until the night became technically morning, although this had more to do with the imperfect labeling created by humans than with any change in the actual nature of the night.

Nilanjana had apparently fallen asleep with the television on. She almost never watched television. She had a television and a cable subscription because it was mandatory for all Night Vale citizens to own a television and pay for cable. Even though she didn't think of herself as a citizen of Night Vale, the law still applied to her. This was fine by Nilanjana, as she didn't mind paying taxes and government fees if they were supporting the less fortunate. Cable television executives had fallen on difficult times in the last few years and were now the most poverty-stricken demographic. So at least the money she paid for cable was going to a good cause, even if she didn't watch it much.

But this morning the television was on. It was the Channel 6 local news with Tim and Trinh. They were identical half insects in identical suits, like all news anchors, and the second most trusted source for news in Night Vale, after Cecil's radio show, which was the heart of the community, and well ahead of the *Night Vale Daily Journal*, which had an editorial stance against differentiating fiction and journalism. Everyone loved

Tim and Trinh because, as many citizens said, "they really speak to me."

And this was true. Tim and Trinh often spoke directly to people who were watching the news. Sometimes a viewer might watch a story in disbelief or smile at a cute feature on animal adoptions or cry because a news item affected them personally. It was in those moments that Tim and Trinh would address that person directly and tell them, "It's going to be fine, Tavin," or "It's not okay but you can only make change in your own life, Diane," or "That dog is cute, right, Earl? You should get a dog. You'd be happy with a dog."

Channel 6 also had the government-enforced power to turn on at any time in any home. Sometimes this was to present important news events, like an Amber Alert. Sometimes it was because ratings were low that period and they needed some "juice." Either way, Nilanjana thought, it was possible that she hadn't fallen asleep watching television. The television could have just turned itself on to Channel 6.

". . . still missing despite the Sheriff's Secret Police efforts to find him" was the first thing Nilanjana processed Tim (or maybe Trinh) saying.

"Police have found no sign of Larry or even his home. Both were reported missing a week ago by a citizen named Erika, who also claimed to be an angel," said Trinh (possibly Tim).

"Hahaha. There are no such things as angels, Trinh," said Tim.

Great, now I know which is which, Nilanjana thought.

"No, there certainly aren't, Tim," said Trinh. "And the police have taken this supposed angel Erika into custody for illegally proclaiming the existence of themself."

"We're getting a report right now that Erika escaped police custody by flying up and away to the heavens using their great feathered wings. Witnesses said they could hear what sounded like a French horn and a children's choir."

"People will go to any lengths to protect their delusions, won't they, Tim?"

"Hahahaha," said Tim, slapping the desk with a human hand. The nail on Tim's right ring finger was three inches long and painted in green and black stripes. "Hahahaha," Tim repeated after a breath.

"If you have seen Larry Leroy, out on the edge of town, please call the number below."

At the bottom of the screen was a phone number. Next to Trinh's triangular face was a photo of Larry. He was smiling, his forehead glistening. The flash was too bright. The smile was the artificial smile of a posed picture, the kind of lip curl that happens when a person calls to the group, "Okay, everybody, say 'broken feet'" and then everyone says "broken feet," and somehow that is supposed to generate a natural happy face.

Nilanjana could see Larry's diorama over on her bookshelf, the diorama she'd found in the desert where his home used to be. The crisp details of Dorothy's face, the accurate texture of the aluminum sides of her war balloon, the fires of what had once been Kansas below her. Nilanjana could almost make out individual houses, children and dogs on lawns. Larry's coloring demonstrated a masterful gradient of an unseen setting sun. Bright yellows and oranges, fading to ocher and mauve with long shadows.

In his art, he communicated life. Journalists and orators must use language to craft their understanding of the world. Nilanjana and other scientists had to use numbers and gather data to form a structure for the universe. Larry used color and strokes and gentle hands to build his worlds. No historian or novelist could, in a thousand pages, verbalize a story quite as rich as one of Larry's shoe-box-size dioramas. Each one a masterpiece, Nilanjana thought. She was crying now. It was fine. She was just exhausted from a nightmare she couldn't remember.

She felt for Larry. She didn't know him. Nobody knew him. He made brilliant art, and it was in no museum, no magazine. He had no children and lived as far from the city as one could live and still live in Night Vale. He had so much to give the world, and no one knew what that "so much" was. It was only in his death—eaten by a centipede? Murdered by the City Council?—that anyone could see what he had made. Not even a body or ruins of a house, just a pit marking where all of that had been buried.

And this diorama, inert and private, in her home. The sole evidence left of his gifts.

She promised when all of this was resolved, she would make sure Night Vale knew who Larry was and what he had created.

"I promise, Larry," Nilanjana said at the diorama.

"What do you promise?" Tim asked from the television screen.

"What?"

"Tim wants to know what you promise, Nilanjana. Did you just talk to that diorama?"

"What? No. I—"

"That's an excellent diorama. Did you make it?" Tim asked.

"No." Nilanjana did not want them to think she had been out digging through Larry's stuff. The pit was a crime scene after all. "I mean, yes."

"Hey, so what are you doing with Darryl?"

"Yeah, what's going on with you two?" Tim asked, forgetting about the diorama. "You make a cute couple."

And here a photo appeared next to Tim's face, showing the couple, both in sunglasses, exiting Nilanjana's apartment building.

"Hey! I'm not a public figure. You can't run photos like that!"

"Sounds like forbidden love, Tim." Trinh grinned (was that a grin?). "Two young lovers, one a logical scientist, the other, a member of one of the most evangelical churches in Night Vale."

"Quite star-crossed these two," Tim added, their one long nail gently caressing Trinh's left hand. Trinh did not acknowledge it.

Nilanjana didn't want to talk about Darryl right now. At her most positive, she tried to think of him as a means to an end, a way to find out what the church was up to. More often, she thought of him as a mistake. Mostly, she tried not to think of him at all.

"Yes, Tim. Wrapping up, in final news, Pamela Winchell, Director of Emergency Press Conferences for the city"—her image appeared on screen—"is holding an emergency press conference about the great, bottomless pit which appeared a few moments ago in the floor of the Night Vale High School gymnasium."

"What?" Nilanjana leapt up.

"Yes. Pamela's quite excited to have a real emergency to hold a press conference about. Most of her press conferences tend to be existential emergencies—bigger-picture issues, less specific to . . ."

"No, the gym! What happened at the gym?"

"We're getting to that. Don't interrupt. Also, we can see you, Nilanjana. Maybe put some pants on," Tim said. She scrambled for the blankets. "Ah, I'm just playing." Tim laughed. "But please put your pants on."

"This morning, during basketball practice, the floor of the NVHS gymnasium disappeared. Several students and faculty disappeared along with it."

Janice was on the school's wheelchair basketball team and was an equipment manager and trainer for the varsity team. What if she had gotten hurt or was one of the missing? And Carlos. Oh, Carlos must be beside himself right now. Or what if he didn't even know yet? She needed to go. She scrambled around for clothes, muttering "shit, shit, shit."

"Calm down, Nils."

"Don't tell me to calm down. And don't call me Nils, Timmy." Nilanjana snapped.

"No, *I'm* Tim," the other one said.

The screen cut to a shot of a student outside the high school being interviewed. The chyron said, "MISTY ALVAREDO, JUNIOR."

"I was in band and felt a rumbling under us. I thought it was great because I had finally pressed down all the valves correctly on my baritone and I thought that had unlocked some great mystery, that perhaps the firmament had split to reveal a face and that face had spoken and the great truths in its words had shaken the ground, just like our old music teacher Louie Blasko used to tell me would happen when I finally mastered my instrument. But the rumbling was something else entirely. It destroyed the floor of the gym," Misty said. "So I guess I didn't press the buttons in the right order. I don't know how brass instruments work."

"Did you know anyone in the gym at the time this happened?" the off-screen reporter asked.

"What? In sports? No. Probably not. Is basketball a sport?"

"Yes, it is," the reporter said. "That's who was practicing."

"Then yes." Misty's face did not change.

Nilanjana had gotten her pants on and grabbed her keys.

"Shit. Shit. Shit," she repeated.

"Well, Trinh, it's a horrible story. Just tragic," Tim said.

"Yes, absolutely. Children are our future, after all. They are a noisy and unruly future, full of unearned self-confidence and silly ignorance. Children are quite an unintelligent future."

"Yes."

"Shit." Nilanjana was trying to call Carlos. She had the phone to her ear as she was pulling on her shirt.

"Carlos, are you watching the news?" she said into his voice mail.

"We already told Carlos, Nilanjana. Why would we not have told Carlos?" Nilanjana couldn't see which one said it. She was already at the front door.

"Carlos, I'm on my way to the school. Please call. Let me know Janice is okay. I'm so sorry."

She let the front door slam shut behind her, forgetting to lock it or even fasten the belt she was wearing. Her bag and hair and shoelaces and belt buckle waved behind her like battle flags as she ran. Her heart pulsed in her ears and she felt the sweat on her upper lip like a cold mustache.

Inside, on the television, Tim said, "For more on this let's go to Emma in sports. Emma? What does a gaping pit in the middle of their practice court and the loss of almost all of the players do to this team's chances to make the playoffs?"

29

Almost the entire gymnasium floor was gone, a deep pit now. Only the bleachers were left, with students scattered across them. Two students were huddled together, their faces puffy from crying. They had their arms on each other's shoulders and were slowly rocking, heads down, and silent. Another group of kids were clearing away the debris, chunks of wood planks and pieces of plexiglas backboard. Several of the Sheriff's Secret Police were conducting interviews of their own for a full report. They were asking students questions like "You didn't see anything, right?" and "You're not that reliable, are you?" Three other students were helping fix a broken wheelchair.

A broken wheelchair. Janice, Nilanjana thought. Her face flushed, her eyes itched, and she involuntarily rubbed her chest as she tried to breathe normally. Janice, she thought again, as she scanned the room. Her eyes fell upon Carlos in the doorway, with Cecil and Steve and Abby. Steve had his big arm over Carlos's shoulder. Cecil had his arm around Carlos's waist while trying to nudge Steve's arm away. Nilanjana hurried toward them as best she could along the bleachers.

"Janice?" she said, as she got to them.

Carlos, too overwhelmed to speak, only let his mouth dangle open, saying nothing, and Nilanjana felt some vital part of her heart snap. Thankfully Abby, who approached life with an absolute practicality and who wouldn't let herself collapse with the trauma of the moment until hours later when she was alone in the shower, pointed to the handball court. Janice was sitting there, staring at the handball wall, not talking.

"She's okay," said Abby. "Or physically at least. The collapse damaged her wheelchair, but some of the kids are working on that."

"I'm so glad," Nilanjana said, knowing it sounded monstrously understated, but not knowing how else to express that she was really fucking glad.

"Us too," said Steve, understanding exactly what she meant.

Immediate concern addressed, she scanned the scene for any new information that could be collected. Among the crying parents and students, and the sand drifting up from the pit, she saw a kiwi bird. She did a double take. The kiwi bird wasn't moving, just watching everyone around the gym. She got closer to examine it. She couldn't be looking at a kiwi, as they are not native to Night Vale, or America for that matter. But she was.

The bird turned and looked at her.

"Hey," said the bird. "It's Josh. From the pizza place."

"Josh! I'm sorry I didn't . . . it's just last time you looked different."

"I've been trying out the bird thing lately. I don't know."

"It looks cool," she said. It did look cool. Birds are cool-looking.

"Maybe." He seemed unconvinced by her compliment, while also happy to have gotten it.

"Are you okay?" She sat next to him.

"I'm fine, I guess. I mean, physically. The team was warming up. A few players were still in the locker room. I was sitting in the stands watching. My boyfriend is on the team, but he wasn't on the court yet. If he was . . . I don't know. That's him over there trying to fix our friend's wheelchair. Hey, Grant!"

One of the boys near the wheelchair looked up toward the bleachers. He kept scanning but could not spot Josh. Josh stood in place, not doing anything.

"Oh, dammit," he said. "I don't have visible wings like this. He can't see me wave. Also when we arrived at school this morning, I was a brown bear."

Nilanjana waved to Grant and pointed to Josh. Grant seemed to get it and gave a slight smile, but then the smile was lost again in the shock.

"What happened to the floor, Josh?"

"I felt the building shaking, and the floor got hot. Scalding even. I was in the bleachers, but it was radiating all the way up. I didn't say anything because I thought it was just me, but then I looked down at the guys on the court and they were all staring at the floor and moving their legs and arms up and down frantically. I panicked and didn't move. I couldn't react in time. I could have saved people."

"Josh, it's natural to not know what to do in a moment like that. Don't feel bad."

"Janice Palmer reacted in time, though—that's her over there. She started shouting at the players to get in the bleachers. She was, like, really on it. Getting everyone she could off the hardwood. And then the whole floor was gone. Janice was right on the edge. I was sure I was going to watch her fall. And Michael Shoemaker—he's the tall one; he plays center—he held out his arm, and she grabbed it and pulled herself up into the bleachers. That's Michael down there with Grant fixing her wheelchair."

"Did you see any movement, or anything else, when the hole appeared?"

"Movement?"

"Like an animal, or machine, or anything else moving underground that could have caused the hole."

Josh clacked his beak thoughtfully.

"No, I don't think so. It happened so fast though. I heard that sound and then the floor was gone."

"What sound? What did you hear?"

"It was like—"

"Josh." A voice came from below. A crying woman in her mid-thirties ran right at them along the third row of the bleachers. "Oh, god, you're okay. Josh. Josh. Come here."

"Mom!" Josh protested as she picked up the kiwi and held it tight to her chest and neck. She stroked his head. "Mom," he grunted.

"I'm sorry. I shouldn't grab you when you are in a smaller physical state like that. Motherly instincts and all."

"I'm not a kid." He was embarrassed to have this happen in front of an adult with whom he had just been having an adult conversation.

"Twice, Josh. That's twice you could have been killed by one of these pits," she said and then turned to Nilanjana. "Hi. Diane Crayton."

"Nilanjana Sikdar. I'm a scientist. I'm researching what's causing these pits. I was interviewing Josh about what happened here."

"I know you. You're from Carlos's lab? I guess we're both lucky today. Thanks for keeping my son company." Diane embraced her son once more, kissing his tiny feathered head. "I know I said you're not allowed to grow wings and fly without an adult around, but if another one of these pits forms, you grow the biggest wings you can and fly far away."

"Okay, Mom. Can you put me down?"

"Promise?" Diane put him down.

"Mom," he whined.

At that moment, Jackie Fierro tore through the gym door and joined the embrace.

"Dude, you're okay," she said. "I'm sorry it took me so long. I'm a shitty sister. I was driving Laura on some errands on account of I offended her a few days ago. Man, I'm so glad to see your feathered ass in one piece."

Nilanjana felt it was better to let them have the moment alone. Also, there was a commotion out on the asphalt.

Pamela Winchell stepped up onto a tall podium for a press conference. Nilanjana walked closer to hear her speech, as did most everyone else. A few camera flashes went off.

"No pictures, please," Pamela said. The cameras stopped flashing. She frowned.

"This doesn't feel right. Something doesn't feel right. There are usually a bunch of bright flashes and clicking sounds when I'm on a podium, but I don't see or hear them now."

Her assistant, a woman named Trish Hidge, loudly whispered: "You told them no pictures. Those flashes and clicks are pictures."

"Ah. I see," Pamela said into the mic. "No pictures, but please make your cameras click and flash. I need the clicks and flashes in order to do this. But no pictures."

A few moments passed as the photographers in the group tried to figure out how to make their cameras do that without taking pictures. Then the press conference proceeded.

"Hello, people of Night Vale. Hello, people of earth. Hello, ghost people of the heavens and hells and in-betweens. Hello, starry gods of the night sky hidden by the bright blue sky and the bright yellow sun. I have called this press conference to . . ."

She paused.

"Why is the sky blue when the sun is yellow? Shouldn't the sky be yellow?" A strong touch of frustration in her voice. "This makes no sense. Trish. Trish! Find out why that is, and get back to me. Interrupt whatever I'm doing to tell me. It doesn't matter if I'm delivering a press conference or sleeping or dying.

"I apologize for that tangent. Where was I? Right. I was at home, then I was in my car. Next, I was at the high school. I'm still at the high school. That helps. See what I did? I examined history to find out more about the present. As the saying goes, 'Those who fail to understand history are doomed, as are those who do understand it.' It was Emma Goldman who said that. And Emma Goldman should know, for she eventually died, and we still don't know what she had to do with today's tragedy.

"Sheriff Sam and their Secret Police are doing a fine job investigating this disaster. They've been shouting at the pit, and I believe Sam has tried shooting at it. The mayor and her staff are also doing a great job. Everyone's doing well at their jobs. You are too, maybe. I haven't investigated you as much as I maybe should have."

Trish leaned to the podium again and whispered.

"I am being told to take questions," Pamela sighed. "Give me some questions, I suppose."

One reporter asked, "What caused the floor of the gym to get destroyed?"

"How would I know? Next question."

"Have any witnesses of the accident described what happened?"

"I'm positive they have. If you were part of something like this, wouldn't you want to describe it?"

"What does the city plan to do next?"

"I can't speak for the city, but I am hoping to finally read Liu Cixin's *Remembrance of Earth's Past* trilogy."

"Speaking for the city is literally your job."

"No more questions."

Pamela spotted Nilanjana in the crowd, and, after a tense moment of eye contact, Pamela gestured at her. The gesture was something like finger scissors, followed by a bobbling of the head, followed by an attempt to touch her neck with her tongue (which she did easily). Nilanjana was clearly confused, so Pamela shouted across everyone, "Meet me in a less populated part of the school yard where I can talk to you secretly.

"What have you done?" Pamela demanded to know, once they were alone. She was leaning sharply into Nilanjana's personal space. Pamela had one finger held out only inches from Nilanjana as if she were about to start poking her in the chest, but the finger came no closer.

"What have *I* done? What have *you* done?" Nilanjana pointed her own finger back. She had had it up to here with this city and most everyone who lived here. "You are trying to stop Carlos from doing his experiments, but is it worth all this?"

"Of course we're trying to stop Carlos. To prevent his relentless poking around from letting that thing into Night Vale."

"The centipede?"

"I don't know all of your big scientific words. That thing the Wordsmith warned us about."

"Darryl?"

"You just said it was a centipede."

"No, Darryl is the Wordsmith."

"Oh, that's right." Pamela slapped her head. Hard. A little bit of blood bubbled above her ear. "Wordsmith was way easier to remember. Darryl's such a dull name. Dull Darryl. Huh. An alliteration. That'll help. Dull Darryl!"

She slapped her head again. There was now a thin stream of blood running down her neck onto her blouse.

"You said he warned you about us. What did Darryl tell you?"

"He didn't tell us anything. He didn't need to. We interpreted the warning. He thought he was there to convert us. Gave us a pamphlet describing the Smiling God. But the City Council, they themselves are otherworldly monsters, so they recognize one when it's described. They understood from the pamphlet that a terrible creature lives in the desert otherworld, and so no one must interact with that place or do anything at all that might let that creature enter our world. What did you call it? Darryl?"

"Centipede. Darryl is a human."

"Whatever. Let that creature be. Let the otherworld be."

Nilanjana had to take a moment to restructure her hypothesis around this new piece of data.

"Wait. You're trying to stop the creature from attacking Night Vale this way? So none of these pits have been caused by you?"

"Of course not," said Pamela. "We're trying to stop giant whatever-you-call-thems from coming into this world. You think I want to see kids eaten by a monster? What kind of person do you think I am?"

"I don't know," said Nilanjana. "I don't know what kind of person I think you are."

"That's terrible if you thought I would do this." Pamela seemed truly hurt.

"But then we're on the same side. We're both trying to stop that creature from doing this."

"Let your government take care of it," Pamela said.

"You've been handling it for two weeks, and people are dying. It's because of how you're handling it that people are dying."

Pamela's face sagged; she was trying to keep herself together.

"You're a hurtful person," she managed after a deep, careful breath and walked away.

What a strange woman, Nilanjana thought. And, she also thought, if the city is also trying to prevent the attacks, then I am left with one possible party with an interest in keeping these events going. The church and its monstrous insect have been devouring Night Vale, bit by bit. It was time to end that, and to end them.

She returned to the gym to check on Carlos. He was leaning into Cecil's chest. It was just the two of them, alone and together. She let them be.

Carlos was particular about how he liked to be touched. Only in certain places. Only for so long. Sometimes it felt nice when Cecil stroked his ears. Then the next day the feeling of anyone touching his ears was unbearable. He could not predict his own responses. In this moment, all he knew was that he wanted to be inside that combination of hair and skin and scent that was Cecil's chest. He put his face right into the breastbone and breathed in. It smelled like home.

"This has to be stopped," Carlos murmured. "Almost Janice. Almost Janice."

Cecil placed a hand atop Carlos's head, a kind of shelter over his frightened husband. Cecil's eyes were closed and his face calm. His voice was soothing and firm.

"Janice is strong," said Cecil. "Stronger than us. She'll be okay. And your science has saved Night Vale so many times. You'll find a solution."

"No matter what," said Carlos. "I've been letting whoever is trying to distract me and sabotage me win. Nothing will stop me from here on out. I won't let Janice down. I won't let you down."

Cecil drew Carlos's face up with a gentle hand.

"We believe in you," Cecil said and kissed his left cheek. "We love you." He kissed his right cheek. "I love you." He kissed his lips.

For the first time in weeks, Carlos forgot his work, his worries, and his world. His universe was a kiss, and he explored that universe thoroughly.

30

As she drove back home from the high school, Nilanjana passed a white van parked a few houses down. It was the van from the Joyous Congregation. When she passed, its engine started and it slid into traffic behind her.

"Goddammit," she thought. "Not this time."

She pulled into the parking lot at Staples ("Life is a hallucination. Buy some pens. Who cares?"). The van pulled in after her. She drove toward the entrance as if going to park, but then pulled a quick U-turn and drove toward the street again. The van, in its slower, bulkier way, turned after her. But she had no interest in losing them. Quite the opposite.

She accelerated toward the entrance of the lot, and just before rocketing out into traffic, she slammed on the brakes and turned the wheel hard. Her car skidded sideways and blocked the van's path. The van stopped. It seemed the driver was uncertain what to do next. There was no other exit back to the main street. The van couldn't leave. Plus she was not behaving in a normal person-being-followed-by-an-unmarked-van sort of way. She turned the car toward the van and gunned the engine. The van started reversing. A car in the street honked at her, trying to turn in to the lot. She gave them a gesture that indicated, in a direct way, that their concerns were not her priority. She let off the brake and lurched after the reversing van.

The curbs around the lot were high, and there were wide planters between the lot and its surroundings. The van couldn't get through that way. Instead it shifted into drive and turned toward the Staples. For a moment, she thought the van was going to drive right through the glass front doors, but they cut left at the last second. She could see them turning in to the delivery lane at the end of the building, which led to the loading docks in back.

Instead of continuing the chase, she decided she could cut them off. She left her car behind and ran into the store. As the doors of Staples slid open, she felt the artificial winter of retail air-conditioning. Inside, the psychological experts of capitalism had created a meandering path that forced the customer through a maze of products to get from entrance to cashier. She didn't have time for that. She started pushing over racks as she ran, heading straight for the back.

"Hey!" shouted Hank, the sentient patch of haze who was floor manager that day. "You can't do that!"

She already had done it. She broke through into one of the wide aisles and tore to the back wall, where she pushed open the door into the employees-only area.

"You can't go in there!" Hank drifted after her. "And you need to move your car."

Her reply was the slap of the employee door closing.

"I hate this place," Hank muttered, sending out a tendril of haze to clean up the racks she had tipped over. "I need to get a job where I don't have to interact with humans."

Nilanjana beat the van to the back delivery area. Behind the store there was a low concrete-block wall, which she leapt over, landing in shrubs and tripping herself onto an asphalt alley road. She fell hard on her shoulder, but scrambled up and ran.

The van had made it around the building, she could see it coming from behind the dumpsters.

Nilanjana wasn't much of an exercise enthusiast. Plus she had had no breakfast and almost no quality sleep. She could feel her leg muscles quivering under the stress and lack of nutrition and regular exertion.

There was a line of young trees that the van could easily plow through to escape into the suburban neighborhood behind the store. Analyzing the data available to her, she eliminated possibility after possibility until she was left with her one course of action. She ran directly into the van's path and stood defiantly. She felt its immense size and speed. A breeze that in other contexts would be pleasant, but here indicated displacement of air from a large, fast-moving object.

She closed her eyes. Her pounding heart and ragged breath gave her a rhythm. The pulse of fear and creeping exhaustion. They weren't going to stop. They weren't going to stop. There was a screech. The van skidded to a stop a few feet from her.

She gasped, trying to regain herself after giving all of her mind and body over to the chase.

The church wanted to get to her? Here she was.

She grabbed the van door and swung it open defiantly. The group of people inside flinched back. She recognized them from her visit to the church. Stephanie. That one with the power drill, Jamillah. And of course:

"Hi," said Darryl. "I guess we should talk."

31

This was it then. The true direction of Darryl's loyalties made clear. Probably the guard from the church was waiting nearby. The pastor too, and her shouty sidekick.

But there was no lunging, no mask placed over her head, no threat to stop her scientific inquiries into the church. Instead, Darryl showed her what he was holding. A huge book, bound with what appeared, to a quick glance from her scientist eyes, to be centipede skin.

"Can we go someplace private to talk to you about this?" Darryl said.

"Just as many monitoring microphones inside as outside," said Nilanjana, quoting the famous line from *A Streetcar Named Desire*.

"It's not the government microphones we're worried about," said Stephanie, from the driver's seat.

"Get in," said Jamillah. "We'll go to your lab."

A trap surely. Or in any case a bad idea.

"Nilanjana," Darryl said calmly. "When the pastor first caught me investigating the church, I went to Stephanie and Jamillah and asked them to help me with a problem. I felt that if there was any chance that any of the leaders of the church were doing something bad, then as members of the church we should be working to inform ourselves. But there was no way to do that on my own without risking being an apostate, a heretic. I told Stephanie and Jamillah everything and trusted them as friends and as fellow believers in the Smiling God."

"How'd that go over?"

"We were all suspicious of your accusations, but we were willing to look into them. I was willing because I trust you. Stephanie and Jamillah were willing because they trust me. When you snuck into services, I texted them to let them know. They did their best to cover for you, and delayed the rest of the Congregation after you pretended to lock yourself in the bathroom. Now, I'm asking you to trust me. Can we go to your lab and talk?"

She opened her mouth. She closed her mouth. She got in the van.

"Remember the notes about the Invocation we found in the office?" Darryl asked. "This is *The Book of Devouring* they mentioned. This is the book the church wants to use to bring the Smiling God into this world."

Darryl kept his eyes on Nilanjana, waiting for a response.

"Turn right at Galloway" was all she said. "We're a few blocks down, in the science district, next door to where Big Rico's used to be."

As they pulled into the alley behind the lab, Nilanjana said, "Inside. Quickly. And then explain yourselves."

The group rushed forward, shutting the door behind them and gathering around a table where Darryl carefully laid the book down, as though it might explode. This seemed sensible to Nilanjana, who knew that while most books are dangerous because of the dangerous information inside, other books are dangerous because they actually explode.

"Thank you for trusting us," said Darryl.

"All I did was let you inside," she said.

She gestured Mark and Luisa over and made hurried introductions. She didn't want to be outnumbered in this situation, and if Darryl had been getting help from his friends, maybe it was time to let other scientists into this besides Carlos.

"We know what the church is doing," said Darryl. "And we don't believe in it. This is our religion. It means everything to us. And we don't want this kind of destruction to be done in our name just because some people in the leadership got the wrong idea about how to worship the Smiling God."

"I've given my life to the church," said Stephanie. "And now they want us to be devoured."

"We want to help you stop them, so that we can take our religion back," said Jamillah.

"We want to worship the Smiling God in peace and with peace," said Darryl, "and that is why we've brought you this."

Nilanjana studied the cover of the book. It had an intricate design made with nails connected by wire. The design had lines going in every direction, most of them silver, but throughout them were gold wires. The gold wires formed a series of interlocking triangles. Near those interlocking triangles was a single golden nail. The design was familiar, but she couldn't put her finger on how.

"What's the cover made of?" Mark said. "It's really shiny and dark."

"Potatoes," explained Luisa.

"That looks nothing like potatoes."

"Well, that's your opinion."

"It's an insect's exoskeleton," Nilanjana said. "Where did you find this book?"

"I stole it from the pastor's office," Darryl said.

"We helped," said Jamillah, proudly.

"We stood watch," said Stephanie. "I've never done anything like that before. It was exciting."

"Her office?" Nilanjana said. "But you already searched there."

"That's true. But when we were in her office yesterday, she told us she wanted to show us the book. She asked us to bow our heads in prayer."

"Gordon made us keep our eyes closed, so we couldn't see what she was doing," Jamillah said.

"And when we opened our eyes, after a short prayer, we saw this giant, hard-to-miss book. It was too big to have been hidden on the shelf, but it must have been kept somewhere nearby," Darryl said.

"Then Darryl commented that the needlework on the wall was crooked," Stephanie said.

"We went back and found the book in a panel behind the needlework," Jamillah said. "I used my drill to open it," she added happily.

"Wow, you three would make a good team of scientists," Luisa said. "I mean, they don't give awards for finding books, but still."

"We all have many things we would have been good at," said Darryl. "But we can only be what we end up being."

Nilanjana opened up the book, examined the writing and diagrams inside.

"What does it all mean?" she asked.

"There's a certain amount of theological debate about that," said Stephanie.

"Yes there is," Jamillah said sharply. This seemed to Nilanjana like it might be a sore subject between them.

"But to summarize," interjected Darryl, who did not want to have to sit through another one of their debates on whether the glistening slime of the Smiling God's antennae was meant to be taken literally or was a metaphorical flourish designed to connect the God to the life-giving nature of water, or perhaps childbirth. "What's not debatable is that this book contains a ritual called the Invocation, which will summon the Smiling God. The pastor is planning on doing this ritual tomorrow evening. We have maybe a few hours before she notices that the book is missing."

"How do we stop her from performing the ritual?" said Nilanjana.

"We don't know," said Jamillah.

"And where is she planning to do this ceremony?"

"We don't know that either," said Stephanie.

"That's why we brought the book to you," said Darryl. "We were hoping with your science you might be able to think of something that could stop Night Vale from being devoured."

"So your religion has created a problem, and now you want science to fix it?" said Luisa, her look of disappointment deepened with layers of disdain.

"Fair question," said Mark.

"Listen, it's not about fault," said Darryl, thinking it may have been a bit about fault. "A problem exists and we all need to work together to fix it."

"And don't get me started on what scientists have done," Jamillah said, and that instigated a prolonged, noisy debate.

While the others argued, Stephanie flipped through the book. Certainly she was interested in the threat that the leadership of their church posed to Night Vale and to everyone she knew. But she was also fascinated by the history of the church. And here was one of its original documents, perhaps even as old as forty years, written in the hand of Kevin himself. She had loved Kevin's radio show, back when he was still hosting it. It was full of happiness, joy, positivity. She didn't know if he had actually gone back through the old oak door to heaven, but she hoped he was still spreading happiness wherever he was.

She was thrilled to see some of his actual writing. Maybe this was the original text he had written after meeting the Smiling God in heaven. She flipped through the pages, yellowed with age, and also with the fact that they were torn from a yellow legal pad.

Kevin had written: "Wow. What a perfectly wonderful, wonderfully perfect super day! I could not be more thrilled. The Smiling God blessed me with Its presence once again. I felt the sand beneath me quake, and Its Maw rose from deep within and greeted me. And I said, 'Hey, I'm Kevin. How's it going there?' And It nearly swallowed me, which was a huge honor. 'Big fan,' I shouted as Its unbearable bulk blocked out all light around me, until it was just me, in the night It had created with Its movement, grinning up at Its darkness. Superinspiring and nice."

Next to this was a smiley face, and a strange symbol. Some sort of geometric design. Had Kevin been doodling in the holy text he had been writing?

("Isn't that just like you religious freaks, you don't believe in science until it's your life on the line and then you come looking to us for answers," Mark was shouting at Darryl. Jamillah was waving her drill.)

Stephanie turned the page, and Nilanjana, uninterested in being part of an argument that no side would win, read along with her.

The same strange geometric design was drawn across the

top, along with some exclamation points and the phrase "Smiling God" in a cartoon heart.

"Boy, life sure is great," the text said. "I've figured out how to tell where the Smiling God will appear next. When It gets hungry, It begins to hunt. And It does these sweeps outward and outward. Always the same way, so I can wait just ahead of It and get a big ol' eyeful of Its nightmare body. Nifty as all get-out!"

Stephanie found the text disappointingly practical. What she wanted to understand was the ineffable majesty of the Smiling God, and instead she was getting the eating habits of a living creature. This cheerful insistence on literality seemed to lower the Smiling God, reduce the mystery and the power of It.

Nilanjana found the text disappointingly prosaic. She wanted specifics, facts, detailed charts about where and when and how this god was supposed to be summoned so she could form some hypothesis for how they could stop it.

("Scientists want to act like they have it all figured out," Jamillah was saying, red-faced, "but no matter how many facts you learn, nothing in your knowledge can tell you what it means. You know but you don't know *why*. Your knowledge is a hollow edifice.")

There were doodles throughout the book, including increasingly complicated versions of the geometric design. Stephanie examined one of the designs closely, trying to make some sense of it, and then, for whatever reason, it clicked into place. She had seen that design before.

Nilanjana recognized the design too, although from a different place.

"Hey, guys?" Nilanjana said.

"FLAT ALL THE WAY ROUND. IT IS FLAT ALL THE WAY AROUND," Jamillah was shouting, her drill running at the highest power.

Apparently the argument had devolved into whether mountains existed.

"Listen!" Stephanie said.

"WHAT?" Jamillah's face was flushed. "I'm sorry. That was loud. What?"

"The design on this cover. It's repeated all the way through the book," Stephanie said. "And it's the same as the one Gordon drew in that smelly paste on each of our necks during the prayer."

"Gross," Mark gagged.

"Churches are weird," Luisa agreed.

Stephanie showed the cover, with its interlocking triangles.

"Yeah, that's the pattern he drew on us," Darryl agreed.

"What do you think it means?" Stephanie asked.

"Who knows?" said Mark. "It's a pattern from the religious book. News flash, all your church stuff is made up."

"Not even a pretty design," disapproved Luisa.

"I think I know," said Nilanjana. "I thought I had recognized it but I wasn't certain."

She gathered them around her terminal and pulled up the video the helicopter pilot had given her. Grainy black-and-white footage, looking down at the desert, where something big was moving.

They watched the flickering image. The thing moving through the sand. Coming out of the sand, moving across it, and disappearing back under it. Then coming back out of the sand at an angle and repeating all over again.

"It's making triangles," Darryl said. "Whatever that is, it's moving in a triangle."

"Interlocked triangles," Nilanjana said. "The cover of your book is a diagram of its movements. It lines up exactly with the video."

She felt a moment of joy as she worked with Darryl, once again on the same side. It was a realization that she was missing something only when it was returned to her, the feeling of partnership when they worked together. She trusted him, even though she didn't know if all the evidence and data added up to that. It wasn't a decision, it was a feeling. She believed that he was on her side, and that made her happier than she understood.

Darryl squinted at the book and then back at the video.

"Then what is this spot?" he said, pointing at the golden nail in the cover.

Nilanjana considered that.

"If we applied that pattern to where this video was shot, and if it continues making the same triangles . . ."

She laid a clear plastic grid on the screen and sketched out the triangles.

"I think that golden nail is . . ." She drew a dot on the grid. "Right here. Oh."

The spot was where Larry Leroy's house used to be.

Darryl nodded, running his thumb absently over the cover of the book.

"I think we know where they're planning to stage the Invocation," he said.

32

There were no feelings of mysticism, just sand, and scrub, and helicopters, and heat, and wind. Before Night Vale grew into a town, much of the area looked like this. This was what was waiting under the town's asphalt, ready to reclaim everything once people were gone and forgotten.

Mark measured the pit where Larry Leroy's house used to be. Stephanie looked through the symbols in the book and compared them to the area. Nilanjana took air-quality samples (dry, speckled). Luisa took samples of plant species (dry, speckled). Jamillah found a small lizard (cute, speckled). Occasionally a Secret Police helicopter flew by, but none that Nilanjana recognized.

She called Carlos to tell him about what they had been researching, and the discovery of the book, mystical and unscientific as it seemed. She asked him if there were any developments on his end.

"Janice looks and feels fine," Carlos said. "But I still worry constantly. Cecil is terrified for me. He said he couldn't bear having to report on my demise. I should stay home. But I can't. This is a crisis. And science exists to solve crises. I've saved Night Vale before, and I'll do it again. I'm going back to the lab."

"At least come take a look at the book?" Nilanjana said, putting her hand on its strange binding. "I think they're wanting to summon the creature where Larry Leroy's house used to be."

"Religious rituals aren't real. Or they are real, but they are real the way modern dance is real."

He sighed.

"I don't know," he said. "Maybe you're right. You were right about investigating the church. But I need to keep doing things my way. I'll run another experiment from the lab. You keep looking into the church."

She got off the phone and told the group, "It's just us. Carlos was no help. We'll need to stop the Summoning ourselves."

"Let's destroy the book," Luisa said, lifting a potato peeler out of a pouch on her belt.

"The Elders memorize sacred texts," Stephanie said. "Because of a general distrust of reading, teaching is done orally. Between Pastor Munn and Gordon, they'll know the entire ritual, book or not."

Luisa lowered the peeler.

"Could we get some planks and then drill them over that pit?" Jamillah asked.

"Whatever's making the holes between the worlds demolished Larry's house, a high school gym, and a pizza joint," Mark said. "Planks won't stop it."

There was a pause, as the group continued to think. They expressed their thinking by staring at the ground and tapping rocks with their shoes, occasionally saying "Um . . ." followed by "never mind."

Darryl finally spoke up.

"Maybe diplomacy is best. I'll take the book back. I'll tell Pastor Munn I took it, that I led us all to this place. But it was not out of weakness of faith. It was out of strength. The Smiling

God is our God, and It has the divine right to devour us whenever It pleases. It is not in the human interest to determine when that is. It is God's will to act as It must. Only It knows the path of Its glory, the path of humanity.

"I might be excommunicated. I might"—he choked up a little, looking at Jamillah and Stephanie—"not get to be around my family for a long time. But it is important that we do what is right. We cannot stop the Smiling God, we can only hope to stop those who wish to bring an end to human lives in Its name."

Nilanjana placed her arm around Darryl. He was weeping. She cradled his head and kissed his hair. She thought of Cecil with Carlos in the gym, and in this moment, she wanted to be a Cecil to someone, as she would want someone to be a Cecil to her.

Darryl had been called the Wordsmith because of his affinity for writing, not speaking. He had trouble demonstrating that he meant what he said. But this was a sincerity she had rarely seen. Even his scrunched, sobbing face was beautiful in that moment.

"Darryl," she said. "Darryl, you would make that sacrifice for us?"

"I would. I would do anything for you." He met her eyes long enough to show that while the *you* here was plural, it was, even more so, singular.

"Anything?" Nilanjana asked softly.

"Anything."

"Because the sacrifice we're going to need to make is much more than that," she said, kissing his cheek and taking *The Book of Devouring* from his hands. "We can't stop the Invocation. And none of you could safely approach the pastor after what you've done. There is only one option left. We need to prevent this thing from hurting anyone ever again.

"And the only way to do that," she concluded, "is by summoning it ourselves."

Stephanie and Jamillah were giddy over Nilanjana's plan. Stephanie had long wanted to conduct a religious rite, and here was a chance to be part of a Summoning. Not just a Summoning, but the Invocation itself.

Darryl agreed. Mark rolled his eyes. Luisa said it was probably going to be disappointing, but that she was happy to do something nonscientific for a change. "Not like I've gotten any awards for what I've been doing. Might as well have fun." Mark tentatively agreed.

After a few errands in town, some of which involved theft from the church's storage unit, they returned to the desert and unloaded the materials from the van. Stephanie had emphasized that any missing elements or errors in the Summoning would make the ritual useless.

There was also a device that Nilanjana had brought from their trip to the lab. It was a large, bomb-like cartridge containing all of the pesticide she had distilled through her experiments with the bacteria. The device was originally intended to spread pesticide quickly over large fields, but it should work just as well on a giant centipede. She hadn't told the members of the Joyous Congregation yet. She wasn't sure how they would take it.

"Mark," Nilanjana said, looking at what he was carrying. "No. Why did you bring that?"

"It might be useful," Mark said through a lot of sweat and strain as he eased his broken machine from the van. "I haven't found a situation where it has been useful, so this might be the one. Anyway, if Luisa gets to bring her potatoes."

"You brought your potatoes?" Nilanjana shouted at Luisa.

"No," Luisa said. Her arms were full of potatoes. "Well, yes. I should if he gets to bring his machine. I'm just trying to help."

Nilanjana decided that her time could be better spent talking to anyone else.

"All good on the ritual?" she said.

"I think so," Darryl said. "None of us know what we're doing, so there's a bit of winging it here." He looked around. "Is Carlos definitely not coming? I would have thought a brilliant scientist would want to see our very scientific deity-summoning ceremony." Behind him, Stephanie poured hot milk into a tray and then scattered teeth over the milk.

"Joking." He grinned and took Nilanjana's hand, spinning her toward him in an embrace.

"Funny," Nilanjana said. It wasn't funny, but it was cute, which was just as good in that moment. She didn't kiss him, but instead smelled him. In all the chaos around them, his smell reminded her of their time together in her bed, and so of being safe and in a pocket of darkness that belonged to her, within the sprawling darkness of the world. She spun herself away from him.

"All right," she said. "We got the hot milk and teeth tray going, let's get this ritual started."

"First," Stephanie said, "we put these on." She handed out fox masks. The fox masks had realistically detailed features. There was fluid dripping from some of them. "The fox represents a lot of things to our Congregation. Its meaning is ambiguous and often debated."

"It represents community," said Darryl.

"I think it represents our relationship with the natural world," said Jamillah.

"Personally," Stephanie said, "I think our founding prophet Kevin just loved foxes."

Mark sniffed his mask and made a face.

"What are these made out of?" Nilanjana asked.

"Oh, these are all humanely and ethically made by scooping all the head stuff out of a fox until only the skin is left. It's harmless to the animal, since we kill them first so they can no longer experience pain or suffering at all."

Stephanie pulled the fox mask over her face. The tiny face of the fox, stretched and transplanted onto the size of the human head, was grotesque.

"And we all have to wear these?" Luisa asked.

"Only if you want the Invocation to work and for us all to not have wasted our time out here," said Jamillah, struggling to pull her own mask on.

Nilanjana put the mask over her head, feeling it, slimy, inching down her face. She held her breath at first, but finally had to take in the smell, which was sudden and fresh. On the positive side, the tiny eyeholes were narrow slits, which made the horrifyingly misshapen fox faces everyone else was wearing difficult to see.

"Now," said Stephanie, "we delicately move the tray of milk onto this altar. CAREFULLY PLEASE. Thank you. Really don't want to spill that. Now we all sway."

"Sway?" said Nilanjana.

"It makes prayers feel more sincere," said Darryl. "See, kind of like this." He gently rocked himself back and forth, and Nilanjana copied him. The movement, the axis of earth and sky back and forth, back and forth, did in fact make everything feel more sincere. Like something important was about to happen, even if she was skeptical that that was actually true. Mark was still struggling to get his mask on.

Stephanie took out a huge square yellow hat from her bag.

"I stole this from Pastor Munn's office," she said. "Snuck back in through the window. I don't even know if it's necessary, but I felt like we could use all the help we could get." She put it on, picked up the book, and started to read from it. Or, not read, mumble. She mumbled to herself. The rest of them swayed. The milk steamed in the sun. This went on for some time. Nilanjana was starting to get tired and hot. It didn't help when Stephanie shouted, "Jump."

"What?" said Mark, his mask half on and half off his face.

"Everyone jump up and down," she said. "Quickly, the ritual is almost done."

They all jumped, sweating into the insides of the fox skins, until the liquid from the fox and the liquid from their sweat smeared thick and horrible on their faces.

"Now smile!" said Stephanie. Nilanjana smiled, more of a grimace as the fox ooze slipped through her teeth and onto her tongue with an acidic tang. "More teeth! Big smiles! Joyful!" Nilanjana tried to feel joyful, but no one had taught her how to do it.

"Pull your lips back. Expose your teeth," explained Jamillah.

Nilanjana looked at Darryl jumping next to her. At least they were doing this silly thing together. And that didn't make her feel joyful, but it kept her from feeling miserable.

"Okay, stop," said Stephanie. "That's it. That should be it."

All of them panting with the exertion, they stopped and waited for whatever it was that was going to happen. But all that happened was the wind chasing the sand in circles, and helicopters buzzing in the sky, and a man in the distance wearing a tattered barber's outfit clipping away at a cactus with scissors. Nothing that hadn't been there when they arrived.

"I don't understand," said Darryl. "This should work."

Stephanie flipped through *The Book of Devouring*. She shook her head.

"Everything seems to be right. Maybe we need to wait longer?"

And so they did, fox masks heavy and pungent over their faces. Luisa tossed a potato from one hand to the other and hummed. Mark, as usual, fiddled with his machine.

Nilanjana looked at the tray covered in warm milk and teeth. Oh no, she thought. Because she could feel it starting to bug her. The teeth had been scattered so that they happened to mostly bunch up on one side of the tray. It didn't mean anything necessarily, although it could mean something. Anything could mean something to someone. But it looked uneven. It was out of place. She wished she could nudge some of the teeth to the other side of the tray, but Stephanie had been adamant about how powerful and dangerous the centerpiece of the ritual was.

Maybe she could tilt the tray slightly. Just to get some of the teeth to the other side. Then it would be more even. It would be no more helpful than before, but it would look neater.

No, she couldn't do that. Manually altering the teeth would be wrong. She sighed. The teeth would be uneven. That was just what the teeth would be and she would learn to cope with that, as she had learned to cope with everything else that she had encountered in her life.

She tilted the tray. The milk pooled on one side but the

teeth stuck to the surface and didn't move. She jiggled the tray a little bit.

Stephanie noticed. "No!" she shouted.

"Nilanjana, put the tray down," Jamillah said. "We can't mess up the ritual. We don't know what it will do."

"She's always like this," Luisa said. "She'll never win even one prize."

"I'm not messing it up," Nilanjana said, more convinced than ever by their annoying warnings that the whole thing was a harmless hoax. "I just . . . the teeth could be neater."

She jiggled the tray again and some of the teeth slid down to where the milk had pooled. She set the tray down. It wasn't even, but the teeth were scattered across the entire surface now.

"See? It looks better now." It didn't, but she didn't want to admit that.

"Please don't touch any of the Invocation materials," Stephanie said. "This is all already beyond my training. We can't risk messing it up."

"I didn't mess anything up," Nilanjana said, and as she said that, a thin dribble of milk dripped from the tray onto the sand.

"The milk!" Darryl ran forward with a tissue, but Jamillah was running forward with her drill, hoping it would be helpful, and Stephanie was trying to lift the tray up out of the sand, and, in the collision of the three of them, the tray flipped over completely. Milk and teeth plopped onto the sand.

"Well . . ." Stephanie searched for what a member of the clergy would say here, what kind of religious quotation or bit of wisdom would fit this moment, and settled on ". . .well shit."

"Oh no," Luisa said. "The unscientific ritual will go from not working to still not working."

"We don't know what will happen," Stephanie said.

"Stephanie's right," Jamillah said. "See? Now the teeth are shaking. That can't be good."

The teeth were indeed shaking, like popcorn that's about to pop. The milk steamed on the hot sand.

"That's weird," said Nilanjana.

"Yes, see, it's weird," Jamillah said, her power drill growling in agreement. "Teeth don't usually do that, I don't think."

The teeth bounced up and down. But there was something more. Nilanjana wasn't noticing something bigger, and she tried to understand what that was.

"Should we try the ritual again?" Jamillah said, pulling her mask off.

"I don't know if we can now that the Teethmilk has spilled," Stephanie said, her mask coming off too. "It takes hours to consecrate that."

"Uh, guys?" Nilanjana said. She realized what she had been missing. "Those teeth aren't shaking."

"It's okay that you feel bad about spilling the milk," Jamillah said. "But you can't deny the consequences."

"Correlation does not indicate causation," said Luisa.

"But it suggests the possibility of causation," said Mark. Luisa glared at him. "What? It's true."

"Nilanjana's right. Feel," Darryl said. "The teeth aren't shaking. The ground is."

Faintly at first, and then more and more, the ground was shaking, like there was a running motor just beneath it.

"Is this supposed to happen?" said Darryl.

"I don't know," Stephanie said. "The book was a little hazy on how the ritual ends."

There was a whirring sound, then a sucking sound. The

ground grew hot. The damp stain of the milk was disappearing into the sand. One by one, the bouncing teeth also popped into the sand until there was no sign of anything having spilled there.

"Scientifically speaking," Mark said, "that was pretty weird."

Then, a few feet in front of them, the ground dropped, like an elevator with cut wires, leaving a pulsing glowing blackness. They scrambled backward. The shaking was getting stronger. Nilanjana strained to see into the hole without falling in. It was bottomless. Or no, there was a bottom. She didn't know how she hadn't seen it before. A definite bottom. In fact, the hole didn't even look that deep. Maybe fifty feet. Or no, thirty. Or. She realized simultaneously that the bottom was getting closer and that it wasn't the bottom of the hole.

"Back," she shouted. "Get back!" as the head of a giant centipede rose from the earth. Its antennae swayed high into the air. Its eyes were vast, empty blanks.

Stephanie fell to her knees and began to sob, although whether this was because she was seeing her God or because her God was a horrifying monster rising from the ground she would not have been able to say.

33

The centipede rose up and up, twisting as it went, and landed with a wide splash of sand. There was a loud clatter from its legs, appendages rubbing against each other, causing a sound like high-pitched thunder that tweaked Nilanjana's stomach and spine.

"My God," Darryl said, and then realized the literality of what he was saying, but didn't know what to replace it with, so said nothing more, just watched as what had always been a point of faith became a physical thing that smelled of mud and tree bark.

Stephanie and Jamillah were on their knees, praying. Mark stood completely still, horrified by what he was looking at, but awestruck by it at the same time. Luisa joined Stephanie and Jamillah in praying, figuring that if this was the way the world was going, she should go along with it.

Useless, Nilanjana thought. But she also couldn't deny the immensity of what they were looking at, and so she allowed herself a moment to absorb the size of the thing, the way its body rolled as it moved, horrifyingly but beautifully, and the hypnotic power of hundreds of giant legs churning in unison. Then, the moment over, she went to the van and began preparing what she hoped would put an end to its threat.

The object of their attention did not seem to care about all the tiny creatures reacting to it. Its antennae, rising up to vanishing points in the sky, waggled, and it rooted around the sand, taking stock of the new area it had found itself in. Nothing about its behavior suggested it was about to devour anyone, for ritual cleansing reasons or otherwise.

"This will just take a few minutes," Nilanjana said, double-checking that everything was working with the device. She only had time to make one, and had no backup plan if it failed. "Everyone just keep their eye on it and try not to get close."

But Stephanie was already rising.

"Thank you, Nilanjana, but that is unnecessary." She had an ecstatic glow to her face, the transcendence of having her beliefs verified in a concrete, enormous manner. "We just have to do the next part of the ritual."

"What? No," said Nilanjana, checking that all the wires on her device were connected correctly. "Don't do that. Don't do anything. Keep praying. I'll be ready in a moment."

"Stephanie, really?" Darryl said, unsure. "Do you think it might help?"

"It won't help," said Mark.

"It might help," said Jamillah.

"It will solve everything," said Stephanie, with perfect certainty. "I didn't understand what the rest of the ritual was for. Why did it keep going after the Summoning? But now I understand. It was made for this moment." She pulled the fox face over her face, hefted up the book, and began bellowing.

"DEVOURER. GREAT DEVOURER. THE SMILING GOD," and so on. The text was repetitive, but Stephanie kept careful track with her finger so that she wouldn't accidentally get the order wrong. She started jumping up and down again, higher than before, tall leaps, with dull thuds on the ground in between.

"This is ridiculous," said Luisa, disappointed in all of them.

The creature slowly turned its enormous face toward Stephanie, drawn perhaps by the power of the ritual, or maybe by the fact that she was shouting and jumping up and down.

"It's working," said Jamillah. "Look, it's coming this way."

The centipede's eyes were black monuments that absorbed the glare of the sun off the hillsides. Its face lowered to the ground and its mouth unhinged horribly. It started to scoop up the sand as it approached Stephanie, shoveling up tons of earth as it devoured its way toward her.

"Or . . . uh," said Jamillah.

Stephanie wasn't certain this was supposed to happen, but she had no idea what was supposed to happen, and so, failing any other plan, she continued the ritual, confident with one part of herself that it would all work out fine, but also with another part of herself terrified and wanting to flee.

"Run!" said Darryl. But she wouldn't. She was trapped in the ritual by panic. "We have to get it away from her."

"I still need a couple minutes with this," said Nilanjana. "Otherwise we can't be sure it'll work."

Mark stepped forward and patted his machine.

"If only we had a way to distract its attention away from her, right?" He smiled proudly. "I knew this would come in handy."

He pulled the switch and there was a deafening bang, followed by a blinding flash. The centipede took no notice.

"Damn," he said. "It still isn't working. It's supposed to be a flash and then a bang. It won't be useful backward like this."

He opened up the machine, poking at the mechanics.

"I just don't understand. I've tried everything."

Jamillah had been pulling at Stephanie, trying to get her to stop, to run, but the noise from Mark's machine had drawn her over.

"I see the problem," she said.

"What?" said Mark. "No, of course you don't. I am a highly trained scientist."

The centipede was closing in on Stephanie. The sun disappeared behind its body. This broke her trance and she started running, but the wriggling monster outlegged her by at least a hundred to two.

"Okay, man, but look," Jamillah knelt down and took her power drill to the machine, drilling through one of the panels. Mark gasped but was too shocked to stop her.

"It's overheating," she said. "That's why you're getting the failure like that. If you just vented it a bit, you'd fix the problem." She drilled more holes.

The sand fell away behind Stephanie, dropping into the cavern of the thing's mouth. Ten feet behind her. Six feet behind her. It was like a treadmill now, her feet slipping against the current of sand.

"See, now this should work if we . . ." Jamillah said and pulled the switch. There was a blinding flash, and then a deafening bang. The centipede turned away from Stephanie and toward the powerful light and sound, moving faster and charging at them.

"You fixed it. You fixed it!" said Mark. He hugged Jamillah. "But also it's coming for us. It's coming for us!"

It was coming for them. There had been nothing more to Mark's plan than the immediate need to distract the centipede from Stephanie, and now he had only succeeded in making him and Jamillah the next targets.

"Hold on for one more minute," Nilanjana said. "I'm almost ready."

The centipede ate up the distance between it and the two screaming humans in a few hungry gulps. They ran, but were no more successful than Stephanie. Jamillah slipped and was caught in the wash of sand moving toward the creature's mouth. Which was when a single, lopsided missile soared through the air and bonked off one of the centipede's eyes. The creature stopped to find the source of the attack, and Jamillah was able to regain her feet and continue running. Another thrown object, a large russet potato, made direct contact between the enormous eyes.

"These wouldn't be useful, huh?" Luisa said. "Take that!"

The centipede veered again, going for its tormentor, who ran in front of it, tossing her potatoes behind her.

"Look at what my potatoes are doing! I'm so proud of them. For the first time, I'm proud of them. This ruins my entire experiment." The potatoes were admirable at keeping the centipede's attention, but did not stop the margin between Luisa and its mouth from decreasing quickly.

"It's ready," Nilanjana said. She loaded the large black capsule onto a sled on the ground.

"Great, let's do it. Whatever it is," said Darryl.

"There's just one step, and it's both simple and difficult," Nilanjana said. "We have to get the centipede to eat this."

"What will happen then?"

"I'm running out of potatoes! So any other plans you have, now would be great. But also I'm still so proud of my potatoes!"

Nilanjana shrugged. And despite their short time together, Darryl was surprised to find himself able to understand everything she was communicating with that shrug.

"You're going to kill the Smiling God?" he said.

Luisa had stopped yelling about potatoes and was now

yelling incoherently. The ground was being devoured only steps behind her.

"What else can we do?" Nilanjana said. "Or do you want to watch people die today?"

Darryl watched Luisa run, and looked up at the centipede, an insect vacancy to its face as it swallowed and swallowed. He frowned.

"You're right. I don't want to watch people die." He took the handle of the capsule and started pulling it on its sled across the sand.

"What are you doing?"

"We caused this problem. My church did this. And now I'm going to fix it." He waved his arms, yelling.

"Hey!" he shouted. "Hey! Over here." He lifted his fist and spun it around. "I believe in a Smiling God. And I am ready for You to devour me."

The centipede slowed, but it seemed done with switching targets and continued toward Luisa, who was now yelling something about burying her with her potatoes.

"I've devoted my entire life to you," shouted Darryl. "You don't just get to ignore me. 'Joyfully It Devours.' Well, I am joyful. See?" He showed his teeth, stretching his lips as far as they would go. "Now DEVOUR ME."

At that, the centipede turned toward him, moving faster than ever before, tired perhaps of this game and wanting to finally eat something. Darryl watched it charge. Nilanjana couldn't watch, hiding her eyes, but then she felt that if this was the last time she would see him, then she should actually see him. That she owed him that. That she owed herself that.

The mouth was upon him. Sand fell around him. He pushed the sled forward at the avalanche and jumped back. The capsule was gone, eaten. But in his leap, his foot caught on the edge of the mouth, and he landed sideways, dragged along as the centipede barreled forward.

His face skidded across the sand painfully. He tried to pull free but was only able to push his leg in farther. He grabbed at the centipede, trying to wrench his way out. But he couldn't get enough of a grip on the creature's face to detach himself.

He was caught, and rapidly slipping in farther, his head pounding against the earth, his nose and throat filling with sand.

He could hardly breathe. He would be torn away and crushed, or suffocate, or slip fully into the centipede and be digested. And maybe that was as it should be. At least he had done the right thing before the end.

But then he saw something extraordinary, something he could not have imagined just a few weeks ago. Nilanjana, beautiful and determined, running toward him, running directly at the mouth of the centipede, and diving forward. Diving forward and extending a hand. Grabbing his arm with that hand, and pulling. His foot came free and the two of them rolled away from the centipede, who had too much momentum to turn in time and thundered past.

They were both panting and sweating, sand sticking to them. She had never looked better. His eyes were watering, partly from her bravery, but mostly from the sand. His lungs were on fire. He had never felt better.

"You're amazing," he said.

She kissed him, a dry kiss full of the grit that covered both of them. It was uncomfortable and awkward and the best kiss they ever had.

"You did a pretty good thing too," she said.

There was a dull pop, heard through several layers of the insect.

"There went the capsule," she said. Gallons of powerful pesticide were released in its stomach. Years of distillation of bacteria by-products and testing. This was it. The creature slowed down, and then jittered and thrashed, sending columns of sand hundreds of feet into the air. Finally it stopped, only its antennae still swaying.

"You killed it!" Mark said.

"Wait, you killed it?" Jamillah said.

"I think I killed it," said Nilanjana.

One of the towering legs twitched. Then skittered a few feet. More legs skittered and lurched. The vast bulk of its body dragged forward again.

"I don't think you did," said Luisa.

It turned toward them. The clatter of its legs became louder and louder.

"What now?" said Darryl.

"I don't know what now," Nilanjana said. "I don't have any other ideas. That was my entire research project I exploded inside that bug. That should have killed a hundred centipedes its size. I think maybe now we die."

The centipede lowered its mouth, preparing to swallow the van and the machine and all of the people around it. Nilanjana grabbed Darryl and pulled him close. But the centipede did not reach them. It stopped again. It noticed for the first time, as the sun had finished its descent below the apocryphal mountains along the horizon, the warm glow of Night Vale's low skyline down the road behind them. A hive of activity and movement, overshadowing the few people standing in the desert.

The ground beneath it collapsed again. A gap in what was

real. The centipede dove headfirst into this gap, disappeared into some other reality, first its face and then leg after leg, until all of its body was gone, and the portal resolved into a shallow pit.

They all took a moment, coming to terms with the continuing existence of their bodies.

"Is that it?" Stephanie finally managed. "Are we safe?"

"We are," said Nilanjana, looking over Stephanie's shoulder. "But Night Vale isn't."

There, from right in the middle of all the fragile lives of Night Vale, came a distant familiar clatter, like high-pitched thunder, and every helicopter in the sky began converging on a single point at the center of town.

34

"In, in, in," Nilanjana shouted as the others scrambled for seats in the van, and then they were tearing back along the road toward town. While she understood on some level that the church would have summoned this monster eventually, and that in summoning it themselves they were only doing their best to protect the city, she still felt like any violence from here on out was on them.

Driving through the outskirts of town, all seemed normal. They passed the Brown Stone Spire, which was humming the latest electropop hit by Buddy Holly to itself. They passed the Ralphs, where shoppers were gathering with paddles since the store had recently moved to an auction-based grocery shopping experience. They passed the vacant lot out back of the Ralphs, where a group of figures draped in tattered and filthy cloth huddled together.

Sometimes it is these normal, everyday things, these things that would ordinarily bring us comfort, that, against the back-drop of calamity, only heighten the fear and the chaos, Nilan-jana thought. How could things so ordinary as these exist in the same world as the horrible devouring god that might even now be rising in the heart of the town?

As they approached the source of the noise, she stopped watching the helicopters. She didn't need to follow them to the source of the disturbance. She knew exactly where it was coming from.

The house that doesn't exist was shaking, as though experiencing a localized earthquake. But there was no earthquake scheduled for this part of town, and anyway, in emergency situations like this, all municipally planned earthquakes would have been canceled. From deep within its windows, beyond the visible living room, there was a bright, white light that made Nilanjana's teeth hurt. A black sedan pulled up across the street. The window rolled down, and an agent with one of the vague yet menacing government agencies began snapping pictures.

Neighbors, used to the weirdness of living next to a house that doesn't exist, came out to their back porches, standing on the concrete slabs set into their dry lawns, and watched their plastic furniture vibrate.

"Should we be worried about this?" one of them, a woman in a flower print dress, shouted at Nilanjana.

"I think so," Nilanjana shouted back.

"Should we?" the woman shouted at the agent in the black sedan.

The agent's eyes went wide, and he frantically rolled up his window and screamed, "We've been spotted! We've been spotted!" Once the window was up, he went back to taking pictures through the tinted glass. The driver never looked up through all of this, just continued filling in a crossword puzzle.

The woman shrugged at Nilanjana.

"I think we're fine," the woman said. "Usually anything weird with that house resolves itself."

Another car arrived. A Cadillac, driven by a familiar man, with a familiar woman in the passenger seat.

"I knew it," Pastor Munn shouted, hopping out of the car.

A long yellow hat hung lopsided on her head, a hypotenuse waiting for the rest of its triangle. It wasn't her normal hat, as Stephanie had stolen that for the ritual. It was some cardboard boxes taped together and spray-painted yellow. "I knew it," she said again. She had not known it. She was completely surprised.

"We knew it," shouted Gordon, circling the car to stand behind her, too angry to keep his arms crossed. He was waving them around to an effect he hoped was threatening but made him look like he was warming up for a baseball game.

"I knew you were betraying your church, your congregation, your community." Pastor Munn spat at them. Even Nilanjana found the force of the pastor's rage frightening.

Stephanie sank down into her seat, and Darryl felt an urge to join her. But now that he had seen and touched the physical reality of the Smiling God, the pastor and Gordon no longer had the same power as before. He recognized them for what they were: humans, who were right about some things and wrong about other things and certain about everything. Shouting humans who didn't know any more than he did.

"I'm sorry," Darryl said. "It had to be like this." Two separate thoughts.

The pastor shook her head, more surprise than disapproval.

"It doesn't even matter," she said. "You don't matter. Only the Smiling God matters. And the Smiling God has come to devour the world. You couldn't stop It, any more than you could stop the sun from making a racket every morning."

"The sun is loud!" Gordon agreed. He hadn't agreed with the right part, but agreeing was the important thing.

Before the conversation could continue, the door of the house blew open. First, a gust of hot air, like the out-of-place suddenness of walking by a restaurant heating vent on a cold day. And then, for the first time since Carlos's return from the otherworld, something emerged from the house that doesn't exist.

First came two thin black wires, springing out. The wires bent and elongated, continuing to emerge from the door. They wrapped back around the house, gripping the stucco sides, cracked the picture window, which is when Nilanjana realized she was looking at legs. Using the leverage of the legs, a black insect face, a monolith of vacuous hunger, squeezed out through the door. The smell of a forest floor after months of rot. Liquid dripped from its face. Once the head came through, the rest of the legs followed. More black wires, shooting out from the door, and pulling along the endless squishy tube of its body. The centipede emerged like a train from a tunnel, more and more legs and segments rushing out from the door, and yet the shape of the door never got bigger, the frame never broke, the house was still a house, albeit one that did not exist.

The centipede turned as it burrowed out, and it slammed into the house to the left. The woman screamed and stumbled back as her house was carried away. Long, spindly legs whipped past her.

"The Smiling God!" the pastor said and sank to her knees. Gordon said nothing. He stared, his mouth open, in too much shock to echo the pastor's words.

Cars began arriving, the Sheriff's Secret Police responding to the call. They piled out, shouting frantic orders at each other, and pointing their guns in all directions. The sheriff themself moved to the front of the group, wearing their cape and bandoliers. They took a moment to assess the situation.

"That's a great big monster," Sheriff Sam shouted. "Let's try shooting it."

They tried shooting it. The sudden cacophony of gunshots did not make the glistening black tube coming from the front door of the house any less terrifying. Luisa crouched in the van with Mark, Stephanie, and Jamillah, and Nilanjana joined Darryl behind one of the wheels.

The pastor and Gordon did not move. They seemed undisturbed by the shooting, already confident that bullets could not harm a deity.

"This is going poorly," said Luisa. She watched the chaos around her with a look of pointed disapproval.

Other than the pastor, the only one completely unbothered by the bullets was the centipede. It continued to barrel forward, pieces of neighboring houses stuck to the segments of its body. It opened up its mouth and swallowed an entire lawn with an aboveground pool. The slab of grass slid in without any resistance, and the owner of the house sprinted away. Sensing the movement, the centipede turned and pursued him, mouth hanging empty and open.

"Help me!" the homeowner shouted as he ran. The Secret Police, not knowing how else to help, continued firing. This did not help him. After a short and simple movement by the centipede, he was no longer running or shouting.

The last of the creature came out of the door with a squishy pop, and, fully freed from its source, it swung its blank eyes toward downtown Night Vale, demolishing house after house as it went, occasionally dipping its head to swallow whatever was in front of it.

"We can't just sit here," Nilanjana said.

"No," Darryl said.

"What can we do?"

"I don't know."

"At least," she said, "we'll do whatever it is we do next together." She ran a hand through his hair. He smiled at her, a natural smile, a smile he didn't even think to go through the necessary steps to make.

"Okay," she said. "Here goes."

She stood and started waving.

"STOP SHOOTING," she shouted at the Secret Police. Gradually they did, mostly because the centipede was out of range. One officer seemed to have really gotten a taste for it and was firing over and over into the ground, until the sheriff took the gun away from him.

"Right, enough of that," the sheriff said. They turned to Nilanjana. "Well, I'm afraid we've tried everything. There doesn't seem to be a way to stop it."

"You only tried shooting it," she said.

"Yes. As I just said, everything," they said. "Terrible blow, but it just seems our best efforts aren't going to be enough. The town had a good run though, eh?"

As they talked, the Moonlite All-Nite Diner, visible down the road, was flattened, its mint green sign sparking wildly against the huge black body of the centipede.

"Hope no one was inside that," the sheriff said. "All right, we gave this one a good try. Let's pack it up and see if we can find some crimes."

"What?" said Nilanjana. She couldn't believe what was happening. She had found herself struggling with belief quite a bit in the last couple weeks, but this was a different kind, a pit-of-the-stomach astonishment that came when a person well and truly let another person down. Then she let the astonishment pass, and concentrated on what was in front of her. A terrible problem, but also just a problem. She would need to solve this problem.

"Back in the van," she said. "We need to follow it."

Mark took over driving, and the others concentrated on tracking the destruction. The road was often torn up and they had to drive on sandy shoulders and over medians to follow the god's relentless path.

"You know, when they talked about having all your sins devoured by the Smiling God, I never imagined something so physical and violent," Darryl said. "In concept, as a metaphor, it was quite beautiful. This"—he indicated the sprays of dirt and asphalt outside the car—"isn't beautiful."

"Speaking of which, it doesn't actually seem to be devouring much," Nilanjana said.

"It's devouring plenty. Look, it's doing it again."

As they neared the centipede, they observed its head dip down and scoop up another lawn.

"It's devouring a bit," she said. "But mostly it's crashing into things. It only eats occasionally. And even then not buildings or people, it's only interested in . . ."

She slapped the dashboard, causing a tense Mark to steer over a patch of road that had recently had a centipede leg through it.

"Please don't do that again," he managed, as he yanked the wheel back around and pulled the van onto more solid earth.

"I know what we have to do," she said.

"Right?" Mark said. "It's obvious. My machine could solve this whole thing. It just needs a bigger input. We could startle the centipede so bad it would simply die."

"I think if I disapproved of it more, like really gave it my sternest face, then it would feel bad enough to leave," offered Luisa. "Did you see how good my potatoes did after years of my disappointment?"

Jamillah suggested her power drill by running it for a moment. But Nilanjana was already on the phone.

"Is this Arnie Goldblum?" she said. "Arnie, I need you to get everyone away from Big Rico's Pizza, if you didn't do that already when you saw a giant bug stomping all over town. I need you to get some shovels and start digging up the bottom of the pit. Overturn all of the soil in that pit. Why?"

She thought about how to explain.

"Because you're going to save Night Vale, that's why."

She hung up.

"You think the Smiling God might be into invisible pizza?" said Darryl.

"It's only devouring areas rich in insects, and especially worms," she said. "I think, despite its size, it's basically a normal centipede, and centipedes eat worms. So we're going to offer it one hell of a tempting meal. But we have to get it to Big Rico's first. It's not going to notice the worms from here."

Already, the monster was turning, its hundreds of legs churning through the asphalt as it moved on toward the library, the opposite direction from Big Rico's. A Cadillac pulled in front of it. Gordon and Pastor Munn, her homemade hat torn and barely hanging on now, hurried out.

"No!" the pastor said. "Some antireligion science nuts are not going to be devoured before me. We have made ourselves worthy of devouring. Joyfully we are devoured!"

"Eat me!" Gordon said.

They ran at the centipede. It turned to face them, and then

stopped, looking down at them with its inhuman face. They fell again to their knees. Gordon dutifully clasped his hands before him.

"What are they doing?" said Darryl.

"You know what they're doing," said Jamillah. "They believe. We were without faith. They truly believe."

The centipede considered the pair.

"I am ready!" the pastor said. "I am—"

The centipede ate them. It was a soft drop of its enormous head, and without a sound the pastor and Gordon were gone.

No one said anything. There wasn't anything to say. The centipede didn't pause, didn't even seem to notice what it had done, just continued skittering toward the library.

"We . . . we need to get it to follow us," Nilanjana said. She was shaken by what she had seen, but it didn't change the reality of their plan.

Mark revved the engine.

"If the pastor and Gordon can believe enough to put their lives on the line," Mark said, "then what am I doing here helping you if I don't do the same?"

"What are you going to do?" Darryl said, but Mark was already doing it.

He jammed down the accelerator with a roar and a lot of screaming from the others in the back, and sped right into the legs of the centipede, bouncing off with a crack. The monster whirled, a broad arc of its body. It hissed, a searing sound that filled the air around it, and made directly for the van. Mark had to do a three-point turn to get the van going the right direction, and by the time he had done that the centipede was already on their tail, scooping up asphalt as it went.

"I think it'll follow us now," he said.

"WHY WOULD YOU NOT WARN US?" said Jamillah, running her drill continuously out of panic.

"That was dangerous. And silly," said Nilanjana. "And exactly the right thing to do."

Fortunately the centipede had not gotten to the part of town where Big Rico's was yet, and so the roads were undamaged. This bit of good luck was mitigated some by the fact that the monster was gaining on them with every mile. Its legs made a constant clicking that was louder even than the van's engine. Closer and closer.

One last right turn and Big Rico's was just ahead. A crowd of employees were there, stirring the bottom of the pit with pizza paddles. Nilanjana was on the phone again with Arnie, telling him to get everyone out of the pit immediately. Mark laid on the horn as he sped at them, and they dropped their poles and sprinted out of the way. He turned too late, and the van skidded at the pit. Two of its tires slipped over the edge. There was a horrible grinding as the bottom of the van slid against the asphalt edge. Mark gunned the engine and banked the wheels hard to the left to get leverage. There was a loud thump as the chassis struck the edge of the pit, followed by a squeal as the tires once again made contact. The van lurched upward and bounced violently into the parking lot, narrowly avoiding the steep fall. The force of the van's leap caused it to pause for a moment on two wheels before falling hard back onto all four.

They all took a moment to breathe, but the centipede was already tearing up the lot, moments from swallowing them. Mark gunned the engine again, but the van faltered, shudders of power with no forward motion. There was no time to get out. The centipede was on them. Darryl closed his eyes and took Nilanjana's hand. She squeezed his hand, and put her arm around his shoulder, keeping her eyes open.

But the centipede stopped and lifted its head again, dirt and pieces of subterranean pipe falling from its face like crumbs. It swiveled its head, and its long antennae swung back and forth. Then it changed direction and dove into the pit with an absolute and passionless greed. As it fell, its mouth opened, and it burrowed into the sea of worms. For several long seconds the rest of its body followed, leg after leg, until the last of it went into the pit. It was curled in there, digging deeper and deeper into the worms, until it hit the concrete of the world government monitoring bunkers scattered deep beneath Night Vale, and it could go no farther.

"Now what?" Stephanie said as they all scattered out of the van. Luisa held up a potato with a helpful look on her face, but Nilanjana shook her head and Luisa went back to looking disappointed in all of them.

Darryl was tired of being the one who didn't have the answers. He had the answer.

"We need to trap it," he said. "Cover the pit."

"That was my idea," Jamillah said.

"We need something heavier than what your drill can handle. I don't know," he said, deflating. "Nilanjana, how do we trap it?"

"I don't know either," she said. And then it truly seemed to them that they were doomed. If Nilanjana didn't know, then none of them knew, then there was nothing to know. In only moments the centipede would finish its meal and rise back up from the pit.

At least I'm with her, he thought.

At least I'm with him, she thought.

At least we're together, they signaled with the way they held each other.

"See, I told you the church guy wasn't bad," said a voice from high above them. They sprang apart and looked up. A fleet of black helicopters, led by a particular helicopter that was familiar to Nilanjana.

"Hey!" she said, waving. "You were right."

"I know I was right," the bullhorn called. "You don't have to tell me when I'm right, I know it. And my ex-boyfriend said I have 'no emotional intelligence.' Ugh. Anyway. STAND ASIDE, CITIZENS."

The helicopters were carrying between them a heavy black tarp, lined on all sides with weights.

"WE WILL NEUTRALIZE THIS THREAT TO SAFETY."

The tarp fell heavily around the pit and draped down over the writhing mass of shell and legs within it. It began thrashing against the material, but with the awkward way its body was stuffed into the pit, and with the concrete below it and the tarp caught in its legs, it couldn't seem to get out.

"Oh my God, I think we trapped it," said Darryl. "Nilanjana, we did it!" He picked her up for a moment and spun her around, a move that would have made him feel self-conscious in any other context but here came as a pure expression of their mutual joy.

"Yeah sure," said the helicopter. "'We' did it. All of us together, and not just the fleet of helicopters keeping you safe."

"This is going to take us forever to clean up," one of the employees of Big Rico's grumbled.

Soon the entire town was crowded around. Sheriff Sam

stood at the front of them, shaking their clasped hands above their head in victory.

"We did it," they said. "Another clear victory for the Secret Police."

"Ugh," said the helicopter. "Come on, guys." The fleet flew away, returning to their endless circling overhead.

"I can't believe it," Darryl said. "The Smiling God is real, and here, and we caught It."

"I don't know about that," Nilanjana said. "But we caught the biggest bug I've ever seen."

Pamela Winchell arrived and spoke through her mic and portable amplifier.

"This monster will need to be killed. For the safety of this town. And also for revenge reasons. Mostly for revenge reasons. And safety."

"No!" Darryl and Nilanjana said together.

"It is sacred," he said.

"We can't kill something this scientifically interesting," she said. With the threat finally neutralized, she saw the vast potential for scientific inquiry.

"We must kill it," another voice said. Carlos came down the parking lot from the lab. His face was grave and determined.

"But what about all that stuff you said? About science and not killing things we are afraid of?" Nilanjana said.

He shook his head. "For the sake of our families, for the sake of our town. It has to die." He met her eyes and she could see how deeply he was shaken. "It almost took Janice," he whispered. He pulled a large tank of gasoline out of the backseat of his car, pushed one edge of the tarp until it fell into the pit, creating an opening, and began to pour the gas into the pit. The giant thing continued to buck against the tarp, more violently as the liquid pooled around it. Then Carlos pulled out a flare, lit it, and tossed it in.

The Smiling God screamed as it died. No one thought a centipede could scream, but it did. It screamed for a long time.

35

Nilanjana nursed her headache with a twenty-ounce coffee. She had stayed up late celebrating. One or two beers to clink and smile over turned into three or four to laugh and swoon over turned into maybe five or six. She couldn't remember.

She did remember that they killed a giant centipede. They killed a religious figure. And before that, it had eaten the leaders of the Joyous Congregation. She hadn't had a conversation with Carlos about the implications of murdering a rare earthly creature. She hadn't talked to Darryl about the death of his god and pastor. She thought about Carlos, whom she trusted above anyone else, and what she would feel if he died or, worse, turned out to be as dangerous to Night Vale as the pastor had. Last night, everyone had been first too wired, and then too exhausted to talk. They just drank and smiled and got sleepy. Darryl stayed at her apartment, and they made love and fell asleep against one another, naked and elaborately entwined: legs over legs, arms across chests, lips against necks, as much skin touching skin as possible.

He was still asleep when she got up. She wanted to get back to work, partially because she liked work, partially because she couldn't fall back asleep, and partially (mostly) because she didn't want to have a conversation yet of deep spiritual implications with Darryl. Nilanjana knew once what they had done the day before—before the drinking and the reveling and the kissing and the cuddling—had set in, he would have a lot of questions to deal with. So would she.

Later. They could sort through those questions later.

Whatever the implications, the bright side of it all was that Carlos was free to continue his experiments, unhindered. The creature causing the incidents was dead. There would be no more rumblings, no more pits. They were not the work of the City Council, but of the church and of a monster. The city had done no more than harass and follow them, which was common governmental behavior in Night Vale, especially toward a group of people as troublemaking as scientists. Besides, they had been working to protect Night Vale from the Smiling God, which wouldn't be an issue anymore. Carlos would receive more visits from Pamela with her strange aphorisms shouted through her amplifier, but Pamela wouldn't provide an actual threat, only scrunched faces, fists on hips, and surveillance vans.

Nilanjana drove to work and carried her coffee and heavy head into Carlos's office. He was sitting in front of a wall-size computer, flipping metal switches, and tapping a monochrome screen filled with long strings of numbers and codes.

"Back at it already?" she asked, smiling. Or she felt like she was smiling, but her face muscles were hungover too, so she was actually scowling. "You don't even look tired."

"Oh, I only had an orangemilk with a splash of club soda last night. I was too excited about getting back to work this morning." Carlos flipped five adjacent switches in quick succession. "Ever since I escaped that otherworld, I have been trying to understand it and protect us from it. I'm so close now." He smiled at her, but the smile wasn't exactly from happiness. There were so many feelings and he didn't know how to order them and put them in sensible, logical words. "I'm so close now" was all he could manage to explain. There was a deep whirring from the machine. Nilanjana's head felt cold. Her body felt warm, but her head was freezing. She pressed her hand to her nose, and her fingers were warm to the touch.

Must be from holding the coffee, she thought.

"So you're back to taking readings from the house that doesn't exist?" she said.

"Sort of. I'm trying something new. I'm going to direct the device to the middle of town first, taking readings on that. Then I'll go in concentric circles outward, taking baseline readings of the entire area. Once I have all of that, I will have some control data from which to compare unusual spots, like the house that doesn't exist, or the Dog Park, or—"

"Don't forget the rec center. There were those pteranodons that appeared from a portal there way back when."

"Yes, of course." Carlos sprang up and wrote "Pterano-dons!!!" on the whiteboard and drew a big heart around the word. "Excellent science, Nilanjana." He drew a second heart around the first heart, and then gave her a thumbs-up. She felt the warmth of approval from a man she respected more than any other person in the world. She also felt warmth through the bottoms of her feet. They were hot. It wasn't scalding, but it was like forgetting your shoes on a hot day on a sandy beach.

"Is it hot in here, Carlos?"

"Oh yeah, I'm sweating," he said. "I need to improve ventilation on the machine."

"My feet are on fire."

Carlos looked at her feet, as if they might literally be on fire, and then, seeing that they were not, turned his attention back to the switches and monitor. In the whirring of the machine,

Nilanjana could also hear and feel a deep rumbling. It's just the machine, she told herself, still a bit traumatized from recent experiences with hot feet and subterranean rumbles from gigantic bug gods.

She heard a sudden startling bang and a crash and then saw a bright flash from the main lab.

"Shit! My invention!" Mark shouted, running toward his device, which had fallen off the tabletop and split open across the floor. Plastic and glass shards spilled out. Some of the plastic looked like it was melting.

Luisa hopped up too.

"Are your feet burning?" Nilanjana called toward Luisa.

"No. Yes. But . . . come look at this." Luisa had gone to the window and pointed out.

Nilanjana followed her and saw a swirling cloud of sand and smoke above downtown Night Vale, several blocks away. And then they heard the muffled boom. Then another distant cloud, but slightly closer, followed by a less muffled boom. Then another cloud, another boom, each one closer than the last, louder than the last. The sights and sounds were getting closer together. The three of them stared in disbelief. It was easy to disbelieve, because they had no idea what they were seeing.

"Ow, god, my feet," Mark said. "Ow, god, my hands," as he picked the broken parts of his machine up off the floor.

All three were alternately lifting and lowering each foot against the heat. It was darkly comical, and Luisa even smiled a rare smile seeing the three of them engaged in such a silly, necessary dance. Then the window shattered. They all dove aside. Shelves and tables toppled over. Luisa watched as her potatoes bounced and rolled across the floor, inches from her face.

"I'm disappointed in that," she said.

From the floor, Nilanjana felt the rumbling coming from deep within the ground. Her body vibrated. Her teeth rattled briefly, and then it subsided. She crawled back to the window and pulled herself up in time to see over half of the Roasted Beans Strip Mall ("It's an entire mall, but just for coffee!") across the street from the lab collapse into a large pit.

Carlos sprinted into the lab.

"Is everyone okay?"

They didn't say anything, only stared through the splintered shards that were once a window. He stepped over to them and looked for himself.

"But it's dead," he said. "We killed it. I killed it."

"Maybe it wasn't the only one," Luisa said. "I mean, consider potatoes. There are lots of potatoes. Literally tons of them in this world. So maybe there is more than one giant centipede."

"We see potatoes all the time," Nilanjana said, "but we've never seen a centipede like that."

"Correlation is not causation," Mark said. Nilanjana wanted to stomp all over what remained of his banging, flashing device and then kick Luisa's potatoes through the broken window.

"No, it's not a second or third centipede. It's something else," she said instead.

"Mark's technically right, Nilanjana," Carlos said, "but I think I agree with you."

"So what's causing this, then?"

"The city." Carlos's eyes were dark. "They're still trying to keep me from investigating that otherworld. It was never the centipede doing any of this. It was Pamela and the City Council."

"They'd destroy Night Vale rather than let us find out anything about the house that doesn't exist?"

Carlos nodded slowly. Everyone was quiet while they thought

through the implications of that. None of the implications were good.

"They lied to us, Nils," he said. "I don't know why I thought I could trust this place—a city that has secret police and vague, menacing agencies, helicopters in every corner of the sky, a dog park that doesn't even allow dogs into it. It's been the city this whole time, destroying itself and its people, placing its secrecy above our safety, pretending it's trying to protect us. It's a betrayal."

She felt the same way. She was just starting to become close to making friends in Night Vale, to maybe finding a partner, to feeling like she belonged here. She had put her life on the line to help, or so she had thought, save the city from destruction. Just when she was thinking of it in terms of a town, a community, that might include her in it, it revealed itself for what it was: an unravelable knot of mistruths and misdirection that would never belong to a person like her who believed in simple scientific truths.

Carlos banged his fist into a wall, the most aggressive gesture Nilanjana had ever seen from him.

"Not this time," he said, retreating to his office. "This time I will finish the experiments, no matter what they do to me. I will science so hard and so fast that they won't be able to stop me. I will be safe from that otherworld, and so will my family and all of you. No one else gets lost. This ends now."

He slammed the door. Nilanjana considered the closed door and then looked back at the pit across the street. She agreed with Carlos's feelings, but his response was rash and unconsidered.

"If the centipede wasn't causing any of this, then did we kill an innocent creature?" Mark asked.

"It would seem so," said Nilanjana.

"We're going to lose our jobs, aren't we?" he groaned.

"That's what I was going to ask," Luisa said. "The city's going to shut us down or blow us up."

"Calm down. Just give me a second, okay?" Nilanjana said. "Let me drink some coffee, breathe, think, get rid of this hangover."

"For a hangover, you should get water, or a banana, or some orangemilk," Mark said.

"Don't bother me," Nilanjana snapped. "Especially over shit like that."

"I was trying to help."

She sat down at her desk, closed her eyes, and rolled back her head. She let out a long breath. She held her coffee with one hand, and rubbed her forehead with the other. She thought through the time line of the destructive attacks over the past several weeks in Night Vale. A new hypothesis occurred to her, one that fit all the available data, but one that also terrified her. It just couldn't be true, she thought, unscientifically. Her stomach rolled. She felt sick and unprepared for what to do if her hypothesis proved true.

She heard a knock far back behind her, at the lab's front door. Another knock. The timing of the attacks. Correlation is not causation, but it suggests the possibility of causation. The knocking continued.

"Somebody get that," she shouted.

More knocking, and then the door opened and Mark was talking to someone. They carried on a bit, Mark sounded like he was arguing. She and Carlos might have been backward in their thinking, their hypothesis based on faulty assumptions, but she couldn't follow her own logic clearly with this noise.

Mark said: "Nils."

"Don't call me Nils."

"Sorry. Nilanjana, I know you said not to bother you, but this guy wants to see Carlos. Says it's important."

"Mark, please, figure this shit out yourself. I'm trying to think through—"

She saw the man standing at the front desk of the lab, past Mark. She knew that man.

"Larry? Larry Leroy?" she asked, quietly.

"From out on the edge of town, yes," said Larry Leroy.

36

There was a lighthouse, he said.

On top of a mountain, he said.

In the middle of a vast waterless desert, he said.

Nilanjana offered Larry some more water. His glass was empty. It had been empty many times.

After returning to Night Vale, he had not gone home because he had no home. He had not gone to the police, because he didn't think they would do anything to help him. He had not gone to see family, because he knew no family. Instead he had come to the scientists, who could maybe help him understand what had happened to him.

He had been living in some kind of desert otherworld, at first alone, and then later with people who began to show up. He had befriended the people, and they were all from Night Vale. They had all had similar experiences to Larry's: living their normal lives when suddenly the ground became hot and gave way, sending them out into a vast desert nothing.

People from Big Rico's Pizza. Big Rico himself. Most of a high school basketball team. Charlie Bair, the weekday shift manager at the Ralphs, who arrived with a huge pile of lactose-free milk.

"Larry, you're one of the only people who saw a centipede attack up close," Nilanjana said. "We thought you were dead. We thought all of those people were dead."

"Well, we may be. I don't know. Rico brought me back to his establishment, but it's no longer there. He told me a handsome scientist fellow named Carlos worked next door and that maybe I should see him about all this stuff."

"How did you get back? How did you live through what the centipede did to you?" she asked. "I went to your house, when I heard about your disappearance. The whole thing was gone, just a sand pit now. All I found was a diorama among the debris. I have it at my apartment. It's of Dorothy."

"Oh, I remember that one." He chuckled while wincing. "I put a lot of work into those. Wish more than one could have been saved."

"It's stunning, Larry. You're a beautiful artist."

He didn't say anything. He wasn't sure how to receive a compliment. He wasn't sure about a lot of things.

"You keep talking about a centipede," he said. "I've seen this centipede, but it never attacked me. It certainly didn't attack my house."

He used to live in a house out on the edge of town. He used to paint and compose and write. He used to water plants and work on his yard. Sometimes he would do crossword puzzles, and often he would read or cook.

One day the floor had disappeared beneath him, along with his art and books and music. The house had fallen away, as had he. There had been no monster. No devouring. Only a sudden pit, and sudden falling. Larry had fallen for a long time, for so long it stopped feeling like falling, but floating. He would imagine, sometimes, that he was moving upward, and with enough concentration he could convince his body of that sensation, switching between falling and rising like an optical illusion that is two different images at once. Eventually he had gotten bored with falling and had dozed off. When he woke up, he was on the floor of an unfamiliar room.

There was no furniture and no sign of any residents, except a picture of a lighthouse on the wall. He had looked at the picture for a long time, trying to decipher it. To him it was meaningful and cryptic, as was all art. But many hours of study and contemplation over the subsequent weeks led Larry to believe it was simply a picture. Of a lighthouse. Nothing more. Nothing less. And, as far as Larry was concerned, that was the most complex anything could be: a pure neutral self, expressing nothing but its own existence.

He had left the house to find he was in a vast desert. Above him was a mountain. He didn't believe in mountains, but there was nothing else there to believe in instead, so he walked toward the mountain. Atop it, he could see a building. He climbed the mountain, seeking out trails and smaller, more climbable ledges. Night came all at once, with no noise or fuss from the sun. It occurred to him that he hadn't seen any sun, only a bright light that came from everywhere, and then was abruptly gone. He had camped out with no supplies in a hollow half cavern of stone and brush.

He had watched the stars. They were not any of the stars he had been used to seeing. Back at home, on warm nights, he would look for Orion the Hunter, with his three-star belt, or Ursa Major, also known as the Big Dipper. There were so many arrangements of long-ago gods and creatures: Taurus the Bull, Draco the Dragon, Buddy the Golden Retriever. But none of those formations had been in this sky. He could not even find the moon. The night was bright but, like the day, had no visible source for its brightness.

That first night, in his semi-cave, he lay down, looking up at the top of the mountain. There was a blinking red light there, and he let its steady rhythm lull him to sleep. The next morning, or whatever time it was when the sky became light again, he went to find food and water, but despite discovering none, and not having eaten in more than a day, he did not feel the need to drink or eat. His body felt healthy, full of energy, and he continued up the mountain to the building.

It was the lighthouse from the picture. Over its door was a pattern carved into the plaster, three interlocking triangles. He made the lighthouse his new home. From there, he could see all of the desert otherworld he inhabited. There was nothing much to see. There was a mountain, which he lived on, a lighthouse, which he lived in, and a little house at the base of the mountain, from which he had come. Other than that: sand and a sky that was a searing blue that felt almost aggressive.

By his count he had lived in the desert for a little over nine months, despite having only disappeared from Night Vale a couple weeks ago. He had used leaves and stems and flowers he found in that world to create his own materials and paints so he could continue his art. He wandered about the desert, but he didn't want to venture too far from the lighthouse. No matter which direction he went, he ended up back at the mountain anyway.

He began drawing maps of this new desert, and then drawing, from memory, maps of Night Vale. The geography was similar. The mountain he was on was similar to the mountain range to the north of Night Vale, which no one believes to be real. There was a tall cactus with four distinct arms, one of which was engorged around its middle, much of the top of it cut away as if by barber's shears. It was exactly like a cactus he had seen for years near his home. The otherworld looked a lot like the desert he had grown up in, except without the buildings or cars or people or hooded figures.

Then one day more people arrived from the house. He avoided them for a while, watching them from the lighthouse. They wandered around the mountain, and argued, and tried again and again to return home through the house they had emerged from. Eventually he stopped avoiding them, realizing they were people he knew from around town. Some of them stayed at the bottom of the mountain, others joined him in the lighthouse. None of them needed to eat or drink either.

From the top of his mountain, he saw movement under the sand. Slithering movements from something unimaginably long. He also saw doors around the desert. Old oak doors, unattached to any building. They did not last long. Each time a door appeared, more people emerged from the house at the bottom of the mountain. The house seemed to be the way into the desert otherworld. Perhaps the doors were the way out. But there was no predicting where a door would appear, and they never lasted long enough for him to get to one. When a door appeared, the slithering under the sand would speed toward it. It seemed like the doors were letting whatever the creature under the sand was come and go from its world. But the creature did not seem to be able to predict when and where the doors would be, so Larry decided it wasn't creating the doors, just reacting to them. Before a door appeared, there would be rumbling, and the creature would be attracted to the rumbling.

"I don't know if it even knew where the doors led," Larry said. "I don't know if it knew anything. I think it felt the rumbling and was attracted to the movement."

Before a door would appear in this desert otherworld, two things would happen. First he could feel a terrible rumbling, and then he would hear an awful mechanical whirring sound. Like gears moving, or like the faint scampering of rodent feet amplified to deafening volumes.

"What do you think was causing those doors if it wasn't the centipede, Larry?" Nilanjana asked.

"I don't know. But I know that the first few I saw seemed to be timed out, controlled. Like someone just pressed a 'Desert Door' button, and it was there for a minute or two and then it was gone.

"After a while, doors started appearing in the old house at the bottom of the mountain too. They would flicker and flash and then disappear. It was like the house was waking up. Like the other doors were waking it. Like the house was alive."

He went back to that house, but it was still empty except for the picture of the lighthouse. He looked closely into the photo. He could see himself in it. It was a photo of him, inside the lighthouse, at the top of a mountain. He stared at this photo of himself inside the lighthouse for a long time, and then he realized he no longer was in the picture. The lighthouse in the photo was empty. But the room he was in was not. There was a coffee table and sofa, photos of a family, old music playing, flowers in a vase, a television. He could smell cooking.

When he walked to the windows, he was looking out into a neighborhood of Night Vale. Cars and people and dogs and bikes and helicopters and spying secret agents. It wasn't a neighborhood he knew, but he was certain it was his hometown. He ran to the front door and opened it, but it opened to the desert otherworld, and when he looked into the house, it was empty again, save for the chair and the picture.

"I did that over and over. Looking at me in the picture until the furniture appeared, and then I could watch Night Vale from the window of the house," he said. "And at first it felt great. I missed my old home. But it started to fill me with anxiety. Because the more the doors appeared, the easier it was to see Night Vale through the house. It was like a boundary there was becoming thinner. The air became hot inside the house, and smelled like metal. I wanted to go home, but I wasn't sure if Night Vale would survive the boundary in the house tearing open. And then I heard about the worms."

"Worms?" Nilanjana asked. "What about worms? We found a bunch where Big Rico's pizzeria used to be."

"Yeah, Rico said he kept worms in his basement. He wouldn't tell me why. He would only say that when anyone else tried to start a pizza restaurant in Night Vale, he would invite the owner over for a meeting. He would take the owner of that other restaurant down to the basement, where they could talk without being interrupted. Then the other pizza restaurant would stop being a problem, and he wouldn't ever see that other owner again. As a result, there was a lot of stuff down there for the worms to eat. Rico winked at me after he said that.

"Then Rico told me that wasn't the point. The point was that as the worms dug more and more holes, the soil had become softer, more aerated, more water and air moving between layers. He said that was maybe sort of like what was happening to the house out there in the desert. The more things that forced their way through into the world, the softer that portal, that house, would become, allowing even more to move through it, with even less effort.

"And then, yesterday, everything changed. The slithering underground thing came right for our mountain, and then it rose from the sand. It was a giant centipede, like you mentioned earlier. The people who had stayed at the bottom of the mountain ran screaming, but it ignored them. It dove right into the house, until all of it disappeared into the tiny building. Once it was clear it was not coming back, we followed it into the house. Its passage had finally torn the boundary of the house wide open. All of the furniture was there, without us having to do anything at all. And the door was wide open. And beyond that door was Night Vale. We all walked through, and came home.

"I thought it was over. I thought we were free. But then this morning, I was going to get coffee before coming to your lab, and I heard the noise again. That whirring sound. And the coffee place in front of me just vanished. That terrible noise, an unbearable heat. I think the boundary between the worlds that broke open yesterday is collapsing."

"And you heard that noise again?" she said.

"Yes. I never figured out what it was, though. I wish I could replicate it for you, ma'am. It's awful."

Nilanjana wanted to find out what Carlos thought of all this, but he was locked in his office, irrational and angry like she'd never seen him, setting up his experiment, and was uninterested in anything else until it was complete. For him, the safety of his family was more important than any truth Larry could give him, but this was important to his studies. She didn't know what to do. She was considering again the terrible hypothesis she had conceived right before Larry arrived, and the thought of it made her dizzy.

As she vacillated about what to do next, she could hear Carlos restarting the machine, preparing for the next test.

She turned back to Larry, and his eyes were wide. His jaw was slack. He was barely breathing.

"Larry?"

He turned and ran out of the lab. She went to the front door to follow, but he was already out to the street and still running.

"Larry, what's wrong?" she shouted, but he wouldn't even look back.

She felt the floor getting hot. She thought again of her hypothesis. The one that she wanted to believe wasn't true, against all available data. And that's when she noticed the whirring of Carlos's machine. An awful, mechanical whirring.

37

The centipede had only ever been a simple insect. The city had only ever been the Secret Police surveillance state it had always been. Neither of them had caused the pits or the disappearing people.

Her hypothesis had become a working theory. She ran with that theory across the lab and pounded on the office door.

"Turn it off. Turn that thing off. Carlos!"

He opened the door, alarmed at her alarm. The floor was getting hotter.

"Not now, Nils. My family is on the line. Only science can save them."

"It's the machine, Carlos. It's the experiments."

"What's the machine? What are you talking about?"

"Carlos." She lowered her voice, forced herself to sound calmer, so that he would not write off what she was saying as an emotional outburst. "Your experiments are what has been opening up those pits. Your experiments have been destroying the town. It's not that the city or anyone else is causing the destruction to stop you. Every time you start one of the experiments, the destruction happens. Our causation was backward the whole time."

Defensiveness is natural, protective. The body's number one objective is to preserve itself. Being told that your actions are bad would seem a threat to your well-being, harming your

reputation, your self-esteem, leaving you vulnerable to re-
taliation, possibly losing your job, which is your livelihood,
which is what keeps you sheltered and fed and alive. In the
quick moment of a single piece of negative feedback, however
catastrophic, the subconscious mind processes all of that far
below the surface. It doesn't make these proceedings trans-
parent to the conscious mind. It doesn't speak to itself in any
kind of human language with constructed arguments for and
against. There is no *Robert's Rules of Order* in the subconscious mind. The subconscious mind is ruled by neurons and
synapses and the deep, conservative demands of instinct.

So while Carlos's reaction to Nilanjana's statement was rich
and complex in terms of physiology and, neurologically speaking, was profoundly interesting, what he said was:

"Oh, come on."

Then he stared at his machine for a long time.

Nilanjana put her hand on his shoulder. He jerked it away.

Therapists will say that the root of much human anger is
guilt, that what makes a person most angry in another person is a reflection of their own recognizable shortcomings. "I
hate it when people are aggressive drivers," says the aggressive
driver. Or just the feeling of guilt can make a person find any
other thing anger-worthy. "I hate it when people are aggressive
drivers," says the person who realized they forgot to call their
daughter on her birthday.

"Go away," Carlos said.

"Just hear me out." She wanted to keep her voice gentle, so
as not to rouse defensiveness, but she could hear the whirring
of the machine, the quiver of the floor. What was intended as
soft and pleading came out as a bark, a command.

* * *

A matinee crowd at Night Vale Cinemas, excited for the opening weekend of *Superman Vs. Himself*, in which immortal screen legend Lee Marvin played both Supermans. Josh was there, human face and long bird legs, wings tucked in beneath him. He favored forms that could fly now, although despite various girlfriends' and boyfriends' (and his sister, Jackie's) constant begging, he found he was only able to get himself into the air. Passengers were just too much for him. He was looking forward to the show. He had never missed a Lee Marvin movie. Growing up, he had always gone to the movies with his mom, but now he preferred to go on his own. Not a negative judgment on his mother, whom he truly loved, but a positive judgment on solitude, which he truly appreciated. So, with Big Rico's closed again while Rico and Arnie figured out the whole smoldering giant centipede body problem, Josh took the opportunity to sit in the back of the theater, away from the other moviegoers.

He scooped up popcorn with his wing and deftly flicked it into his mouth. He smiled at the dexterity he was developing with his new forms, but his smile fell into a curious frown as he began to feel a certain strange warmth beneath his talons. He examined the floor, which looked no different, but felt warmer and warmer with each passing moment.

Carlos turned, his eyes deep and angry. "Pamela lied. She stopped us at each turn, followed us around each corner. We killed that monster they were trying to keep out of our reality, and still. Still it's not enough for them. If they want a fight, I will show them a fight. I will protect my city. My family. My lab. Our lab, Nilanjana. I will protect you and everyone here."

"By destroying the town?"

"I'm not . . ." He snorted and kept his eyes hard on Nilan-jana. "I'm not destroying the town. I'm doing science. Science is helpful. That nutty church, those nutty religious people, they tried to destroy this town. I'm going to save it."

"Larry Leroy came back," she said. "He wasn't eaten like we thought. It wasn't the centipede doing any of this. The centi-pede never touched anyone until we started attacking it."

"Out!" Carlos stood, his voice hard, his eyes harder, and Nilanjana reflexively backed away. Taking the opportunity of the space ceded by his fellow scientist, Carlos closed the door, Nilanjana on the other side. She heard the lock.

Josh had no time to worry about the warmth from the floor because the movie was starting. Or, of course, the pre-movie messages and previews. There was the usual one about buying snacks or adopting a dog from the concession stand, so that you'd have something to munch on or a beautiful puppy to pet during the show. Josh kind of wished he had thought to adopt a dog on the way in instead of just getting popcorn, but he was afraid that, if he went out now, by the time he had filled out all of the adoption paperwork and had the required inspection of his home to make sure it was a healthy environment for a dog, the movie would have already started. Instead, he sat through previews for the latest big alien invasion documentary from Werner Herzog, full of the usual explosions and wisecracking good guys keeping earth safe, and the preview for Lee Marvin's next superhero film, *Superman Vs. Nobody*, in which Superman finally found peace.

The floor was going from warm to downright hot, but he was distracted from that by an even more annoying issue. He would think that a movie theater, on the opening weekend of a major blockbuster, would properly calibrate their audio system, but, over the sound of the previews, people in the room could hear a low rumbling and an annoying mechanical whirring. He had made his ears larger than normal to better hear the movie, and so he was especially put out by the sound problems. And the floor just got hotter and hotter, so hot he had to lift his feet to avoid getting burned. He felt a sense of terrifying familiarity in what was happening, but before he could process this, the movie began.

"Nilanjana, you're alive!" Darryl stumbled in. "I was so worried."

Darryl moved to her, his eyes damp and sagging. He wrapped his arms around her. Between the violence of the slammed office door on one side, and the empathy of Darryl on the other, Nilanjana went stiff. Sandwiched by two different kinds of aggressive passions, she wanted to collapse to the floor.

"Are you okay? You were gone when I woke up, and I wasn't scared at all, but a little confused that you weren't there, but then the TV came on, and—"

"Darryl!" Nilanjana put her hand to his face. "Shut up."

She kissed him. Quick and soft.

As their lips parted, she said, "This isn't about me or you right now. This is about Carlos."

"I don't know what you mean," he said by scrunching up his face.

"You don't have to understand right now," she said by actually saying it.

The whirring of the machine got louder. She banged hard on the door.

"Please let me in. Carlos." Her violent knocks were fading.

She could feel her energy waning as well. "Carlos, if you could just pause your experiment, for a second. If you could only hear me out. Hear my hypothesis. I think once you understand the science of the situation, you—"

Carlos opened the door. He was crying. She had never seen him cry. He was overwhelmed, and unsure of how to express his emotions, since he usually only did so in carefully worded sentences, not with water from his body.

"The science of the situation?" he snarled. "That otherworld. I was trapped there, Nilanjana. I couldn't see Cecil. For ten lonely years, I was kept away from the people I love, in that desolate place where you never get hungry, and you never have to drink water, and so you never live. It is a place that devours. It is a place that is empty. That is the science of the situation. And I study it. So I can fix it. Only I can do that. Only these experiments can do that. I'm sorry, Nilanjana. I'm not going to stop so that you can tell me what science is."

Josh didn't fully comprehend all that was happening at first, only that people in the front of the theater were getting up and shouting. This wasn't polite behavior in a movie theater, but he didn't feel like having an argument about that. It wasn't until the standing people started running back toward him that he got up too, concerned. He looked down at the floor, which had gotten unbearably hot, and he remembered how the floor of the gymnasium had felt. The screams of the cinemagoers, the screams of the basketball team.

A hole had opened up just in front of the movie screen. It was small at first, capturing a stray empty cup that rattled over its side, but it was expanding quickly. Josh fluttered up into the air in panic, and took stock of how bad the situation already was. As the crowd scrambled back from the edge of the hole, its bottomless depth had cut everyone off from all exits. The people could only retreat toward the back wall of the theater, until there would be no more theater to retreat to. The hole was already a crevasse. Row by row, empty seats littered with popcorn and bags that had been left by fleeing people were tipping forward and disappearing into the darkness.

Josh eyed the exit. He still could fly down there, get out the door, keep himself safe. But he looked back at the panicking crowd, shoving each other as though there were anywhere to go but where they already were, and he swooped down to land among them.

"I know how much you believe in what you're doing," Nilanjana said. "But the pastor believed in what she was doing. So did everyone at the Joyous Congregation who went along with what they did. Belief is not enough. Not in a god. Not in science. We were wrong, Carlos. Science is not inherently good. It is just a method of thought that works to find truth. But the thoughts within that method can lead to good or bad places. It's not enough to believe in science. You also need to listen. Listen to other people. Please let me tell you what happened to Larry."

"Please let me tell you what happened to me," said Larry. He had run a few blocks, but then he had turned and come back. His legs were shaking in terror, but he was a man that cared more about the legacy he left than at what age he ended up leaving that legacy. And without a Night Vale, there would be no one to receive his art. He would be forgotten, not after two generations of children, but all at once, in a single falling motion. So he had come back to do what he could, whatever that was.

"Larry," Nilanjana said. She was overjoyed to see the man she thought she'd never see again. This was the second time in only a few minutes she'd felt this way about Larry. "Tell Carlos what is happening."

"I know what is happening," said Carlos. "Don't lecture me about—"

Larry stepped cautiously to the door, and Carlos went quiet, reacting to Larry's calm demeanor. Larry's hands were old, the skin hanging off thin bones, knuckles ashen, nails long and yellowing around the cuticles.

"You don't know me, young man," Larry said, his voice still a bit weak. Nilanjana could barely hear it over the machine. "My name is Larry Leroy, and I think you might know something about a lighthouse. On top of a mountain."

Carlos opened his mouth, and then closed it again.

There was hardly a theater left to stand in. In front of the audience was a wide nothing, growing wider, and before that was Lee Marvin, intoning masterfully that Superman must be stopped, and the only person that could stop him was Superman. Josh felt pressure and then a crushing as everyone compressed into a smaller and smaller island of safety. And then he heard the cries and caught the eye of a man, a father maybe, or an important member of society, or just a person who got on with his life, just a normal person who didn't think his life would end today, as the man teetered backward and then with one terrified yelp was gone into the abyss.

Josh thought again of flying away, but knew that he couldn't. He thought of what his sister, Jackie, would do. Jackie, the bravest person he knew. Probably she would fall into the pit and die.

Sometimes bravery isn't enough. Sometimes you need the right tools for the situation. He flapped his wings experimentally. It wasn't going to work but he would have to try. He turned to the woman next to him, Maureen, whom he recognized from Dark Owl Records, where she often hung out.

"I think I can lift us," Josh said to her. He grew human arms to go along with the wings. "Let me try." He held his new arms out and moved his wings to indicate what he was going to try to do.

"No way," Maureen said. Two more people fell screaming. The math was simple: the same size crowd, less and less floor.

"Yeah, okay," Maureen said.

Josh and she hooked their arms together, and he flapped as hard as he could. He flapped until his shoulders burned. He bit his lip in the exertion, and tasted blood. He tried to find more in himself, but there was nothing. It was no good. He couldn't do it. And it was as he was thinking this that he realized his feet were no longer touching the ground.

"Oh holy shit," Maureen said.

He wasn't that high up, but he didn't need to be.

"Okay, I'm going to drop her off, and then I'll come back to get each of you," he said. But as he dropped Maureen safely at the exit, another couple fell into the crevasse. He knew there would not be enough time left to save all of them.

"There is a lighthouse on top of a mountain," said Larry. "From that lighthouse, you can see all of the desert, not this desert but another desert. And in that desert is one other structure. It is a home. It is a home with a photo of that same lighthouse."

Larry tilted his head.

"You've been there, haven't you?" he said.

Carlos reached over and shut off the machine. The whirring faded down to a faint hum.

He looked empty now, without the fire of a scientific solution to a crisis to fuel him. Science could not fix this basic fact: His method had not been wrong. All of the science had been correct. But still the results had been, morally, bad. It was an equation he was still struggling to comprehend.

"It's nice to meet you," said Larry.

"Hi, I'm Carlos." His voice was weak but steady. "I'm a scientist, for better or worse."

"You hear that?" Larry asked.

"What?" Carlos asked. "I don't hear anything."

"Me neither," Larry said, smiling now.

"What's your—"

"Hang on, son," Larry said. "Just listen."

There was nothing. No rumbling. No heat. The vast crevasse that once was a theater was still there, but the crevasse wasn't getting any bigger. The crowd found stable positions on the bit of floor that was left. As moments passed, and nothing continued to happen, they realized they were going to survive. Most of them started weeping. One woman just started swearing, as many words as she could think of. She didn't even know why. Delayed fear, maybe. Or a celebration of the existence of her lungs.

Josh looked around. He had only been able to carry a few people to safety, but now that the crisis was over, or at least paused, he felt a surging satisfaction that he had found it in himself to do even that.

"Let's keep this going," he said, testing out the power of his wings. They felt good. They felt strong. "I can just take one person at a time but I'm going to get you all out of here."

There was nothing. Or there were many sounds: helicopters and sirens, near and far. Wind and leaves and traffic. The slight sound of the sunrise, lingering on into midmorning. Breaths and heartbeats of the people in the room. The low grumble of a jet plane somewhere near the stratosphere as it released helpful psychotropic chemtrails. The constant clicking of the camera held by an agent from a vague yet menacing government agency that was in the room, monitoring them. The sounds of day-to-day life. The sounds of everything. And so, nothing.

Carlos had been causing disasters by trying to stop the disasters that he was causing. A loop that could only be broken by just holding still. And now he could hear his own inaction, and it sounded like the safety of his family.

"It's quiet, Carlos. Do you hear that?" Nilanjana stepped toward him slowly, respecting his space, but Carlos inched back toward his office. "Listen."

"Listen," Luisa said.

"Listen," Mark said.

"Listen," Darryl said.

Nilanjana smiled and touched Carlos's hand. He flinched but did not end the contact.

"Come here," she said.

Carlos looked at each of them. They were all smiling, albeit tentatively, except Darryl, whose lips were pulled completely back, teeth exposed, as his church had taught him. Carlos paused for a second on Darryl, but then finally moved his eyes to Nilanjana.

Carlos cried and cried. A lifetime of physical emotion that

he hadn't expressed, all coming out of him. It felt like illness, but it was only existence. Nilanjana was crying too, crying for her town, which had come so close to not existing anymore. And crying for her mentor, who had done everything right but gotten it all wrong. She pulled him in and embraced him. Luisa and Mark followed, then Darryl and Larry too. They did what all scientists do when following proper scientific method: (1) hypothesis; (2) argument; (3) fight; (4) cry; (5) hug.

And though this moment didn't fix the town, it saved it.

38

They had gone to the house that didn't exist. Carlos insisted on going in alone. He had started this. He would end it. He led everyone he could find in the otherworld back through the house, into Night Vale. He couldn't find everyone. No grave mistake can be fixed completely. Carlos wanted to keep going back, to keep going and going, but Nilanjana wouldn't let him. Past a certain point, it would stop being about helping others, and instead be about punishing himself.

Even though the pit at the theater had happened less than an hour before, survivors that he led out reported they had been in the otherworld for six weeks.

On their last trip through, Cynthia—the woman who lived in the house that doesn't exist and, by extension, did not exist herself—protested. She shouted at these strangers barreling through her home, not wiping their feet.

"I'm sorry," said Carlos. "No one will be coming through here anymore."

"I'd certainly hope not," said Cynthia. She huffed into the next room and promptly disappeared, because she did not exist.

Carlos closed the door as he exited.

"There's no need for us to try to open this door, or look into these windows anymore," he said. "The otherworld will stay where it is. I'll keep my eyes on this world, where all the people I love are."

Cecil, who had waited anxiously outside as Carlos did his rescue missions, swept him into a kiss.

"I would trade all of Night Vale for you," Cecil said. He kissed Carlos again, a lengthy kiss that smashed their lips and hurt a little. A kiss that expressed not just love but anxiety and relief, all the worry of the past couple weeks pushed into a kiss. Breaking off, he added, "But I would really prefer not to. You stay away from desert otherworlds."

All of this was broadcast on the radio. Cecil broadcast almost everything he did on the radio, to the gentle exasperation of an understanding town.

Luisa and Mark had dismantled Carlos's machine. Mark used one of the scrap mechanical parts to improve his own machine. It now made a bright flash, followed by a loud bang, followed by a puff of smoke. Mark knew he could now apply for some quite prestigious scientific research grants.

Luisa used the giant metal frame of Carlos's machine to build a potato garden. "These are going to be the most disappointing potatoes I've ever grown," she said. Mark agreed with her, and she thanked him for supporting her efforts.

"Maybe we could get a drink sometime," Mark said. "Like, I mean not a date, but a date."

"I'm sorry," said Luisa. "I'm only interested in potatoes."

"That's okay," said Mark. "Grab drinks as friends?"

Luisa smiled.

"No," she said. And then she went back to being disappointed in her potatoes. She was genuinely only interested in potatoes.

Nilanjana had gone with Darryl, Stephanie, and Jamillah to check in on people who had lost their homes or businesses. Stephanie—appointed a Church Elder through an emergency vote by the Congregation—had set up a Joyous Congregation

Fund for Rebuilding Night Vale (or JoCoFuFoReNiVa for short). They sent out several church and community volunteers to help rebuild Big Rico's, the high school gymnasium, the coffee shops, and Larry Leroy's home, among many, many others.

Several local businesses gave contributions—including a nice donation from the Last Bank of Night Vale, with a little urging from bank employee Steve Carlsberg. Larry would have to start over on his creative legacy, but now that there was an awareness of his artwork, he converted part of his house to the Larry Leroy Public Museum of Art, Out on the Edge of Town.

After a long day painting the exterior walls on Larry's new house, Darryl and Nilanjana collapsed, exhausted, at her apartment, which was still only her apartment, but had a growing number of Darryl's books and clothes and toiletries in it.

She leaned back into Darryl's outstretched arms and sighed. He sighed too. They were happy, tired sighs.

"Thank you," Darryl said.

"For what?" Nilanjana murmured.

"I haven't really said this, since, uh, since the centipede thing, but it's been tough trying to understand what I'm doing with my life, what my church has brought me to."

He paused, trying to find the right words through the haze of sleepiness and alcohol.

"When we killed that thing, I was happy because we were safe, but I also knew we killed a god. We killed the god of our religion, and, I don't know. I couldn't see it as a metaphor anymore. I couldn't go back to that thinking. And then there was the fact that my pastor, who I trusted, who I followed, was trying to destroy Night Vale.

"I've been in a bad way over this, wanting to leave the church, because it just didn't mean anything anymore.

"But this rebuilding stuff. It's given me meaning. Or not me. It's given the church meaning *for* me. Our god is dead, but lots of gods are dead. It doesn't make them . . . you know, less. What matters is the people who are alive and there with me, working toward a common cause, following a common set of values. Stephanie and Jamillah. They still believe. I don't think I believe anymore. But I also don't think I have to. Religion can be something you do, not something you believe. And that can have just as much meaning."

He took a sip of wine, more out of self-consciousness in conversation than actual enjoyment of what was a mediocre cabernet. He had meant everything he said, and it had come out as earnest and sincere. In coming to new terms with his religion, in dropping the necessity of absolute belief in divine joy, he had connected to something in himself, and he no longer came off as sarcastic or false.

"It was meaningful that you joined me, Nilanjana. Thank you."

"That's sweet. You're welcome." She nuzzled his armpit with her back with a happy wiggle.

"I know you aren't religious and especially not into the Joyous Congregation, but you've been so supportive of me these past weeks. And whether you know it or not, you've made me better. A better person, I mean."

She turned and looked at his face. She had a hypothesis. Or no. Something solid and backed by all available evidence. A theory.

"Darryl Ramirez. I really like you."

"I really like you too." His face flushed with warm blood and mediocre wine.

"Stephanie, and Jamillah too. I like them so much. You have

great friends, and I feel like I do too now. I'm not joining the church. I hope that's cool with you. It's the same way I wouldn't expect you to learn science and join our lab. We have different things. But we could do those different things side by side, in parallel, you know?"

"I think if there's one thing we learned these last couple weeks, it's that both of our things are pretty interesting," he said.

"Right? Maybe it's just the stress of all the danger recently. And having survived that danger together," Nilanjana said. "But having a person in this town who could be with me when I'm not working, who could be with me after the pesticides and disappointing potatoes and otherworld dimensional rifts. Who could make me laugh and let me cry and . . ."

Darryl grinned.

"I know. I know. It's hokey. Fine. I'm hokey."

"Are we doing this, then?" Darryl asked.

"Sure. I'm not that tired." She began to unbutton his shirt.

He laughed. "No. I mean are we doing this? You and me. Are we together? Differences and all. Are we going to make this work?"

She leaned in and kissed him. His lips were soft, warm, and sticky sweet. They kissed for a long time. She was too tired to think of centipedes or churches. Inside her mind was the deep black of the night sky. No stars, no moons or planets, just an infinite darkness from well before Creation, from long after Entropy.

In that darkness there was only Darryl's smell, and the feel of him. His breath, his skin, his hair. The soft, warm lips, purple with a $9.99 cabernet from Ralphs. Nilanjana ran her tongue lightly along them as she pulled away. The wine tasted better that way.

"Of course," she said.

They looked into each other's eyes, smiling, giggling, palms on each other's cheeks. They were kissing again. Time passed and neither of them knew how much. She reached across him and turned off the television, the last light left that night. And in the dark, just against his ear, she whispered: "I'm glad this all worked out."

39

It didn't work out.

That's a simplification. Just because something eventually doesn't work out doesn't mean it never worked out. It was working out fine until, not much later, it wasn't working out at all.

Happiness is not canceled out by unhappiness. A relationship is not canceled out by its end.

But try telling that to either of them, who, while still friends in a shaky, tentative sort of way, regarded the connection they had as an anomaly, a closeness brought on by shared danger mistaken for a true and lasting romance.

There were a few weeks when it had seemed like it would really work. The sex was good, the conversations were interesting and involved a lot of fascinating disagreements on the nature of science and religion and existence. They went on dates and, even more intimately, didn't go on dates, sitting on her couch or his couch and watching trashy but addictive reality television, like *Orbs!* or *So You Think You Can Slowly Freeze to Death?* She would put her head on his shoulder, or he would put his head on her shoulder and one of them would sleep on the other, and they were both warm, temperature-wise, which feels quite a bit like love.

Then there were a few weeks when it seemed like it would

maybe work. The sex was still good, but the fascinating disagreements were just arguments now, ones that circled around the same subjects and fractaled out in all directions, encompassing topics that had not been related to the conversation until they were suddenly being disagreed upon, and neither of them knew why. And they had watched every season of *Orbs!*, and he wanted to go on to *SphereZone,* but she thought it looked like an uninspired spin-off. Still, though, there was warmth and shoulders and it seemed wrong to drop something so promising, which had recently felt so intense, just because the intensity was harder to find.

And then there was the week when it would not work. They tried to make it work, and it didn't. The disagreements were everywhere, no matter which way they steered the conversation, and they annoyed her so much that she didn't want to watch TV with him, and it was still warm on that couch together but maybe the warmth no longer felt like love but just like human closeness when sometimes she wanted to be alone. The sex was still good but it wasn't enough. And she said exactly that to him. It was right after they had had sex, so the timing was awkward, but it was also true, and he knew it was true. He said he knew it was true, and they were both agreeing that it was true, and then they realized that meant they weren't dating anymore. They were naked in bed together and no longer a couple, and it was weird. And he got dressed and left.

"How's, um, science stuff going?" he asked.

They were having coffee at the Spikey Hammer. It had been a few months, and they both wanted to be friends and were doing their best to make it happen. Because it was no longer a date, they no longer had to go to fancy places with disappointing drinks. Instead they could go to their favorite coffee shop and order their usuals. Darryl even got the barista to smile at him, after complimenting the coffee in a genuine, warm tone.

"The science stuff's been good," she said. And then she realized it actually had been good, even though she had only said that on reflex, and so she said it again. "It's been really good actually. I was promoted to be Carlos's main assistant. He says that he can't let himself lose the context of the science he's doing anymore. Science is only a tool, and, without knowing why you're using that tool, you can accidentally do terrible things. He wants me to help him not do terrible things. Which is a pretty great job. Plus I get to do my own little hobby projects still. Like the pharmaceutical work and the pesticides. I don't want to end up, you know, being disappointed in potatoes, trying to win awards, and feeling like that's all there is to a scientific life."

"That's fantastic, Nilanjana," Darryl said. He waved his fist in the air, part celebration, and part a knowing parody of his usual move. She laughed, which made him laugh. The conversation felt easier.

"What about you?" she said. "Still thinking of taking over Gordon's job?"

"Yeah," he said, thoughtfully swirling around the pebbles and moss in his Americano. "There's a lot of administrative stuff to deal with. I mean, the pastor was misguided, but she was good at making that whole machine move. A church is a business that can't feel like a business to anyone but the people running it. That's a tricky thing. Stephanie's been great at holding services though. She and I have been"—he paused, gauging Nilanjana's reaction—"seeing each other, actually."

"That's great," Nilanjana said and meant it. "You and her are perfect for each other. Is it . . ." It could be a terrible question. "Is it weird to pray to a Smiling God when you know we killed the Smiling God?" It was a terrible question. "I'm sorry."

"No, it's fine," he said, and it was. His faith was solid, and so there was no question that could bother him. "I know I said that my God was dead, but that was right after. I was still so confused. I realize now that we didn't kill the Smiling God. We killed a giant bug. Maybe some of our prophets, like Kevin, mistook that bug for the Smiling God. But I know in my heart that our God is not a hungry centipede."

Nilanjana nodded. Now that she had no stake in Darryl's beliefs, and his life did not intersect with her life, she was able to say, sincerely, "Okay. Cool."

"I mean, look at the pastor. She believed in the literality of the Smiling God and it got her eaten. We're not going to repeat her mistakes."

"Carlos and I actually had an argument about the Smiling God. Because I was there when we summoned it. I saw the Summoning ritual work. He says that it was a coincidence, that his machine opened a hole into the otherworld, which the centipede came through, and that just by chance it happened as we were doing a meaningless ritual."

"He could be right," Darryl said, shrugging. "It's not my thing, but your science hits on correct answers more than not, even if it doesn't know what to do with those answers."

"There's a lot of data that supports his view. But, I don't know." She poked at the metal shavings and cinnamon on her coffee with her spoon. "Some part of me believes that the ritual worked. I don't have any numbers, but I was there. I just know in my gut that we did it."

"Looks like a little of my faith rubbed off. Anyway, hard to say either way if the ritual happened simultaneously with Carlos's experiment." He winked. "Time is weird, right?"

She didn't know whether to grin and acknowledge his flirtation or roll her eyes and acknowledge his hokey joke, so she hedged her bet and did both. There was a long pause in their conversation. Because they were navigating a brand-new dynamic, this particular silence felt dense.

Pamela Winchell sat at the table next to them listening to their conversation. She still followed them, but only as a friendly gesture. Friendly gestures are thoroughly subjective things. She raised her mug.

"Here's to the moon," she said through her amplifier. It was never quite clear what she meant by anything.

They raised their mugs back, and then looked at each other and laughed again. And it was right then that they both realized that, though they had failed to have a relationship, they were, just then, starting to succeed at having a friendship.

"Interloper!" shouted a man in a yellow trucker hat who had been quietly having a latte by the window. He wasn't pointing at Nilanjana. He was smiling a natural-looking smile.

"Nice to see you again, Kareem," she said.

"Nice to see you, too, Nilanjana," he said, returning his attention to his coffee. He was cute. She would go talk to him after Darryl left.

She imagined myriad possible outcomes, from a friendly shout of "Interloper" and a welcoming smile to a partner like Cecil who would sleep next to you, worry about your safety, hold your hand, make dinner, do chores, take vacations with you, raise dogs or children, and accept all facets of your being.

Looking at Kareem, she had no expectations, only knew now that people were worth meeting. Everyone in that coffee shop was a member of the same town as she was, a town she was not remotely close to understanding, but whose weird messiness she was starting to accept.

Not everyone believes in mountains, yet there they are, in plain sight. They ring this desert like the rim of an empty dinner plate. Scattered sparsely along the flat middle are small towns with names like Red Mesa, Pine Cliff, and, right in the center, Night Vale, believing none of it.

As they say, seeing isn't believing. Smelling and touching aren't believing either. Strangely, hearing *is* often believing.

Much of this story is hard to believe, even for the people who experienced it. After all, to believe in the black helicopters that circle overhead, monitoring everything we do, that is easy. To believe in the distant, flitting UFOs that use our world as their laboratory or, a more horrifying possibility, their playground, that is simple. But to believe in a giant centipede, worshiped as a god, arriving here from some other desert world? Well, that is a lot to ask.

Of course, for some involved, this story was easy to believe. They had grown up believing it, and so it was only a manifestation of what they already expected of the world.

What is experienced and what is believed are not often related. As a qualified scientist like Nilanjana could tell you, correlation is not causation. She could also tell you that feeling close to someone is not the same as love. And that what is felt completely in one moment becomes a flat memory of that feeling in the next moment, easy to recall but difficult to re-create. Her qualification as a scientist would not be why she could tell you this.

Darryl could tell you that experience is irrelevant to belief. Because experience is only life, while belief is happiness. After all, what is the harm in a fanciful belief if it carries a person happily from the start to the finish? If they die thinking incorrectly that the world has been good to them, would it have been better for them to die knowing that it has been indifferent and random? What is, he would ask, the sound argument for seeing the world as it is if it is possible to see the world as it isn't? Then he would do that circling fist thing in the air.

And here is where Nilanjana would sigh, finish her drink, and leave.

Take any person from Night Vale, and try to convince them of mountains. Tell them about altitude. Try to explain to them the feeling of cold air, of breath turning to steam, of red cheeks and noses. Tell them stories about people who have gone to high places, for good reasons and for silly reasons. Tell them stories of people who have lived their entire lives among the highest places, and of others who came great distances to die on top of some mountain they had never seen before. Tell them about mountain passes, about armies crossing them, about invasions and the turning of civilizations. Trace for them the history of the world, and how often it has been shaped by literal peaks and valleys. Show them a mountain. Point to a mountain and say, This was here before you, it will be here after you, it doesn't need you in order to exist, and when you die the contour of its rocks will not be changed at all.

Be cruel or kind. Reveal more than you should. Tell them anything you like.

It doesn't matter. They won't believe you anyway.

WANT MORE NIGHT VALE?

This is the end of the book. "*It Devours!*? Oh yeah, I've read that book" is now a thing you can say to friends, or even to complete strangers on the street, as those strangers try to ignore your sudden unprompted assertion about a book you once read.

If you enjoyed this novel, we recommend you join us in our ongoing *Welcome to Night Vale* podcast, which has been telling stories about this strange desert town since 2012.

Our podcast comes out twice monthly online and is completely free. You can download it to your computer or listening device through iTunes, Stitcher, SoundCloud, YouTube, any of the hundreds of free podcasting apps, or by going to welcometonightvale.com.

All of the episodes going back to the very start are available to download right now. Or if that sounds like too much time investment, just hop right in wherever we are now. You'll be in the swing of things in no time. Well, some time. It will take longer than zero time.

Interested in more stories from us? Visit www.nightvale presents.com to listen to *Alice Isn't Dead* and *Within the Wires,* new serial fiction podcasts from the team behind *Welcome to Night Vale,* plus a bunch of other new podcasts we are making with artists we love. Check back regularly to see what's launching.

We also do live shows all over the world (more than two hundred shows in sixteen different countries at the time of this writing). These live shows are full evenings of Night Vale story-telling, with live music and guest stars, designed so that you do not need to know anything about the podcast or novel to enjoy.

Keep an eye on welcometonightvale.com to join us next time we pass through wherever you live. (Wherever you live is our favorite place to perform.)

See you there.

ACKNOWLEDGMENTS

Thanks to the cast and crew of *Welcome to Night Vale*: Meg Bashwiner, Jon Bernstein, Desiree Burch, Adam Cecil, Felicia Day, Emma Frankland, Kevin R. Free, Mark Gagliardi, Angelique Grandone, Marc Evan Jackson, Maureen Johnson, Kate Jones, Erica Livingston, Christopher Loar, Hal Lublin, Dylan Marron, Jasika Nicole, Lauren O'Niell, Flor De Liz Perez, Teresa Piscioneri, Jackson Publick, Molly Quinn, Em Reaves, Retta, Symphony Sanders, Annie Savage, Lauren Sharpe, James Urbaniak, Bettina Warshaw, Wil Wheaton, Mara Wilson, and, of course, the voice of Night Vale himself, Cecil Baldwin.

Also and always: Jillian Sweeney; Kathy and Ron Fink; Ellen Flood; Leann Sweeney; Jack and Lydia Bashwiner; Anna, Levi, and Caleb Pow; Kate and Derek Zambarano; Rob Wilson; Kate Leth; Jessica Hayworth; Holly and Jeffrey Rowland; Zack Parsons; Ashley Lierman; Glen David Gold; Andrew Morgan; Eleanor McGuinness; Hank Green; John Green; Patrick Rothfuss; Cory Doctorow; John Darnielle; Dessa Darling; Aby Wolf; Jason Webley; Danny Schmidt; Carrie Elkin; Eliza Rickman; Mary Epworth; Will Twynham; Erin McKeown; the New York Neo-Futurists; Laura Brown; Janina Matthewson; Christy Gressman; Julian Koster; Gennifer Hutchison; Kassie Evashevski; Katharine Heller; Brie Williams; Dr. Rudy Busto, who first got Joseph interested

ACKNOWLEDGMENTS

in the intersection of science fiction and religion; the Book-smith in San Francisco; and, of course, the delightful Night Vale fans.

Our agent, Jodi Reamer; our editor, Amy Baker; and all the good people at HarperPerennial.

ABOUT THE AUTHORS

Joseph Fink created the *Welcome to Night Vale* and *Alice Isn't Dead* podcasts. He lives with his wife in New York.

Jeffrey Cranor cowrites the *Welcome to Night Vale* and *Within the Wires* podcasts. He also cocreates theater and dance pieces with choreographer/wife Jillian Sweeney. They live in New York.

Find out more about Joseph Fink and Jeffrey Cranor by registering for the free monthly newsletter at www.orbitbooks.net.